Ch

Tesser was so wet it was indecent. She felt heavy, sensual and voluptuous next to Kevin, who was well-hung, fresh-faced and eighteen. He couldn't believe his luck, and he jumped to it, as if Tesser might withdraw her offer if he thought about things too long. Tesser felt like hot chocolate fudge to his citrus: she was indulgent, experienced, corrupted; he was transparent, fresh, and virtuous. But willing to be corruped. And that was all that mattered.

Other titles by the author:

RIKA'S JEWEL

For Justine –
the cheapest trick in town

Cheap Trick

ASTRID FOX

BLACK
lace

Black Lace novels contain sexual fantasies.
In real life, make sure you practise safe sex.

First published in 2001 by
Black Lace
Thames Wharf Studios,
Rainville Road, London W6 9HA

Typeset by SetSystems Ltd, Saffron Walden, Essex
Printed and bound by Mackays of Chatham PLC

ISBN 0 352 33640 4

Chapter One

Was Tesser the only one who'd ever noticed it about the Starbucks Coffee logo? It was a mermaid, right, but a mermaid who had her legs spread – or, rather, her tail split. She held up each side of her scaly and now forked bottom half in each hand. It was corporate pornography. A cheerful grinning siren exposing herself like a flasher – here's my nice juicy stuff, wet with the liquid I've sold you; drink me up and I'll show you more, you'll get a bit of tail this time, that's for sure . . .

Tesser shut her legs tightly and looked away from her latte for a moment. She was so hot for it she was fantasising about goddamn coffee. Jesus Christ! The drink was a bit of a splurge, anyway, 'cos she was soooooooo broke. But, hey, she had to kill some time and she figured sitting down for ten minutes would give her space for a little reflection. Time for a little cool-down. Because, if she didn't get screwed soon, she was gonna shove her hand down under the waistband of her forest-green skirt and rub herself dizzy right here in the middle of a Liverpool Street Station coffee shop. Her pussy already felt sticky and *she-was-dying-for-a-shag*.

'Shag' was an interesting word. Tesser had learned it within a week of moving from Seattle to London. She found the addition to her vocabulary list quite useful. In fact, she'd spent the first few months in London going from shag to shag, from great shag to bad shag, from one-night shags to three-night shags, from dirty, thrusting, furtive alley shags to slow, quasi-romantic, clit-on-fire build-up shags. She had even had a monogamous relationship based entirely on shagging. Aside from that, she had been shagged upstairs in terraced houses, shagged downstairs in council flats, shagged behind the back wall of Islington Tesco Metro, shagged in the middle of Brockwell Park, shagged in the middle of a Glastonbury crowd and shagged within the hearing of eighteen subtle and eavesdropping masturbators in a youth hostel that slept twenty per room.

In short, she had thought she was shagged out.

Then she had met Jamie.

And now she was as horny as if she'd never been licked or fucked or fingered since she'd shown up in ol' London-town. As if she hadn't spent her acclimatising months pressing her own sweet pussy on to thick hard cocks of every description, as well as brushing up against a few lovely pussies in the bargain. She felt like a goddamn nun, though by that she meant the kind of nun who's desperate for it, the kind of young, innocent, fragrant nun that takes off before vespers because she's breaking out in a sweat and has to get to the confines of her own cloistered cell so she can grind herself to a filthy, secret orgasm and smell her fingers when she sneaks back into evening prayers. That's the kind of nun Tesser meant.

That was the way Jamie made her feel.

And now she had decided to get her mind off him. So, when she'd woken up this morning and had that ghost-walk feeling again, she figured she'd indulge herself with a little manhunt. She had rung up a number listed in *Break-Time* and there had still been a place left on the walk.

One of the most successful manhunt methods Tesser had yet discovered was the ghost walk, a.k.a. a weirdo-cum-historical supernatural hike advertised in the cheap ad sections of weekly guide magazines. She had already done *Jack the Ripper* and the *Wives of Henry VIII*, and she was looking forward to spending some time with *Prostitutes of Hoxton Village*, if it meant she would be able to get Jamie off her mind. Some fresh new meat, a young twenty-two-year-old student: studious, randy and into indie music would be just the ticket. Yep, she'd pick him up and shag him back at his student housing – or maybe they'd linger behind during the ghost walk itself, and then fuck in one of the stately haunted rooms and she'd blow him and he'd finger her and, that way, she'd make sure that she got Jamie off her mind.

She sent a quick text message to Kitty, who was always amused by Tesser's predatory nature – THE HUNT BEGINZ. T NTENZ 2 SCORE – and took a long, lukewarm draught of her in-house latte. Yeah, right. Forgetting about Jamie had so far appeared to be as easy as avoiding him. It didn't help that they had the same quirky interests – lo-fi gaming, ghost walks, no-budget Super-8 films, local jumble sales, free classical concerts at Christ Church, charity shops –

Jesus Christ! Tesser choked on her coffee. At last she'd pinpointed it. The thing she and Jamie had in common was being cheap. For a moment she paused and surveyed her whore-red fingernail polish and her torn sky-blue fishnets, and caught a glance of her short, bleached-blonde pixie cut and violet eyeshadow in the Starbucks wall mirror. She had always considered her unique style funky, but maybe what it truly was was cheap.

Cheap, cheap, cheap.

3

She was a cheap girl. *Poor*. But surely that meant Jamie – outsider artist and current darling of the alternative press – was a cheap *guy*. Hell, yes. And he was slumming, whereas Tesser lived cheap out of necessity. He had shown his face last weekend at the Conway Hall concert (not free, but still under six quid, which made it – well, let's face it . . . *cheap*) and Tesser couldn't avoid noticing the fifty-pound note that he tried to get changed from one of the musically inclined anarchist octogenarians who ran the concert series. Fifty pounds was more money than she had seen in a month. Well, screw him. She had to make her own fun. She'd be damned if she'd sit home whining in a bedsit the way all the Brits did when they were broke, when there was actually plenty to do and see for practically free if only you had a bike and could make it out of your bed in the morning. There were museums, weren't there? The only problem was, last week at the National Gallery, Tesser had had the ill luck to run into Jamie in the Sainsbury Room. And then at the Saturday morning jumble sale at Hackney Methodist Church. And then the next day at the Conway Hall concert.

They'd been civil to each other, of course. As was proper between two people who had experienced together a night of absolutely mind-blowing sex, but who had also agreed the next morning that they would 'just be friends'.

And therefore everything would have been fine, if only Tesser had been able to stop thinking of Jamie's lanky, trim body and his sexy, droopy eyes that managed to look both doelike and wickedly perverted at one and the same time, and the way he had run his fingers through her then red hair and the way the two of them had kissed when he slid his cock into her that night, slowly, just good and easy, and the way it had taken her heart a good half-hour to stop beating triple-time after he'd taken his long, graceful fingers and massaged her

4

to a fucking incredible come. If only Tesser had been able to stop thinking about those kinds of things.

But she hadn't been able to, and now she had to get laid. She was dressed for it, after all. She checked out her reflection in the coffee house shop-front window. Hell, she looked *hot*. She wanted unknown flesh against her own, the spontaneity of a one-off fuck, just to cool her down a bit. Just to give her a bit of relief. And the ghost walk trick was the best trick she knew. Forget the meat-market clubs and bars – you want to get screwed by a nice sleazy guy, you go to a ghost walk.

Matter of fact, the walk would be starting soon. Tesser rose up, took one last slurp, wiped her mouth with a serviette embossed with mermaid porn and picked up her overstuffed backpack, shoving past the thirtyish corporate bitch who was jabbering into a mobile the size of Tesser's thumb, and who refused to move out of the way.

Tesser earned a glare from the businesswoman. But she drew her pride together and with a sense of reverse *noblesse oblige* she ignored the yuppie tart and walked out of the coffee house into the greater glare of the station, clattering on her red platform heels. The electric light was hard on the eyes. She shielded them, while at the same time looking for the Bishopsgate exit. She always felt turned around at Liverpool Street Station, and a couple of times she had ended up exiting the opposite way from the direction she had intended. But this time she got the right exit and there was the group, meeting near the news-stand as planned. There were the usual American tourists (unlike myself, Tesser thought with heavy irony – I'm an American *traveller*, of course!), several husband-and-wife teams, one nuclear family complete with 2¾ children (well, at least a very small third child) and two young men who fully met her specifications.

Oh, she was having a lucky day today. Fuck Jamie!

5

That was what she thought. She was going to get hers and she was going to have a good time doing it. What, did he think roses grew out of his dick? I don't *think* so, buddy.

She had-had-had to stop thinking about stupid, sexy Jamie. So back to the boys. One of the ghost walkers was Tesser's usual tall, gangly type – studenty, looked like he wrote bad poetry on those days when he skipped class, and then enforced it on impressionable female freshers that evening at the pub. Hey, she knew his game. He had floppy, strawberry-blond hair and big pale-blue eyes and he looked up at her underneath his lashes. Oh, yeah, she knew his game all right. Sensitive in order to screw. That type can be fun if you treat 'em right.

Potential Fuck Number Two was different. He was not a tall man and kind of stocky. It looked good on him. He had a cute ass and black eyes and real dark hair. He was looking at Tesser, too. Had his eyes stuck fast on her cleavage, which admittedly Tesser was flashing rather a lot of through the vintage charity-shop 50s basque she was wearing. She had him collared as a Canadian tourist, though – a trust-fund kid skimming through Europe, in London for only a day and wanting to do something a little quirky. That was why ghost walks were such great pick-up places: they always attracted people who were by nature a little peculiar and unconventional, and therefore not always beholden to the restraints of comfortable, predictable couple sex, and also those people who were breezing in and out of town – ripe for one-off sessions, which incidentally were Tesser's favourite kind of sessions. Until she met Jamie, that was.

But enough about him.

The dark-haired guy – Potential Fuck Number Two – seemed nice. She hoped he knew how to fuck, and she also hoped he had a hotel room. She had no intentions of repeating that youth hostel episode.

'Hello! Is everyone on the list here now?' The guide's voice broke in on Tesser's dirty thoughts. 'I'm expecting sixteen! Are you all here?' As the birdlike older woman, complete with a sticky label that read HELLO, MY NAME IS CAROLYN began to count up the group total, Tesser found herself looking from Blue Eyes to Black Eyes and back to Blue Eyes again. Oh, yeah. It was going to be a *fine* walk this afternoon. Her clit was already stiff and her panties were so moist that she'd probably catch a cold if she didn't get that fuck real soon. But with which one? Tesser ran her hand through her short blonde hair and tugged at one of her bright fishnets and smiled. Maybe both. Hell, why not? After all, two young men were smiling at her, and it was obvious that they had noticed each other's presence too, since they both were beginning to shift their feet and glance about in a sort of jealous, bristly way. She'd enjoy playing them off against each other.

Tesser smiled slyly back at both boys in turn.

'Tesser? Tesser Roget?' The guide pronounced Tesser's last name the French way, but Tesser didn't break her concentrated staring at all when she answered back. She didn't even turn around to face the guide. She just kept smiling.

'Roget. Rodge-it. Rhymes with hobbit. Or it would, if hobbit had a "j" in it. It's not pronounced fancy. You know how uncultured we Yanks are.'

The guide cleared her throat, evidently embarrassed by Tesser's smart-alecky ways and evidently unsure whether she should agree with the statement. Tesser imagined the older woman's internal struggle: Of course, Americans have no irony! Is the girl joking or not?

But Tesser still didn't turn around to check the lady's reaction. She was moving quickly: she had already lowered her gaze to Black Eyes' groin, a nice packet encased by an equally nice pair of upmarket corduroys. Week-end-slacker cords. She could sense that Blue Eyes was so infuriated by her displaced attention that he was considering whether to throw a punch at the young man with the beautifully dark eyes and the admirably thickening crotch.

'I'm Alistair,' said Blue Eyes, making Tesser's eyes jerk upwards at the interruption. He stuck his hand out in an introduction. 'And you are . . .?'

Grudgingly, Tesser shook hands with Alistair. Black Eyes was still staring at her. 'Tesser Roget. Rodge-it.'

'What kind of name is Tesser?' Now Black Eyes was forcing himself back into the arena. That was fine with Tesser. Nothing like a bit of healthy competition. He was North American; Tesser had guessed right.

'It's short for Contessa, which was my grandmother's name. I hate it, actually. I've gone by Tesser since I was eight.'

'Well, I'll certainly bear your preferences in mind, Tesser.' Black Eyes gave her an insinuating smile and for a split second Tesser felt an urge to slap him that was almost as strong as her urge to fuck him senseless.

'Who are you, then?' she asked, rudely.

Black Eyes glanced over at Alistair in a manner that Tesser interpreted as territorial pissing regarding her favours. Then he said, 'Eric.'

'You guys been on a ghost walk before?'

Eric shook his head and said no, but Alistair admitted he had been on one once before in Cambridge.

'An Oxbridge man?' Tesser batted her heavily mascara'd eyelashes ironically, but Alistair just nodded and mildly affirmed her statement. 'And you're no doubt Canadian,' Tesser continued, turning back to Eric. Trust-fund kid on a short-term holiday. He had to be.

'I'm from Maine.' Minus one point for Tesser's psychic ability. 'Just here for the week. Just passing through town.' Plus one point. She'd call it a draw. 'You from the States, too?'

Tesser groaned inwardly, but gave a brief history of her time, filling them in that her dad was British whereas her mom was American, and though she'd grown up and went to film school in Seattle she had dual citizenship and had been hanging out in England for the past five months, just to see what it was like. They both listened politely, and the animosity between them seemed to have cooled off a bit, which for some reason rankled Tesser. She wasn't into that whole jousting white-knights crap, but she knew for sure that a nice piece of ass like herself was worth a *bit* of a duel . . .

'OK, ghost group – let's get started!' Carolyn the leader had a sort of geriatric Girl Guide enthusiasm, and she directed the ghost walkers down Bishopsgate for a good quarter of an hour's walk to Hoxton, pointing out various historical reference points on the way, but not many spooks. Tesser listened half-heartedly as Carolyn tried to drum up the possibility that the plague pits they were walking past were no doubt haunted, but the suggestion seemed a bit desperate. In fact, Tesser was beginning to feel a bit pissed off about the whole thing – both Alistair's and Eric's interest in her seemed to have waned since she had introduced herself. They were talking to each other about the achingly straight-boy topic of football and ignoring her entirely, so it didn't seem as if she was going to get laid after all, and now there weren't going to be any proper haunted mansions, either. Maybe she *should* give Jamie a call. He had given her his number written on a travelcard, but of course she'd never really considered using it until now. Because now she was getting desperate. Not desperate enough for him in *particular*, of course. Just desperate for a shag.

But just then Carolyn stopped the group in front of a dilapidated but still impressive old building, which had faded stone letters carved above its door that read THE CORNUCOPIA MUSIC-HALL.

'This,' Carolyn said with some pride, 'is a former residence of the famous actress and woman of pleasure Hettie LaFonche. You may have remembered her from your studies as a royal paramour. Well, she was much more than that. She was a fine actress in her own right and her ghost is said to haunt still this very theatre, a tale upon which I will elaborate as we go through this rather fabulous old building. It was called the Bainbridge Playhouse in her day, of course, and was only renamed the Cornucopia in the 1890s.'

Despite her horniness, Tesser found herself surprisingly interested in Carolyn's anecdotes as all sixteen of the ghost walkers trouped dutifully up the marble stairs. The stairwell interior was decorated with lavish ruby-red curtains and on every flight there was an overblown and ostentatious statue whose concept must have originated in a Classical aesthetic and then gotten lost in Victorian hubris along the way. But the steps were also endless and Carolyn was heading the pack like some relentless Head Girl on speed, oblivious to the fact that the children were whining and the adults were panting. By the third floor, Tesser hung back. She *knew* she had been smoking too much dope lately. Her lungs weren't working right. She had to get her breath back.

Interestingly, when Tesser paused, Alistair and Eric seemed to hang back as well. And it was apparent they were discussing her, though she couldn't make out what they were saying. Hey, hey, hey. Maybe she'd get that double-header after all. Bingo. At last.

No sense in pussyfooting around. She'd lay her cards on the table.

So she stalled completely and gave them both a coy smile. Alistair smiled shyly, then glanced quickly back at Eric for his approval, though God knew why. Tesser's heart started to beat joyfully again. They might think they were going to be in on some kind of macho gang-bang threesome, but this session was going to be on her terms. Oh, yes.

Tesser looked back over her shoulder with her best demure look, and nodded towards the door on the flight of stairs on which they now stood. Carolyn hadn't mentioned this floor at all, as she'd seemed eager to sprint upwards to the fifth and final floor, where apparently there was a prostitute's bloodstain that reappeared every morning, no matter how many times it was scrubbed away. Tesser put her hand on the brass door-knob and twisted. The door worked. Tesser walked in. The boys followed, the door slamming shut behind them with an audible bang.

It was a bare and dusty room, one where all the furniture had been removed. But due to the dusty paintings on the wall and the marvellously ornate cornices it still had an air of opulence. It looked like it might have been a sitting room of some sort – perhaps those celebrated actors and actresses who had lived in residence had once entertained their friends here. And to be fair, it wasn't a total wreck in terms of hygiene. It could have been dusted and swept, but it was not by any definition filthy. In fact, Tesser thought, this room really defines the term 'faded glamour'. This impression was lent credence by the fact that it was very bright; the sun was streaming in through all the uncurtained windows and making odd shadows even in the furthest recesses of the room.

The three of them stared at each other. If she spoke first, Tesser knew she would get the upper hand of the situation. But instead she moved first, her pulse beating fast, her hands going dry with nervousness. She stepped close to Eric, who was nearer. He was staring at her, as frozen and blank-eyed as one of those hallway statues. Tesser ran her eyes down and up his body. He didn't flinch. Then she flung her zipped backpack off to the

11

side, got down in a squat – one that resulted in her skirt riding up – and unzipped his cords.

Oh, thank-you-Jesus. She was going to get laid after all. She felt so eager that she was shaking with anticipation; she was afraid to speak, because she might say something wrong and right now it all seemed to be going perfectly to plan. Having sex in a stately, haunted room, just as she had intended to when she woke up this morning. But Eric was pressing on her shoulders and she sank down further, down to her knees. The cheap fabric of her green skirt tore as she spread her thighs apart and leaned forward, curling her fist round his cock. It was a beauty: fat, thick and hard as concrete. Tesser's mouth was watering. She gave him a couple of pulls, worked her hand down the whole length of his prick, her red fingernails against it making quite a pretty if pornographic picture. It looked really sleazy: a thoroughly private, furtive handjob. He must have thought so, too, because he groaned loudly when he looked down.

Behind her, Tesser could hear Alistair fumbling around with his flies, evidently badly in need of a wank. She herself felt filthy. Filthy, sleazy, naughty and free. She had a man's cock in her right hand and it was like a rock; he could pound out nails with that thing, that was how stiff he was. Tesser swallowed hard, pumping her hand on him, feeling her forehead break out in a light perspiration, her mouth going dry, her armpits going damp. Everything was getting reversed – he was the one who should be swallowing in anticipation. Not her. Him. Still, she didn't give a monkey's ass. She wanted to open her mouth wide and take in that thick cock of his until she gagged. Before she did so, though, she licked the whole length of it from base to the juicy plum of its head and, above her, Eric started to tremble. Tesser's hands were shaking too, but she had her wits about her so she looked up at Eric like she was in control, even though

12

she was on her knees. He in his turn was looking down at her with an expression that looked like desperation. He couldn't even speak.

Tesser stared him out for a few seconds, then she dropped her head, moved her mouth to his stiff cock and then deliberately ran just her lips against it, leaving a smear of scarlet lipstick. Oh, he was a marked man, all right.

He groaned again, and at last Tesser took him within her lips, gliding his cock into the warm, red, juicy cave. Immediately, he began to thrust into her, and she screwed her eyes shut and sucked just as hard as she could; fuck, she was wet, she could taste her raspberry-flavoured lipstick still on his cock, and taste the musky beast scent of him. He was moaning words, but it was like Tesser had somehow gone deaf or something, because there was this roaring in her ears. Her mind and mouth and throat felt full of cock. This was what she was born for. Oh, fuck. She sucked harder, and Eric thrust into her like a goddamn piston, pumping into her mouth. Tesser started to shake so much she thought her knees were about to give way. Her pussy was slick, her clit was as hard as the cock she was sucking and she had to get off. In fact, she had to get off *now*.

She shifted and rammed one hand down under the waistband of her skirt, straight down to her crotch and, as she swallowed him as forcefully as she could manage, she moved a finger up and down over her clit. The harder she bathed his cock with saliva and suction force, the more frantically she rubbed herself. He shoved himself into her. She tried to draw even more of him down her throat by sheer power of her lips alone. She did it so hard she thought her hand was going to fall off.

Tesser wanted more. Each time she stroked herself and each time her mouth went back and forth along his prick, she felt sharp pleasure in her groin. She felt like her tits were swelling as big as a porn star's; she felt her thighs trembling with effort to support her position; she felt the blue knotted strings of her fishnets strain and then snap. She sucked up all that raspberry lipstick from him, and just as he shot his load in her mouth and she began to swallow it greedily, thirstily, just as she began to swallow down the very come that she had coaxed to this climax, just as he sprayed in her mouth, she felt her own finale spiral towards her. Her hand jerked furiously up and down over her clit.

'Fucking hell!' Tesser muttered. Then she grinned.

And then she made him let her get up so that he could get down and lick *her*. She pulled his T-shirt off him as he did this, and he paused to let her disentangle it completely. He had a lovely back and she observed it with approval as he obediently knelt there in his turn and worked away at her very wet pussy. His flesh was brown and taut and he had some kind of weird tattoo with an upside-down heart on his upper arm. A flexible tattoo, one that rippled when his muscles moved as he got down to business and served her properly.

All of this time, out of the corner of her eye, she could see Alistair jacking off, glancing from her to Eric and back to her again. She was wet and dizzy with sex as she pressed her back against the wall and held her skirt up with both hands so he could push aside her pale-blue nylon panties and really get in a good lick. She nearly forgot about Alistair then, to be honest, so after she came this second time and while Eric was wiping her sweet juices off his mouth, Tesser motioned for Alistair to come in a little closer.

'He's not gotten off yet,' Tesser informed Eric. 'Though you've been trying very hard, haven't you, Alistair?'

Alistair drew nearer but didn't say anything.

'I thought maybe you boys could give each other a helping hand.'

Tesser watched them eye each other tentatively. Eric

14

was already stiff again from going down on her. That's how you can tell if a guy really likes pussy – if he gets hard when he's eating you out. A pussy-licking-induced hard-on is a beautiful sight to see.

Now, Tesser knew what most straight guys were like. They'd rather shag their own grandmother than another man – when they were sober. She also knew what most straight guys were like drunk. Their inhibitions fly off and they gag for it regardless, cock or cunt. It doesn't matter. You better believe it: alcohol is the great bisexual equaliser. *In vino veritas*, and all that. Maybe people should all be drunk, all of the time. Baudelaire was right.

These boys weren't drunk, but they were definitely sex-stoned, and that was even better.

Sure enough, Alistair moved in on Eric. At first Eric looked like he was going to bolt, but then he closed his eyes as Alistair put his pretty mouth down on his cock and he moaned with the pleasure of his second blow-job of the afternoon, lucky boy.

As the guys started grooving on each other, Tesser took a step back. They made a mighty fine sight there in the bright afternoon sunlight, their faces intermittently tense with anticipation and then slack and sleazy with pleasure as the next wave of desire kicked in.

In a weird way, it looked very 1940s documentary, kinda like Henri Cartier-Bresson took a B/W still of Julian Sands blowing a young Marlon Brando. In an alternative universe, of course.

Tesser rearranged her damp panties, pulled her skirt down over her hips and tried to knot a few diamonds in her frayed fishnets, still keeping an eye on the action. With their eyes closed, the two young men looked evocative – epic, even.

It was beautiful. She *had* to get it on film. She edged over to her backpack, unzipped it and quietly removed her Super-8 camera, her fingers momentarily brushing over the jackknife she always carried with her. She was pretty sure the Canon camera had plenty of battery juice left. And Alistair was still working away on Eric, too; they were rocking back and forth in this kind of steady rhythm. Eric was moaning again and his face was kind of screwing up and Tesser could tell he was close to coming.

She began to film. She attempted to use the split-image rangefinder, but there was a problem with the reflex focusing. Eric was making so much noise now, panting and huffing, that for a half-minute Tesser thought she was going to get away with it all. But then there was one of those slight pauses, the kind that always occur right before you really start to go for it. It's a tension, actually, as opposed to a pause. Unfortunately, the moment of quiet between the two guys emphasised the whir of Tesser's camera.

Eric jerked out of Alistair's mouth so quickly that Tesser thought he was in danger of getting his jewels bitten off.

'You fucking bitch!' he screamed, grabbing up his cords and pushing Alistair out of the way so that he could get to Tesser.

That was when Tesser had to run for it. Breasts heaving, still half-covered by her black 50s bodice, skirt riding up, one shoe on – Tesser shoved the camera into her backpack and made a bolt for the stairs. She had a bit of a lead, because Eric was still doing up his trousers, so she kicked off the remaining bright-red platform heel (they matched today's lipstick, natch) and ran stocking-footed, slipping down the stairs as fast as she could manage, towards the grand Victorian door of the music hall, through whose windows Tesser could detect the natural light of the great outdoors!

Escape.

'Bitch!' Behind her, maybe about a flight up, Tesser could hear Eric as he rushed down the stairwell, bare feet thudding and slapping on the cold marble steps.

16

And now, fuck it, finally she was at the door. She grasped the knob and pushed outwards, panicking, trying to make it outside and trying not to drop the backpack swinging from her shoulder. She had only a few seconds to glance around. To her right, she could see the tail end of the ghost-walk group heading round the corner. They must have left the building in the interim. Conscientious Carolyn apparently hadn't noticed that three of her charges had gone AWOL. To the left, there was nothing. Tesser headed left.

She circled the corner, ran for three blocks, then decided to head back to where the ghost group had started the walk, by the Hoxton council estates, since it was unlikely Eric and Alistair would double up on retraced steps. She was still running, though, backpack on one shoulder, shoes in one hand, dishabille in the big sense of the word. She was still breathless, *completely* winded. What was more, she was still panicking – and, strangely, still horny.

Then she rounded the corner and ran smack into Jamie.

Chapter Two

'Jesus Christ! What are *you* doing here?' Tesser was panting from the sprint, and she leaned back against the brick wall and looked up at Jamie, trying to catch her breath properly. He didn't look too surprised to see her.

'Umm . . . well . . .' Jamie's voice trailed off. He looked down at Tesser, his tall frame in stark contrast to her own limited height. Even in three-inch heels she was only five foot five. 'I guess I wanted to see you,' he admitted in a rather sharp tone. Tesser looked closely at him, trying to read his expression. His dark eyes were glittering behind his specs, and now his words seemed clipped, like he was edgy or nervous or something. Maybe he was.

Then the implication of what he had said hit her like a smack in the gob. She looked up, a half-smile stealing over her face. For a second, she ignored the fact that she was being pursued by other once-admirers. 'You *have* been following me around, haven't you? Admit it.'

Hell, outsider artist Jamie Desmond, following her all over town. It *was* kind of flattering.

Jamie observed her from his vantage point. Once

again, Tesser couldn't read his expression. He could be furious or he could be curious. Then Jamie cracked a wide grin, one that lit up his whole face. 'I admit it. You're irresistible. The blonde thing you've got going on looks great.'

Last time she had seen him, she had been a redhead. Blonde was a vision that had come to her yesterday afternoon and she had borrowed a bleach kit from her squatmate Jana and made that vision come true.

'Come on, Tesser, I'll treat you to a coffee to calm you down and you can tell me why you're rushing about in such a hurry.'

The plan sounded good – maybe. She glanced nervously around the corner. There was no one there.

'How about continuing on this way, away from Spital-fields Market?' Jamie suggested. 'There are some cool old buildings and supposedly haunted theatres we could check out, too. Didn't you tell me you were into that kind of stuff?'

'Nah, I've just come from that direction,' Tesser said quickly, as she steered Jamie back in the direction from which she'd just arrived. It was an old detective trick: when in flight, double back and trail your pursuers. Or retrace your steps entirely. They'll never catch up. 'That haunted-theatre crap is just a bunch of people trading in on the whole Jack the Ripper thing. It's old hat, that kind of sham. A couple of murdered prostitutes still haunting the area and so on. Pretty standard stuff, really.'

'If you say so.' Jamie took Tesser's hand in his and they walked back along Bishopsgate, but turned off at one point and headed towards Old Street. She had to admit it felt nice to be walking along with him, particularly when he squeezed her hand. She looked up at him, and he winked.

* * *

The Old Street coffee house was upmarket and pretentious, full of slumming *nouveau* Hoxtonites recently emigrated from west London. She queued politely in line, holding her head high and pretending it didn't matter that the other female customers were scanning her entire person for designer labels and finding them severely lacking. She decided that she would be happy to take Jamie at his word and therefore let him purchase her coffee when it came to the crunch. So she told the woman taking orders that she'd like a large, expensive cappuccino, and then concentrated instead on pulling down her skirt and patting her hair flat, because she sensed it was sticking up in wild blonde spikes. Jesus. She could use some freshening up after the afternoon she'd had. She made a mental note to step into the toilet as soon as she had a chance and check out the state of her lipstick: she had a feeling it was smeared all over the lower half of her face.

'Over here, Tesser,' Jamie said. He had picked up both frothy cappuccinos, balancing them as he stepped through the crowded café, and was looking mighty fine with his short dreadlocks and heavy-rimmed specs – sort of Malcom X does angry-young-independent-filmmaker. There had been that sycophantic spread in the *Sentinel* last weekend all about Jamie Desmond – 'The Outsider Artist Who Hasn't Sold a Single Painting' – and because of it Jamie now seemed to have hit some sort of recognisability factor, because a couple of laydeez who had been shooting Tesser judgmental looks now seemed to be looking at her with new respect: like maybe she was his East End muse or something, with her jumble-sale clothes.

'Excuse me,' said Tesser, as she shoved her way past and accidentally on purpose stepped on someone's Italian-leather-covered toes. The owner of the foot in question yelped, but Tesser didn't offer a second apology. Those slumming 'It' girlz just didn't *get* it. Rub their toffee-noses in dress-down grunge and they'd still come up shining as polished and personality-free as this very coffee house. It had happened with every street-fashion look so far – punk, grunge, gangsta rap, you name it. The expensive Prada boots on this one were a dead giveaway, despite her carefully faded jeans. The woman gave Tesser a dirty look, but Tesser refused to be obsequious to her upper-middle-class mores. If there was one thing she couldn't stand it was the constant 'I'm sorry, I'm sorry, I'm sorry' litany of the British when a simple 'excuse me' would suffice. Bitch shouldn't have had her pretty feet in the way, regardless.

'I'm followin' ya,' Tesser told Jamie, and pushed her way past a couple more chickie-babes in dress-down jeans and Manolo Blah-blah-blah-nik shoes. She was a Manolo Refusenik, personally. Jamie had found, miraculously, a spare table, right towards the back, and Tesser followed along in his wake. Jesus, Jamie looked great from behind. His ass was a work of art. He wore a pair of designer denims as enticingly moulded as the muscly curves of a Fiorentino nude. The thought of homoerotic art quickly made Tesser remember the boys back at the music-hall theatre, and she felt herself blushing as she reached the table. She grabbed a chair and pulled it close into the table. Jamie's long legs were sticking way, way out. My, oh, my, Tesser thought, I do like a lanky man.

'You look a bit flustered,' Jamie said. 'I'm not making you nervous, am I?'

Tesser couldn't tell if he was giving her a hard time.

'No, no, no,' she said. 'I've just had an . . . interesting afternoon, that's all.'

'Interesting in what way?' Jamie shifted, and Tesser couldn't help but be aware of the lovely way his jeans strained at the crotch. Nice.

'Interesting in a hot way. In a three-way hot way.' She looked Jamie straight in the eye. She wanted him to get the clear picture that she was not girlfriend material,

21

that she was a free agent, and that she was going to fuck who she pleased, when she pleased. Even if at the moment she wanted to fuck *him*. Even so.

'Yeah?' Instead of looking jealous or put out, Jamie's eyes were shining, and he leaned closer. On second thought, maybe a *little* jealousy would have been a bit more flattering. He seemed completely nonplussed regarding Tesser's cheerful admittance of her own prom-iscuity. 'Wanna tell me about it?' He looked deeply into her eyes, and then pointedly lowered his own until he was taking a prolonged survey of her cleavage.

Tesser blushed even more deeply as Jamie continued to gaze at her tits, pushed up by the black, barmaid-style bodice, and she really shouldn't have been blushing at all. She shifted a little. Then she got a hold of herself. She had the sexual upper hand in this non-relationship, right? He was the one who tracked *her* down, not the other way around. And now he was trying to score control points. Making her feel uncomfortable. Tesser ran her fingers through her bleached hair, leaned forward and licked her lips. Jamie swallowed hard, and she stifled an impulse to shove her tits right in his face, 'cos two could play this game, right? Instead she sat tight, and made her voice slow and overcasual. 'We-e-ell,' she said, dragging the word out in a Texan three-syllable, which was quite an affectation for a West Coast gal like herself, 'we-e-ell, I happened to meet a pair of really nice men on one of my ghost walks today.'

'A bonded couple?'

Tesser blinked. 'Why would you say that?'

'I just wondered. I've learned not to assume across-the-board breederness. Let's just say I'm a sensitive guy, attuned to such matters. Go on.'

He looked a little too casual and serene, and this made Tesser determined to give him an unedited account of what had happened. He needed a bit of a shock. 'They weren't at all a couple, actually, Jamie. They were a pair of straighter-than-straight young men, men just like your fine self –'

'Black men, then. A couple of straighter-than-straight upstanding, middle-class black men, just like my fine self.'

'Come on, Jamie – do you want me to tell the story or not?'

'Accepted. Continue.'

'Anyway, mid-ghost walk, I sorted out a situation where I found myself with not just one, but both of these fii-ii-iine pieces of ass in a deserted backroom of a haunted theatre.'

'I've heard about these backrooms. I thought you said that whole haunted-theatre thing was crap. And I thought you said these men were straighter than straight.'

'It is. They were. At least until I manipulated the situation so that they ended up blowing each other, and let me tell you, mister, *that* was a beautiful sight to see.' Tesser sneaked a glance at Jamie to see whether he looked jealous, but he just looked keenly interested.

'And you took off before there was case of homosexual panic, so as to avoid any tertiary queer bashing? Nice one, Tesser. I always had you figured for someone who looked out for herself.' Tesser couldn't gauge whether his voice was sarcastic or admiring. Maybe she hadn't got that British irony thing worked out quite yet, after all.

'Actually, no, I'm not that callous. I wouldn't stir up the latent emotions of a couple of super-straight straight boys and then just take off. It was more a case of artistic curiosity.' Tesser took a sip of her cappuccino, and then took a big breath so that she could launch right in and tell Jamie the whole deal with the camera and the subsequent chase. 'See –'

But right then Jamie moved really close to her. 'Just shut up for a second, OK?' He shoved his hand right

23

under her left thigh, so she felt it pressing her fishnets into her flesh.

The cheek! Tesser hated it when people told her to shut up, even as part of erotic foreplay repartee. 'I *won't* shut up, OK?' Jamie's hand was now just skimming the hem of her green skirt, his fingers gouging into the diamond pattern of her fishnets. It felt good, and she closed her eyes and enjoyed the sensation. 'If I shut up,' she added, 'it's because I choose to.' Damn, but his hand felt nice there on her leg, stroking and stroking.

'OK,' said Jamie.

Tesser closed her eyes again, so she could really concentrate on how Jamie's hand felt, concentrate on the warm friction against her thigh. She was still pretty turned on from the episode in the theatre, and she was in that weird anything-feels-good head space, so she kind of rocked her thigh closer to him, smelling his aftershave – she thought it was Old Spice, but surely not – in order to give him more access to her own perked-up pussy.

She opened her mouth to say something, but then decided that she wouldn't give him the satisfaction of hearing her speak. But Jamie just kept rubbing his thumb over the fishnet strings, and it was kind of tantalising and kind of irritating. Like, get on with it! She wanted him to slip his hand all the way up her leg. She wanted him to push aside her panties, take one of those sexy, drawn-in breaths and just plunge his hand into her. She was so wet and she wanted to rub herself all over that strong hand of his.

'Cat got your tongue? What happened to the breathless kiss-'n'-tell account? You all right?'

Tesser raised her lids and looked straight at Jamie. His eyes were twinkling. The bastard!

'Hey, I'm fine!' Tesser answered, willing herself not to jerk her hips forward so that her pussy touched his hand. Damn it, her breathing was getting kind of fast now, too. With utmost decorum, she leaned over and picked up her cappuccino. She balanced it carefully in her hand, but her pussy was singing out bad 80s music: Touch me! it screamed, Touch me now! Jamie couldn't hear the cheesy Samantha Fox lyrics; he was looking straight at her, watching for any change in her facial expression, waiting to observe any quiver or tremble. Tesser wasn't going to give him the pleasure. She took a long, long draught of the foamy beverage. The coffee nearly burned the roof of her mouth, but it was worth it to retain the appearance of outward self-control. 'The coffee's not bad,' she said to Jamie in a conversational tone.

'Oh, yeah, it's not bad at all,' Jamie said, equally unflappable, and then at last he moved his hand further up her leg, his fingers skimming along her pussy lips. If he was surprised that she was wearing panties, he didn't show it, even though Tesser reckoned chances were she probably hadn't been wearing any the last time they shagged.

Damn him. He wasn't even properly touching her – just rubbing along the edge of her pussy like he had been rubbing at her leg. Tesser took another drink of coffee and this time she gulped it too fast.

'Hey, watch it there,' Jamie said, with a look of mock concern. And at that moment he shoved his fingers up into her hole and when she gasped he smirked.

He had got her very wet and very hot. Tesser held her cappuccino carefully, not spilling a drop.

At that exact moment, to Tesser's horror, the melody of a Britney Spears song drifted into her mind.

Hit me, baby, one more time!

She hated that song. Her mind was betraying her. Her body was betraying her. She was in thrall to her own wet pussy, and to Jamie's probing hand.

She had her back to the other customers, and Jamie was sitting fairly close, so Tesser didn't think anyone could see explicitly what was going on, but then again she wasn't sure this was the case. Ah, Jesus! I don't care, she thought. Yeah, yeah, fuck me, she thought, get your fingers all nice and wet and finger-fuck me, Jamie. Hey, how about it?

I-yai-yai, will-always-lo-o-ove you-oo-oo-oo-oo-oo –

Now Whitney Houston was invading her brainwaves. Would the torture never stop?

'Push your fingers in!' she hissed violently to Jamie.

But, instead of coasting along nicely deeper into her, Jamie's fingers kept up the weird tickling rhythm that now was not only familiar, but also very irritating.

Tesser held her breath and waited.

At long last his cool fingers moved into her wetness again, smooth as whipped cream. They glided on in there and she gasped, pushing herself down on him, bearing down. He grabbed her with his other arm and pulled her towards him in a kiss, probably so that the other customers wouldn't see him fingering her, Tesser figured. Instead of immediately fucking her with his hand, though, Jamie teased her clit lightly, over and over again. And all the while he kissed her like anything, his lovely full lips pressed against hers, his hot red tongue seeking hers out. Tesser's pulse was banging out a drumbeat nearly as fast as his thumb worked her clit. She felt like she was melting inside. It wasn't supposed to feel this good, this . . . emotional. Not with someone whose only connection with her was a one-night stand. She was going to drop her coffee. She was going to drop her coffee.

Their bodies were so close. Tesser's corset, and, by association, her tits, were smashed up against his beige short-sleeved shirt. She found herself noticing unexpected details of her surroundings, like the smooth acrylic texture of that vintage Sta-Press shirt of his. Like the way the chocolate sprinkles were dissolving on the white fluff atop a mocha belonging to the woman sitting

26

some distance to Tesser's right. Like the blue vinyl padding on her own chair, which was pulled right up next to Jamie's. Despite these snippets of clarity, she drifted off in a super-sensual haze, and every time his fingers rubbed at her she kind of floated off again, but then a sort of crescendo would occur, because she was getting more excited with every second that passed, and soon she was wiggling on the blue padded seat and now half of Jamie's beautiful brown hand was pumping into her wetness while his thumb was still spinning magic between her legs. The porcelain coffee cup was jiggling in her hand, in danger of smashing to the floor.

Tesser just closed her eyes and let him french her and felt his fingers moving down inside her – creaming her up soooo nice. She concentrated on the spicy scent of his aftershave and on the stubble on his chin kind of grazing against her own chin and pretty soon her mind's eye was flashing pornographic pictures of what her pussy looked like right now – all pink and hot and juiced up. His palm was soaked with her come and intense, needle-sharp pleasure was spiking out from the spots where his fingers touched her flesh and it was just sexy, sexy, sexy. He kissed her even harder and, just as he did so, Tesser orgasmed on his hand: on his clit-rubbing thumb, on his fingers thrusting deep into her, snug and forceful.

As the last tremors of her climax faded away, Tesser groaned a deep, drawn-out groan, and then at last she set her cappuccino back down on the table. She tried to ignore the fact that her hand was shaking like her favourite vibrator at full speed. She took a deep, steady-ing breath.

Jamie was sitting there looking at her, the thickened line of his cock visible through his jeans to the rest of the café as he leaned there against the wall. Tesser reckoned that the other customers had to have heard her groaning, but you never know – you get caught up in the moment and you're not really aware of how little or much noise you're making.

Tesser had the feeling she had been making a lot of noise.

She sneaked a look at Jamie to see whether she could tell if this had been the case from his expression, but Jamie himself didn't look like he'd give a flying fuck if they had been observed or overheard. He was lolling back against the coffee-house wall with his thighs spread wide apart, daring someone to make some comment about the thick, aroused cock underneath his jeans. No one said anything. But people seemed to be glancing away, looking anywhere but between Jamie's legs, even the posh totty who'd clocked him as he'd first walked into the café. Tesser didn't even know what the female equivalent of such in-your-face arousal would be – maybe the real-life version of the Starbucks mermaid? Legs spread, underwear soaked, visibly *wet*. Nah, it was too threatening – because if she sat back against the wall as Jamie was doing now, hiked up her skirt and parted her legs, stretching the lurid blue strings of her torn fishnet stockings so she could show off her bits, if she were to let the damp arousal on the crotch of her panties glisten for all to see, she'd never get away with it. Still, it was a tempting thought.

'Are you ready to tell me what happened now? What's on your mind?' Jamie asked calmly, as if he wasn't sitting there splayed with a big thick bolt of an erection in full view of the Sloaney tarts behind Tesser's back.

In a way she valued his good opinion, so she couldn't share what was *really* in her mind and nearly on her lips, which was that she was on the brink of humming some Phil Collins ballad, in a sort of cooldown way. It's my pussy putting these bad songs in my head, Tesser thought. My pussy quite likely has the worst musical taste in the known world.

No, she'd much rather admit to her public-exposure

fantasies, or at least recount what had happened back at the Cornucopia Theatre.

She started to giggle. 'All right, then,' she said, 'I'll tell you what happened earlier this afternoon.' And she did. She couldn't help noticing Jamie shifting a bit, particularly when she got to the part about blowing the American guy while the other guy stood there and watched. Tesser exaggerated her prowess a little, making out that she was actually a lot better at giving head then she actually was. Then she went hurriedly back to the narrative, realising that Jamie already had her fellatio-ability details on file. From three weeks ago. From the first time they fucked.

'– and so,' she concluded rapidly, 'not only did I get caught secretly filming them, but I damn near got clobbered, because at least one of the guys got pretty pissed off about it.'

'Bloody hell,' Jamie said when Tesser had finished telling him, 'that was pretty hot.'

Tesser was taken aback. She thought all straight boys had a real problem with gay male sex. So she asked Jamie if this was indeed the case.

'What makes you think I'm straight? That's pretty presumptuous.'

'Well, you fucked me, didn't you? Listen, honey, I know when people are faking. And believe me, Jamie, you weren't faking.'

'That's true,' said Jamie. 'I wasn't faking a bit.' He smiled and pulled Tesser closer to him so he could kiss her. He tasted wonderful – like cinnamon. Or maybe that was his aftershave again. Tesser guessed it didn't matter. The end result was that Jamie smelled, tasted and looked nice. Maybe a little too nice, actually.

'Your treat next time,' said Jamie, as he took out a five-pound note and paid for their coffees, just before they walked out of the coffee house.

'What makes you think there's going to be a next time?' Tesser asked. 'That's pretty presumptuous.'

They made it back to Liverpool Street Station with Tesser seeing neither hide nor hair of any member of the ghost-walk team, including those members she'd had sex with. They didn't hold hands this time, she and Jamie, and that was fine with Tesser, because, let's face it, it was all getting a little too nicey-nicey cosy-cosy, and if they kept up this way Jamie was going to be begging her to pick out china patterns at Heals or something.

They walked past the huge multicoloured and vaguely anthropomorphic metal sculpture that stood guard outside the station area. The sculpture always reminded Tesser of how she felt after a heavy weekend: split into pieces, one eye by her toes, the other perched on her ear. She didn't break her pace, but for a few seconds she gazed up at Jamie: he looked nonchalant and was humming something quietly – it sounded like that Samantha Fox song, actually, and this made Tesser redden because she hoped desperately that she hadn't been humming it herself. To Tesser's dismay, Jamie caught her looking at him and he smiled, lips closed, and gave her his customary wink. Tesser didn't grin back and instead quickened her tempo, her red platforms banging out a speedy rhythm on the pavement. Great, she thought, now he probably thinks I've got a crush on him or something.

But as she walked along, instead of feeling calmed down, she felt more and more horny. Admittedly, she could feel randy at a funeral, but today she was insatiable. She could only imagine how Jamie must be feeling, considering that he hadn't got off at all. But he seemed to be keeping his cool.

'Do you have any shows coming up?' Tesser asked as they drifted down on the escalators that flanked the train station – mainly to steer a conversation away from her lusty thoughts.

'I have, actually,' Jamie said. They stepped off on to the speckled marble floor of Liverpool Street Station. 'It's in two months. It's about hybridism and the morphing of cultural icons.' He seemed distracted.

'Tell me more,' Tesser said in a faux-coquettish voice, as she clattered behind Jamie towards the ticket hall, trying to get a better look at his ass.

'"Cyborg culture, old myths and a spit in the face at facile postmodernism" – that's from the press release.' The way his narrow waist gradated up to his nice firm back, that almost-swagger that made him look as cocky as teenager . . .

'Huh?' said Tesser.

'Never mind, it's a bunch of old bollocks, anyway.'

The way he swivelled round to face her – intense, searching. That genius flash in his dark eyes . . .

'Look,' Jamie said suddenly, 'I have to be honest here, and you can tell me to piss off if you want to. I just really, really, really want to fuck you right now. I can't think of anything else. I feel as horny as hell.'

For a fleeting second, Tesser considered whether she should act all maidenly and demure, and then decided it wasn't worth the effort. Prim girls never got off. She looked around herself wildly – up at the Tannoy, towards the trains, towards the chain bookstore where she had once tried to pocket a copy of *No Logo* and had then been apprehended by a security guard. She looked everywhere but at Jamie, yet at the same time she was well aware that he was staring hard at her. There was tension in the air.

Then she spotted the sign. The one at the head of an escalator that led down to a burrow of facilities a floor below. The one that said TOILETS CURRENTLY CLOSED FOR CLEANING. Jamie saw it at the same time as she did and immediately pulled her down the steps of the escalator.

31

They were both half laughing as they hurried down. Another yellow plastic mini-sandwich board that read CLOSED FOR CLEANING was still in place at the foot of the escalator, as well. They pushed through the turnstile towards the men's toilets.

'Hello?' Jamie called out, but there was no one else around as they walked across the slick, newly washed tiles. The whole place smelled of disinfectant and Tesser wasn't sure whether it was even legal for her to be in the gents'. Well, she wasn't trespassing, was she? But in a way she actually was: trespassing on men-only space. It reminded her of the feeling she used to get when she was a young tomboy eleven years old and had played in the otherwise all-boy Little League baseball team. She had thrown the meanest curveball in the league, too.

Now that she found herself positioned in the men's lavatory, she felt that old sweet rebellion all over again. She liked the feeling. Because men's toilets were fascinating by virtue of their sheer foreignness, Tesser always wanted to take her time checking out the alien features – the lack of tampon dispensers, the urinals. But maybe the close examination of urinals, at least, was kind of sick. Thank God the ones in this place seemed to have been scrubbed clean recently. Like she had noticed upon entering: the whole room smelled of disinfectant and bleach. It wasn't a bad smell – just very clinical, and the vapours made her nose itch. Her eyes caught Jamie's in the mirror, and he flashed her a grin.

'Shall we?' he said, nodding towards one of the stalls.

Tesser caught her breath. They were about to shag in the men's toilets. Well, that was why they had come down here, anyway. It wouldn't be the first time she'd shagged in a public loo. She'd done it before. She glanced quickly from left to right – just like I'm trying to cross the bloody road, she thought – and then darted into the cubicle, behind Jamie. He was rough when she joined him in the toilet stall, and she hadn't expected

32

that he would be. He grabbed her towards him and bolted the door behind her. She dropped her backpack. His hands were already all over her tits, already down the middle of her basque.

'Jesus!' Tesser commented. 'Hold on a second, will ya? Let me catch up to speed.'

But she didn't have a chance to say anything more because Jamie's tongue was halfway down her throat and he had grabbed her hand and pressed it between his legs, rubbing it over and over the outline of his erection like it was he who guided her hand's motor functions and not she. She took a close look at him. His eyes were glazed and his breath was coming quickly.

'All this because you didn't get off!' Tesser smirked and then ran a hand over the back of his neck. She nuzzled nearer to his throat, her warm breath stirring the tight curls at his hairline. He smelled of spices and coconut hair oil and ever so faintly of perspiration. It was a combination that made Tesser go weak at the knees.

'Don't mess with me, Tesser. I mean it.'

'Oh, yeah, a man's libido is a dangerous thing.' Jamie's eyes met hers. He wasn't smiling. But, once she'd started talking, Tesser couldn't stop. 'I don't think so, Jamie Desmond. 'Cos you've yet to come head to head with the full force of my *libida*, so to speak.'

Abruptly, she kissed him, and when the tips of their tongues touched, she felt like someone had kick-started her cunt. *Pow!*

She grabbed at the crotch of his jeans, and squeezed the bulge there. At the same time, he thrust his hand up her skirt and fingered her through her panties, and she sank back against the wall of the cubicle and sighed. She spread out her fingers over the straining denim, then closed them firmly together. His prick felt tight and urgent, pressing up against his jeans, and it turned her on even more. She stroked her hand over his groin, rough and hard. She was vaguely aware of someone else entering the room – probably the cleaner – but she couldn't pay attention properly because Jamie bit her lip, and she groaned. 'Jesus fucking Christ!' Her pussy was already getting *so* wet.

'Shut up!' Jamie hissed in her ear. So she shut up and unzipped Jamie's flies, and began to rub the base of her hand along the length of his prick inside his thin white boxer shorts. She looked in admiration at his flat stomach with its fine smooth contours, at the sexy contrast between his coffee-dark skin and the luminously pale boxer shorts he was wearing. He looked hot. She immediately wanted to strip him of his smalls and just give him a nice long suck. Her mouth was already watering as she thought of his stiff cock, and she lowered her head accordingly, already prepared to indulge herself in the act.

'Mmm.' She looked at Jamie and fluttered her lashes like a drag queen.

'Will you be quiet?' Jamie whispered in her ear again. Tesser could hear someone walking across the tiles of the floor, towards the stall in which they now were. So what? She opened her lips, ready to give him a Tesser Special, but to her consternation Jamie was lifting her up by the hips, and Tesser stifled an urge to scream out. He sat back on the closed toilet lid, still supporting her by the hips – so she guessed it was a good thing he was such a tall man and that she was such a slight li'l flower, a good thing in terms of the balancing act they were now performing, at least. She bit her lip to keep from cracking up, but instead of laughing she gasped, because Jamie shoved the gusset of her panties aside and sat her straight down on his prick. She was well juicy, but being impaled on his cock was a shock to her system. She winced, and again Jamie mouthed the word 'quiet' to her.

Tesser at first felt ludicrous, with her platform heels

planted firmly against the opposite wall of the loo, her knees bent, and with Jamie supporting her firmly with his hands so that she didn't fall off him on to the floor. But then suddenly she got in the swing of things, and she began to rock back and forth on his lovely thick cock, back and forth, just a little bit. The position made it a nice tight fit and Tesser quite liked the fact that she was the one controlling the movement and the thrusting. Ooh, yeah. He looked so cute there, panting, holding her up, his hips just thrusting up a little bit every time she bore down on him so that he could savour the full slick glide up into her cunt. One of her tits had come loose of the corset and was now bouncing up and down just as she bounced her hips up and down on Jamie, and she was so horny and so juicy, sliding up and down on his pole.

'This is fucking great!' she stage-whispered to Jamie.

'I mean it, Tesser.'

She could hear that there was definitely someone else in the room, no doubt about it, but she was just starting to get in the groove, just starting to get going, and his cock was just the ticket. He – it – felt delicious. And, despite his protests, it was obvious that Jamie too was caught up in the spirit of the moment, because, when Tesser looked down at his face, his eyes were scrunched shut under those trendy black frames and his short dreads were swaying with the movement of his head and, though his eyes were closed and his open panting mouth was silent, he appeared to be willing Tesser to slide down further on his cock, further and tighter and deeper. She did so. This time it was he who groaned.

'You all right, mate?' a man asked, from over by the urinals.

'Yeah, yeah,' Jamie managed to say, 'stomach trouble, that's all.'

'It hits the best of us,' the voice said, and Tesser heard the sound of a zipper being done up.

'Deeper.' Jamie leaned forward and whispered in Tesser's ear. 'You're so wet, love.'

Tesser flushed at the thought of her pussy juice making his cock go all slick, all the way down to its root. She heaved down on him, her blue fishnets tearing once again. They'd taken a beating today, that was for sure. She'd probably have to throw them away. Mmm. Jamie's cock felt bloody nice. She slammed her pussy down on him, her red juicy wet cunt encasing his prick all – the – way – down. It was the fuck equivalent of swallow-it-all blow-job. And Jamie was digging it, that was for sure, because his face was going all tense and then slack, each time she slithered her pussy down on him. She knew she ought to be making an effort to be quiet, but whoever had enquired after Jamie's wellbeing had evidently gone away and, besides, there had been only one pair of legs visible to someone standing outside the cubicle – Jamie's.

'Your pussy is so wet,' Jamie said again.

The prettiest pussy you'll feel all month, Jamie Desmond, that's for sure. *Let's talk about sex, bay-BEE. Let's talk about YOU and ME.*

In her mind there began the faint whispers of bad music again, but she managed to block them out.

Jesus, her thighs were trembling. Her mouth had gone dry and she reached a moment of revelation where it was apparent that the only thing to do – the only thing that mattered, really – was that she came, and came soon.

Fuck world hunger, the environment, a President-Bush-induced nuclear arms race – she could worry about those things in an hour or two – right now the *only* thing that really meant anything to Tesser was the tight throbbing itch of a potential orgasm. She was wound tighter than a broken watch. Jesus, his cock felt so good. Jesus, he had a sexy mouth, all full and pouting and dark red. Jesus, she loved to fuck him.

Risking her balance, Tesser glided her hand along her pussy, her fingers feeling for a moment the push-push-push movement of her cunt enveloping and then releasing Jamie's cock. Her hand got to experience the thing her eyes never could, at least not without a mirror or a camcorder. She closed her eyes and concentrated as she shoved her fingers down on herself and began to make hard circles around her clit, pressing violently, grinding her fingers against her flesh. That felt nice, too. That felt very nice. She was going to come in a matter of seconds. She could smell the disinfectant in her nostrils, reminding her that this was a forbidden place for her, a place all for the boys – but fuck 'em, she was here anyway; she was Tesser Roget and she had invaded this dominion and, with her fingers rubbing between her legs and with a nice fat dick between them, she was well on her way to bliss. She had nearly forgotten about Jamie, that was how wrapped up in her own pleasure she was. Mmm. His cock was lovely, though. She came – groaning, rubbing her own clit frantically, pushing down as hard as she could on Jamie's prick.

He was still pumping away. His eyes were closed and there was a light sheen on his skin, and he kept rocking his prick into her. He was breathing heavily, but in a puffing kind of rhythm that resulted in his gasps coming more and more quickly, so Tesser knew that he was ready to shoot pretty soon. As quickly and smoothly as she could, she fumbled down inside her backpack with one hand and drew out the pocket knife she kept there. Her pussy was still buzzing with pleasure. With Jamie's eyes still shut tight and his cock still a-fucking, which was still feeling pretty damn nice, she quickly brought the blade down to hip level. It was a good thing that Jamie had pussy on the brain, because, if he had opened his eyes, Tesser reckoned it might give him a shock to see the knife so close to his family jewels. As it was, she swiftly cut through the few remaining threads of the crotch of her fishnet stockings and then the sides of her underwear.

She clicked the knife shut, deposited it tightly and snugly in her bodice between her tits, and then pressed the fragrant damp blue fabric underneath Jamie's right hand, which was at the moment gripping tightly on her ass. As his fingers touched the moist material, his eyes flickered open. For a moment he stared down at Tesser's panties, unsure why she had done this. But he got the picture pretty quickly, and brought them up to his nose, inhaling the scent of her arousal, licking at the damp oval her pussy juice had left on the crotch itself. It made him thrust his cock even harder into Tesser's sex, and his genuine horniness was a beautiful sight to see. It had the effect of turning Tesser on all over again. She rode him as hard as she could, and managed to slip a sneaky finger down on her clit to enable a surreptitious second orgasm on her part. Orgasmo, part deux. Not bad, not bad. This time the sensation was bittersweet, and flooded her whole body with painful pleasure.

But Jamie was bucking underneath her more and more quickly, his nose and mouth draped with the torn blue nylon panties, groaning, and Tesser made a hasty decision. In a single movement she managed to lift herself off Jamie and brought her legs back down to the floor.

Jamie was so stunned that he just gave a weird sort of yelp and let his jaw drop. He looked pretty funny, with his wounded eyes peeping out above the underwear, like some kind of alarmed pervert with a Lone Ranger fetish. Had the situation been reversed, Tesser knew that her thoughts would not have been peaceful ones. A couple of former lovers had tasted the wrath of her tongue after 'unfinished' episodes, as she did not suffer the female equivalent of 'blue balls' gladly.

As it was, she didn't give Jamie a chance to really ponder the shock to his system, because she immediately got down on her knees and swallowed his hard cock, taking it all the way to the back of her throat. And then she pushed her wet lips back and forth along his erection, back and forth, back and forth, nice and easy, and Jamie slumped back and groaned loudly, completely giving himself over to her attentions. Tesser wondered whether there was anyone left outside in the wider washroom space, as now her legs too were visible to an onlooker, and Jamie was emitting a sort of steady moan, at last oblivious and uncaring as to whether anyone discovered them. She wondered, and then she sucked harder.

It didn't take long. The combination of her wet underwear and her mouth working his cock made Jamie jerk his hips more intensely towards her lips, and at the last moment he sat up, put his hand down to his prick and wrenched it free, spraying his come over her cleavage, his creamy jism showering all over Tesser's pale cleavage, making her *décolletage* look glossy and obscene, like polished and wet white china.

'Give those to me,' Tesser whispered, and shoved her panties into her backpack as Jamie tried to zip himself up. All the activity made things difficult. Tesser on her part stepped out of her trashed fishnets, wadded them up and shoved them into her backpack, too.

'Can't I at least keep your knickers? A little reminder of you?'

Tesser looked him in the eye suddenly. 'Give me yours,' she hissed.

'What?' His voice was as quiet as hers.

'Give me your underwear.'

He shook his head wonderingly, but he still smiled and lowered his jeans until they were bunched around his knees. He was ready to take off his shoes, but Tesser stopped him. She removed the now rather sticky knife from between her tits and, while Jamie looked down with some trepidation, she cut through the leg holes on

39

each side. She held the material, formerly an item of underwear, close to her face. It was clean, freshly laundered and, while it didn't smell of sex especially, it did smell faintly of cinnamon. She didn't want to have it for particularly pervy reasons – although that was an idea – but for some reason she liked the idea of having a token of some sort, a little spin on that whole boy-takes-girl's-panties thing. Wait. The word 'token' was too close to some jousting knight's romantic love thing, wasn't it? Call it a trophy, instead. That's right. A trophy.

Jamie pulled her close to him and spoke into her ear in a low, low tone. 'I won't need a reminder.' Her naked, stocking-free legs pressed up against his G-Stars, and this made her feel all sensual and slippery. His body felt great. It felt nice to be held, to be held so closely and firmly. 'Ready?' He looked at her before he unbolted the door. Tesser nodded.

They tentatively exited the cubicle – there was no one in sight – and Tesser quickly made her way to the sink. She deposited the jackknife safely inside her backpack once again and splashed her tits with cool water, then caught sight of her flushed expression in the mirror. She hadn't actually been too worried that they'd get caught. In fact, the whole time they'd been screwing in the toilet, in the back of her head there had been a faint titillating hope that someone *might* be listening. Coupled with the minor thrill of being in a male-only space, the whole setup had been arousing. Bravo, Jamie.

She turned around to share these thoughts with him, but he had his back to her, and was staring at a cubicle – not the one from which they had just exited, but one on the other end of the wall. From the partition was the clearly audible sound of someone wanking, the moans becoming faster and faster as whoever it was reached his climax.

Tesser rapidly finished washing – her cleavage was now rosy and glistening – and just then the man in the cubicle groaned loudly. There was a slight fumbling, a flush of a toilet and then the man in question exited. He was a really good-looking young white man, slim with closely cropped hair and green eyes. At first he exited with a smirk, but his smile faded when he saw Tesser, and then he only looked shocked.

He looked from Jamie to Tesser and back again. Then he gave a little laugh. 'I was listening the whole time. I thought you was two blokes,' he said, 'but I guess a bird is a pretty good blow as well.' He gave Tesser an appreciative once-over, which rankled slightly. 'You look a little like my girlfriend, love. And you, mate –' he turned to Jamie, '– you look like a fucking wet dream. Have a nice rest of the day, kids, whatever you do.' He whistled and walked out of the room without a backward glance.

Tesser and Jamie looked at each other and both started to giggle.

'Come on,' said Jamie, taking Tesser's hand, 'we better get out of here. I'm not sure if the next bloke in need of a piss is going to have that degree of polysexual tolerance. Plenty of guys are going to resent a pretty girl in the gents'. Makes it hard to concentrate.'

'Speaking of polysexual tolerance,' Tesser said, as they made their way quickly up the stairs to the main station area, 'think of those two men I messed around with earlier. Funny, isn't it? They were so up for it at the time, really into it, but then the American one goes all extremo, just 'cos someone films him having sex with another man. Go figure. People's prejudices run deep, even unto themselves.'

'Maybe he just resented being filmed having sex without first giving his permission,' Jamie suggested in a mild tone. 'I have an old video camera and I know how it is. People can be touchy about these sort of things.'

'Nah, you should have seen this guy. He was pissed off big time. Closet-case case study. I'm tellin' ya.'

'Hmm.' Jamie made a noncommittal type of noise.

Tesser walked him to the tube entrance and waited while he purchased a ticket. She was going to have to walk back to Hackney herself, because she had blown all her spare change on that Starbucks latte earlier in the morning. It would be a nice hour's walk, anyway. She was in a good mood.

'So,' Jamie said, as they stood there, awkwardly looking at each other.

Tesser was getting nervous, getting itchy to get away.

'Umm,' she said.

'So am I going to get a chance to see you again, without chasing you over all the low-rent events in town?'

Tesser wasn't sure if she took exception to his turn of phrase or not.

He was still looking at her. 'How about it?'

'How about what?'

'How about we meet up for an all-you-can-eat-for-four-pounds vegetarian curry in Chapel Market next week? Sounds up your street, doesn't it?'

As a matter of fact, Tesser was a devotee of those all-you-can-eat Chapel Market curries whenever she had the money, but she wasn't going to admit it.

The three-shag rule, Tesser. Remember the three-shag rule. The one she had developed since Noriko, the one that stated that she must never fuck someone on more than two occasions, because, after the third good fuck, inevitably, people start to bond emotionally, regardless of their previous reservations. They had now shagged on two separate occasions – the night they met, and now today.

'I'm kind of busy next week,' she said abruptly, looking away so that she didn't have to meet Jamie's eyes.

'With what?' He was standing his ground, not yet put off.

'I have to finish a film. For the Geyser Independent

42

Film Festival in two weeks. I'm going to be very, very occupied with my muse.'

'Who's he? Or she?' Jamie added as an afterthought.

'Very perceptive,' Tesser said. 'No, I really am going to have my head full of splicing and camera angles.'

She looked up at him. He was smiling down at her in a kind manner, as if he had expected all these excuses and wasn't insulted in the least. He smoothed a hand over his short dreads and grinned even more widely.

'OK!' Tesser felt exasperated but flattered. She would keep to the three-shag rule, but there was nothing wrong with being platonically friendly. 'It would be nice to see you there. The opening day of the festival takes place on the thirteenth, in Stoke Newington. Actually –' she dug through her backpack '– here's a flyer. My stuff's being shown around eight thirty, I think, but these things never run to schedule.'

'I'll definitely try to make it,' Jamie said, and he leaned down and planted a quick kiss on Tesser's cheek. 'If I'm not occupied with a muse or two, that is.' He grinned and walked away, whistling a tune that sounded suspiciously like 'Reach for the Stars' by S-Club 7.

Tesser stared at Jamie's back as he inserted his journey card into the ticket machine and swung his tasty ass through the turnstile.

For some reason, the thought of his having a harem of muses ruffled her feathers more than she would have expected it to.

She kept thinking about Jamie, with and sans muses, all the way home to Hackney, which totally went against the three-shag rule. Tesser was well aware that she hadn't given him the blow-off she'd normally dole out to a one-night stand. *Au contraire*, Tesser thought, and she stumbled a bit on her platforms as she climbed the steps that led first to the kitchen and then up to her cluttered boudoir. *Au contraire*. She'd given him a blow-*job*.

Chapter Three

*T*hrough the door, up the stairs, past the communal kitchen.

At a snappy pace, Tesser hurried past this social hub of the squat, managing to avoid inconsequential chat with her fellow squatties, managing even to ignore her two closest friends Kitty and Jake, who along with several others were perched around the kitchen table drinking lukewarm tea. The radio was on too, KLKR – the Hits of the 80s, 90s and the New Century, which was the station that had brainwashed Tesser into humming inane schlager-pop all day. Besides, there were some things she had to get straight in her head and she wasn't sure if she wanted to pick it apart in a crowd setting. So she marched onwards to her own room. There, she stripped herself of the green skirt and bodice. Even though it was summer, the walk back through Hackney had caused her bare legs to shiver with cold, so the next stop was the bathroom and a hot bath. She had dumped Jamie's underwear in a communal skip that she happened to walk by, because, to be honest, souvenirs weren't really her thing. It was all in the moment, wasn't it? But it had been a hell of a moment. While the water ran, she painted her toenails with Quik-Dry bright-blue sparkly polish and then sighed with relief as she finally stepped into the foam. She lay back in the steamy bubble bath, filled with gratitude that the council hadn't bothered to have the water and the gas heating turned off yet.

There was nothing like a good soak to clear your thoughts.

But the more she lay there contemplating in the bath-tub, naked and cosy, staring up at the ceiling with her arms underneath her head, the more she realised that she didn't have a fucking clue what to do about Jamie. She wasn't even sure how she felt. She liked him. She didn't like him. She wanted freedom. She wanted his arms around her.

The word, she believed, was 'ambivalent'.

Someone was rattling at the door. Probably Jana.

'Tesser! Time's up, don't you think?' Right on the money. Tesser resolved to enjoy the hot water for a few extra minutes. But then, the more she thought about Jamie, the more confused she got, until at last Jana started banging on the door and whining about getting in to use the shower because she had plans for the early evening, and Tesser hadn't come a whit closer to solving what she was now starting to think of as the Jamie Dilemma.

So she sighed, scrubbed herself quickly, got out of the bath and dripped all over the floor – which was *sure* to piss Jana off, and made Tesser wonder why Jana both-ered living in a squat in the first place. Free rent, probably, since Jana was such a miser. A hundred times, Tesser had watched her at theoretically informal house meetings trying to tot up on a calculator who actually ought to be paying for the tea bags that week. Her attitude went against the whole ethos of community living, actually.

'All yours.' Tesser stalked out of the bathroom with as much dignity as she could muster, towel wrapped tight around her. On the bright side, she was deliciously fatigued from the effort of five orgasms earlier in the day. She wriggled with pleasure. There's one thing I know for certain, she reflected – but her thoughts were interrupted by a shriek down the hall.

'I smell nail varnish!' Jana yelled from the bathroom. 'Did you use my blue nail polish again, Tesser?'

Tesser feigned deafness, hurried to her bedroom, locked her door – which also went against community ethos, but such double standards never bothered her – dumped her towel on her bed and walked over to the radiator and turned it up full blast. The one thing she knew for certain: the three-shag rule was a true one. Jesus, even she had fallen victim to it, once with Charles, years ago, and recently with Noriko. She had gotten all squishy and romantic and, in the latter case, had had her heart totally broken. She wasn't about to fall for it again, no matter *how* cute Jamie was. No way, nohow. Nope, my friends, find another fool this time.

She started humming 'Why Do Fools' – her mental soundtrack was improving – and pulled on a sleazy peach-coloured 1970s negligée that reached all the way to the ground, covering the blue sparkly varnish shel-lacked on to her toenails. Jana seemed to have quietened down – for the moment, at least. Tesser got her 814 XL Electronic camera out of her backpack. Jesus! Just think of the lovely visual delights that camera held inside. She couldn't wait to send it off and get it back from devel-oping. But hold on . . . Super-8 processing centres prob-ably looked askance at developing what was, essentially, porn. She had heard rumours that you couldn't even *get* porn developed if you weren't a bona fide (!) porn production company. And there were so few Super-8 developing centres, too. If she got blacklisted, she would never be able to get *Chain of Lurve* made.

Her ultimate Super-8 goal, *Chain of Lurve*, for which *The Passion Flowchart* was but a miniature warm-up. Her important, artsy, impressionistic Super-8 project, a sort of six degrees of sexual separation, detailing the happy daisy chain of modern romance where you've slept with your lover's ex-boyfriend's girlfriend. Tesser had decided to give Eric and Alistair a starring but anonymous role, making judicious use of their fine-muscled torsos and tight asses. Best not to risk it. But she could eventually splice some of this boy-on-boy stuff into the *The Passion Flowchart* short all by herself.

Tesser began to lay out the pans and poured the developing fluid, taking care not to let it splash on her negligée, for which she had paid all of twenty pence at a boot sale a couple of months back. She drew down the shades and blocked them off with cardboard before carrying the pans to the closet she had converted to a darkroom. Then she pulled out the film reel and slowly, slowly unwound it in the liquid. In a weird way, it was a rather sensual, even erotic process, this concentration of practice and skill in the darkroom. She knew the procedure by heart. She could do it blind.

Paint. Sex. Paint. Sex. Paint. Sex. There were only two things on Jamie's mind. He had been itching to get painting all the way home on the tube – for shagging always got his creative juices going, too. Now back in his Islington flat, he took out a Stanley knife and cut out a great long rectangle from the cardboard refrigerator box he had found behind the appliances store down the road. He wished he could gesso it, like for an oil or acrylics painting, but he had used up his last tub of the white goop. His dad had halved his allowance last month and Jamie was finding it necessary to limit his expenditure on such supplies. Besides, in a way it didn't look right for a self-described outsider artist to use such a conventionally expensive paint primer. But maybe he could just cover the flat brown cardboard with a base of matte house paint. Yeah, that ought to work. And then he would have a blank canvas on which to begin his next work. Cardboard: the poor man's canvas.

The intercom beeped. Absent-mindedly, Jamie walked over and pushed the button.

'Hello, my fine feathered friend,' Trevor shouted up. Jamie buzzed him in.

By the time Trevor pushed open the unlocked door, Jamie was carefully beginning to lay pages of last week's *Sentinel* down on highly varnished wooden floorboards. The flat, which belonged to Jamie's dad, was such a posh place that Jamie usually didn't even bother locking the main door to the flat once he was inside the larger complex, since there hadn't been a robbery here for twelve years.

'Caught you at a bad time?'

Jamie smiled briefly. 'Nah.' His stepbrother was looking his usual scruffy self, a bandana tied tight over his skull, nu-metal style. Trevor really tried too hard. Jamie suspected Trevor tried to drop the fact that his stepbrother Jamie was black into every conversation, scratching for that little bit of cred.

'Nice write-up in the *Sentinel*, bro.'

The Americanism was grating. Jamie tried not to feel irritated and glanced over at the wall opposite, the wall on which thirty completed paintings were leaning – some framed, some not. Thirty imaginative, colourful, highly detailed paintings, born of skill and energy and passion and love. Not a single one had been sold.

Not one.

'I see they made the most of that "never sold a single painting" crap,' Trevor mentioned casually. His ability to read Jamie's thoughts was often alarmingly spot on.

'Well, at least they didn't say I lacked talent.' Jamie slowly began to cover one side of the cardboard flat with pale house paint.

'Hey, give yourself some credit. You're wonderful. You've been praised – actually *lauded* – in 'zines across

48

Britain, you know.' Coming from anyone else, the comment would have been sarcastic. But Trevor idolised his stepbrother and the flattery was sincere.

'Don't forget my Yankee fanbase,' Jamie added self-mockingly, and just for a moment his thoughts flickered on the subject of Tesser.

'True! You're a starlet artist. Soon your day will come, Jamie Desmond – *soon, soon,*' Trevor intoned.

'Maybe.' To his half-horror, last month Jamie had discovered three US fan websites devoted solely to his work, though that was probably because he had created front covers for a cluster of counterculture paper 'zines in the mid-nineties, before the Internet hit critical mass in 1997. 'Somewhere in the shady underbelly of corporately thieved subversive photocopied publications, I developed a following of underground miscreants and freaks.'

'Anyway, it's not true that you've never sold a painting. You traded one to me for a copy of *Shogun Assassin.* Don't you remember? And the werewolf painting, for that stack of CDs.'

'Trading doesn't count.'

'In my new world order, obscure Japanese techno CDs would be an accepted form of currency.'

Jamie finished blanking out the difficult corners of the cardboard.

'Does giving paintings away for free to beloved and admiring friends and relatives count?' Trevor asked tentatively.

'Nope.'

'Does bartering them for paintings you admire by other artists count?'

'Nope.'

'Then they got it right, bro. You've never sold a painting.'

'Please stop calling me "bro",' Jamie requested.

'It's bloody amazing. Because you're good, br – You're good, Jamie. You really are. I'm a fan, at least.'

Maybe Trevor was right, thought Jamie. After all, that gushing write-up in the arts section of last week's *Sentinel* had waxed prolific about his use of 'subversive media', his 'extraordinary talent' and his 'alarmingly ingenious Boschian vision'.

'A lot of good that sort of acclaim does me,' Jamie said out loud, more to himself than to his brother.

Trevor flopped down on the big beanbag and took out a spliff. 'Depends on what you're after, whether you want respect from arsehole art critics or respect from peers that you admire.'

Jamie supposed he *had* experienced quite a few pints and congratulatory slaps on the back last weekend from his mates down at the Damaged Loon, the local Islington goth pub he occasionally dropped into. That was something, anyway.

Respect. Who knew what it meant?

When Tesser finished looping in the film, she closed the closet door and tiptoed away from her makeshift darkroom. She would never be able to explain it, but she always felt a bit of reverence for this act, for the magic of pictures materialising on bromide and silver. Developing film was like being at church, and it demanded its own rituals and respect. So she quietly picked up her camera and a couple of rolls of film and closed the door to her room behind her. She wanted to fix that fiddly reflex focusing.

She was halfway down the hall before she remembered her scant clothing. For the second time, she antisocially passed by the kitchen, but no one called out to her, nor did anyone say anything about her (lack of) apparel. They were well used to her walking about in crazy get-ups.

'Hello, Kitty,' Tesser hollered out to her friend – it

was a phrase Kitty was familiar with – and kept heading down towards the basement of the squat, where she unlocked the door and turned on one of the portable heaters. It was fucking freezing. She was shivering like a foal in the snow but the plug-in heaters should soon kick in. The building was a former working men's clubhouse and this basement was vast. It was kind of spooky down here, but it was nice to be alone. She moved closer to the window to take full advantage of the light. Jana had made the point at the last house meeting that they ought to try to make it less obvious that they were siphoning off the electricity and hot water. For once, Tesser reckoned she was probably right. She personally wanted to enjoy the luxury of nice long steaming baths and a working refrigerator for as long as she possibly could.

She ran her fingers over the camera and discovered the problem. It was easy enough to fix and she rectified it quickly. She pressed the start button to test it and then, at a loss for things to film, she hitched up her negligée and filmed down at her blue toenails. Yep, rangefinder functioning A-OK. The entire camera seemed to be working fine.

The late-afternoon light was still bright, and Tesser looked out the window for a moment. Jesus, what a day she'd had. All go-go-go on the action front and all this before the sun dipped low in the sky. Then she peered more closely out the window. She thought she could see movement from one of the back windows of the houses opposite.

She could.

Jamie looked at the now milk-blank piece of cardboard, glistening with lacquer. It would take at least an hour to dry properly.

'OK. Maybe I have the wrong attitude,' he admitted.

'Exactly!' Trevor said, excitedly. 'After all, it's fame

and notoriety you want, not money. If you wanted big cash, you could have sold your soul and entered the netherworld of corporate art.'

'Dad didn't cut you off last month, too, did he?'

'Uh, no.'

'I knew it. He's trying to encourage me to get a proper job – preferably as a bank manager or something similarly spiritually rewarding.' He pounded the lid back down on the white paint tin with the heel of his hand. 'Man, I wish I could be like this girl I hooked up with today.'

'Who?'

'Oh, just this girl. She's a creative type, too, but she doesn't seem to care whether or not she receives any accolades at all for her work. She just does it, point-blank. I've never met someone like her before in my life.'

'Sounds pretty cool,' Trevor said in an encouraging tone.

'She is cool. She's also cute and sexy and a real wildcat – and not just in the sheets, either. She said something about wanting to make a thirty-minute film on some dinky little camera of hers. And you know what the crazy thing is? She's going to succeed at whatever she wants to. She's amazing. If she were in business like Dad, she'd be lethal.'

'So, if she's so amazing, then why isn't she over here now, and why are you moping around on your own?'

'I dunno. She follows her own star. And I'm following *her* around like a bloody puppy.'

'You're *stalking* her?'

'Um. I'm not sure. For the past month, I've been lurking around every spot she mentioned the night we first copped off: specific charity shops, Conway Hall, the main Hackney shopping street, all in the hope of seeing her again.'

'A bird with expensive tastes, then.'

Jamie gave his stepbrother a pained look, and continued: 'Sometimes I was lucky, sometimes I wasn't. But when I did "run into her", she was friendly. Too friendly – casual. Like I was nothing but a minor distraction.'

Trevor was staring at Jamie with disbelief. 'Bloody hell, bro, you've got it bad. So she gave you the brush-off. She's blowing hot and cold. Oh, man, Jamie, don't waste time on those mind-game frigid types. They're not worth it. Believe me.'

'Well, I wouldn't exactly say she was cold. No, "frigid" is not exactly the adjective I'd use.' Jamie thought of her in the stall in the gents' and he began to grow stiff again. She was lusty and uninhibited. She was feisty and endearing. 'She doesn't sell out,' he attempted to explain. 'She doesn't care about social approval.'

'You seen her work?'

'Not yet.' Jamie hated this pretentious use of the word 'work', but Trevor was his stepbrother, so he didn't say anything. 'I hope I'm not going to be disappointed. I don't think I can deal with it if her stuff turns out to be crap. Or worse, boring. Maybe it won't even matter if it is.'

'Man, you have such a crush on her that it doesn't matter? You're hung up on her, that's all I'm saying.' Trevor walked into the kitchen, released the fridge door without asking, extracted and then cracked open a beer.

Jamie stood in the middle of his living room, staring at the paintbrush in his hand. He *was* hung up on her. And he still didn't have her phone number or even her address – apart from the fact that she lived in deepest, darkest Hackney. He wanted her. He wanted to hold her. He wanted to lie in bed on Saturday mornings and giggle with her. He wanted to fuck her until even the insatiable Tesser Roget cried ''nuff'.

Eventually Trevor took off. For the next two hours Jamie paced around his flat, until he started to get a little stirred up. He wasn't sure if he was horny or if he just needed to paint something. Because every time he started to think of sex he would think about the curve of Tesser's hips, or the way she bit her lip, or some romantic foolishness like that. He sat down at his desk with a feeling of helplessness. He had to stop thinking about her. Maybe his attraction was merely a question of aesthetics. Maybe he was itching to paint. That was what was bothering him. That had to be it.

He took out a pencil, some brushes and some old tubes of acrylic colour. Carefully, he put his hand down on the cardboard he had smeared with white paint. It was dry, crisp to his fingertips. He started to sketch idly. He didn't have any idea what exactly he wanted to represent, but like a tarot-card reader, he hoped that something would come to him. Then he realised he was drawing the tilt of Tesser's slightly freckled button nose. That was her pout starting to form there on the board. And he wasn't even intending to do a portrait. He had thought he'd probably do some imaginative landscape, surrealist and weird. Not some lovesick caricature.

He had been crushed when she had turned him down at the railway station. He was so sure she would say yes. Her face had been flushed from sex with him, her eyes had been glowing. And he had felt joyous, optimistic – like things were going really well. He had assumed she had felt the same way, until she turned him down and made that snotty comment about being occupied with her muse. Yeah, Jamie just bet. Jamie wondered how the poor sucker was going to be feeling when she threw him out on his ear. Probably like he'd been kicked in the gut.

Jamie knew the feeling.

To hell with her. He'd been dissed, and it hadn't been pretty. Now he felt bloody angry about the whole thing. He fired his pencil hard across the room – *smack!* – and then threw himself into his favourite beige beanbag. He couldn't make art in this condition. He couldn't even prep a sketch for painting. Seriously unbidden images popped into his head: looking down at Tesser's blonde spiky hair as she sucked away at his cock; Tesser checking him out as they walked towards the station; Tesser holding tight on to her coffee as he slipped his fingers between the lips of her wet, hot pussy. Fuck, fuck, *fuck*! He was angry. He was horny. He was both. He looked down at his jeans and even there was a reminder – several short flaxen hairs, like he'd been curling up with a spoiled blonde Persian cat. He shifted and got up. His cock was hardening, becoming tight and thick as it rubbed against the bare denim of his jeans, a painful reminder of the missing trophy underwear Tesser had taken as her tithe. He pulled his shirt up over his head. He was hot and sticky. His skin felt heavy over his bones. He would have a wank. He would have a shower. And then he would start to paint.

He gripped his stiffening erection through the crotch of his G-Stars as he leaned against the tiles of the bathroom wall, his heart beating quickly. Tesser wasn't the only one who could summon up muses at a moment's notice. He thought of her wet, warm mouth, and he began to touch himself.

Tesser couldn't believe what she was seeing! She stood dumbfounded at the window, drinking in the sight. She didn't even worry about getting caught looking, because the couple she was observing weren't too concerned about it themselves. It was obvious that they had their minds on other matters.

She leaned up against the windowsill, her camera still in her hand. The man was shoving it into the woman – really hard, from behind. He had no hair, but she could see he was a young man. He probably shaved it. It looked good, like he was some young techno hardcore stud. She squinted and tried to see if she could make out any body piercings on him, but didn't see any – that didn't mean anything, from this distance. He had a couple of tattoos, though. The woman was leaning against the window, her hands spread out on the glass, whitening from the pressure. Tesser could observe this detail even from where she was standing. The woman had long red hair and she was obviously enjoying being fucked like this, taking it from behind, with a little exhibitionist thrill of being shagged against the glass thrown in for good measure. Tesser could imagine how good it felt. She loved getting fucked from behind, with a big fat cock or strap-on pounding into her, making her go breathless from the penetration. She loved it. She'd tighten her pussy around the hard length and shove back hard herself, getting fucked more and more deeply.

She wondered whether the woman got as wet as she did. She wondered how it felt for the man to be fucking this woman, forcing out this joy and lust while the redhead's pussy squeezed hard round his cock, back and forth, in and out, oooh . . .

Tesser started to feel slightly horny again. She watched the couple as they shagged there in profile, the bald man's thick cock gliding into his lover's pussy with a lack of inhibition rivalled only by that of beasties on the Discovery Channel. Tesser's own skin was starting to feel tingly under the stretchy acrylic slip she was wearing, her nipples tightening under the thin beige material.

She had never been a fan of porno films. If she had to state a preference at all, magazine images got her going more than a movie did – which was weird when you considered her cinematic obsession. She was sure her former film teachers at university would say she had a need for the static, controlled image to be fetishised, or some such psychobabble. On the other hand, these same professors would have a problem with chicks looking at pornography in the first place. It was all that male gaze/female gaze bullshit: ultimately sexist PC intellectualism.

The fact was, women looking at sex was threatening. Pictures were men-only enjoyment. Her perusal of such images mucked up the aim of the market economy itself.

She herself was not partial to skinny airbrushed blondes with too long fingernails and silicone tits, but the real juicy ones in the sleazier mags with the fleshy hourglass shapes, who looked like they actually enjoyed fucking. The ones with oil glistening on their natural huge breasts and come dripping on their tongues and their asses exposed to the harsh glare of the camera lens, their gazes meeting the reader head on, unapologetic and proud. The ones that made you want to fuck them. That was what she liked. She had once wanked off to a *Saturday Sportlife* newspaper picture of a famous chesty blonde, a rear-shot photo: the blonde's tan, plump ass spread wide for the onlooker. When she had masturbated Tesser had imagined what it would be like to fuck her from behind herself. She hadn't been the target readership, she was sure of that. So, paper porn had its appeal, but live-action stuff never rolled her socks up.

But now, watching this redhead get fucked by the bald man, knowing that this was really going on and wasn't just a staged money shot for some sleaze merchant, well ... this was a little different. She put the camera up to her eye and used the power-zoom lens. Even better: she could almost feel the heat coming off the couple as the woman started to masturbate with the man still plunging into her from behind. Tesser squinted so that she could better see the lovely, silky wetness glistening on the man's cock whenever he pulled out a bit. The woman's skin was succulent, juicy and smooth like the polished skin of a ripe nectarine. There was a thin layer of perspiration on her brow; her hair was now hanging down over her face and the heavy auburn mass kept Tesser from seeing her expression. The guy's bald head was shining. He had a rock-hard, pale, muscled body. Upper-arm tattoos seemed to have made a comeback, Tesser noted, thinking of Alistair – or was it Eric? – back at the music-hall theatre. No, she couldn't even see the vague outline of the woman's face, but there was little doubt that she was enjoying it because she had begun to push her fanny back against each thrust the shaven-headed guy delivered, and also had begun to move her fingers more and more rapidly over her clit. Jesus, she looked hot. Her clit was probably stiff and wet; her pussy was probably drenched. Tesser wanted to drink her up.

She wished she could make out their faces more clearly, but, other than the general idea that the man was bald and the woman had long red hair and they were both fit and horny as hell, she couldn't discern the finer details. Still her camera whirred away. Maybe she should consider a career as a pornographer – they made a lot of money, didn't they? – but that industry was as plastic as the music business. And talk about stereotyping! She'd never have the stomach for it.

Their window was open. She wished she had a tape recorder running, because this particular camera, her baby, actually had a pulse generator for synchronous sound. In this instance, her little darlin' was deaf. She wondered whether she would be able to hear the sounds they were making if her window, like theirs, was open. Why not try? She balanced the camera in one hand, unlocked the window and carefully, slowly slid it up. 'The camera as voyeur', she *could* hear one of her former professors saying in her head. At least it wasn't Phil Collins this time. And she could hear them! The man was groaning loudly and the woman was making some sort of high-pitched whinnying moan, and there was that obscenely juicy slap-slap-slap noise as they fucked, like their genitals were glued to each other like a well-lubricated piston, easing back and forth, a sex machine oiled by wetness, perspiration and lust.

Get on down, like a sex machine!

And there was little chance they could hear her camera, which suited her to a T – it would suck if she were to be caught filming a couple for the second time in one day. Hey, maybe she ought to become a pornographer after all. Nah. Besides, she could finish up this B/W film and develop it herself in time for the festival, at the same time sending off her tamer colour footage to a developing house, and maybe splice both sex episodes, boy–boy and boy–girl, into her current short, in an artsy, lyrical kind of way. Tesser adjusted the power zoom, feeling slightly idiotic for filming in her nightgown in broad daylight. But there you go.

Oh, man. He was really starting to go for it, now. Tesser kept on filming, stretching her arm out at first to get a better view and then carefully refocusing. She felt desperately aroused as she watched the man's hips slam into the woman, and again she didn't know which of the two she would rather be. Impatiently, she pulled up the hem of the negligée, so that she could seek out her pussy with her free hand. If – she – could – just – touch – herself ... Lovely. She was so wet, all slippery, and Tesser fondled herself while continuing to film; continuing to capture the lovely, slurpy, pounding fuck opposite. She began to shake as her wanking grew faster and more intense, and just before the film ran out she saw the woman arch her back, her hand between her legs, and saw the man give a huge lustful push into the redhead. Tesser sank down on the cold concrete of the basement floor out of view, leaned back against the wall and rubbed herself silly. She rather hoped that no one would enter the basement at this point and find her sunk down on her ass with her legs spread wide, stroking herself between her legs so quickly that she fancied her hand was a blur. But, even if someone were to come in, Tesser knew she wouldn't be able to stop. She'd look up at them with her flushed face, groan and then go straight back to rubbing her pussy as she was doing

59

now, rubbing herself briskly and sweetly towards a climax.

The camera lay forgotten to her side, but the images it contained were still clear in Tesser's mind as she masturbated, fingers plunging quickly and wetly in and out of her pussy, fingers rubbing up and down over her clit. It – felt – so – fucking – good. The images were very clear indeed.

Afterwards she went and took another bath – which was sure to piss off Jana – and had another wank, this time thinking of Jamie. To her irritation. She had assumed that the earlier afternoon session had meant that she would get him out of her system.

'Besides,' Tesser added to the conversation she was having with Kitty on the numeric value assigned to a man's cuteness in determining his put-up-ability quotient (Tesser's opinion: a high numeric value), 'I have more important things than Jamie to worry about.'

Tesser was sitting in her bathrobe in the kitchen later that evening, chatting and nursing her cup of PG Tips tea. It was the third time around for the tea bag in question and the beverage was starting to look a bit anaemic no matter how hard she pressed the bag against the side of the mug with her spoon. Thank God they had more potent stimulation in the form of a fine skunk spliff that Kitty had generously donated to the festivities.

'Such as?'

'I need to get some dosh. How else am I supposed to fund *Chain of Lurve*?'

'*Chain of Lurve*?'

'The follow-up to my soon-to-be-celebrated short, *The Passion Flowchart*.'

Kitty handed the joint to Tesser and switched immediately over to taking a swig from the whisky flask she always carried around. 'When you say funding, how much are we talking?' Tesser suspected Kitty might have a drink problem, but had always felt nervous asking her about it, in case her friend brained her with the small chrome-plated flask.

Tesser took her time answering, inhaling the grass deeply and holding it until her lungs were bursting. She blew it out and then spoke. 'Each reel costs thirteen pounds, developing included; each reel is only about three minutes, and to make a colour thirty-minute film means the budget has to be in the region of a hundred and fifty pounds, minimum. Allowing for mistakes, dodgy acting and the like.'

Kitty swallowed hard and smacked her lips, screwing the lid back on her flask again and hiding it back in one of her jacket pockets. 'That's madness. You should switch over to DVD, like everyone else. Even video. Especially old-format video. It's cheap.'

'Yeah, I know, but I'm a purist. And I like the Super-8 aesthetic. Besides, there's absolutely no way I could afford the equipment.' She took another quick puff off the spliff.

Kitty seemed rather unsympathetic. 'We're all of us skint, Tesser. I'm a mature student, for chrissakes. I hear we're in for another recession soon. I haven't even recovered from the last one.'

'Look, I'm having cash-flow problems even at subsistence level. Even the bag of potato crisps I'm eating at the moment was acquired by dubious means.'

'Yeah?' Kitty's interest had been piqued at last. 'I figured you just pilfered them from Jana, as usual. And hand over that spliff, by the way.'

Tesser reluctantly proffered the joint back to Kitty. 'This carbohydrate-rich snack is the result of the semi-legal exchange of a ten-pound book voucher I received as a winter solstice present from Jake, who in turn had received it as a complimentary perk of his job in the museum bookstore. I went to Waterstones and bought one of those sixty-pence Penguin mini-books – *The Diary*

61

of an Opium Eater, on your recommendation, actually – and then pocketed the subsequent change. And even that windfall came about only because I flirted with the till attendant. Nine real pounds and forty pence to spend as I please. Minus the thirty-five-pence price tag on this crisp packet.'

'I see the problem.'

Tesser was irked by her friend's tone. 'Honestly, Kitty, I am trying my best to make ends meet.'

'Hmm – sounds to me like you've been indulging in a few luxuries, judging by the morning you had.'

'OK, OK, OK.' Tesser knew Kitty was right. 'I shouldn't have squandered my bus money on that fucking latte. I know Starbucks means multinational exploitation and all that. It's just that they do pretty nice coffee, and I needed a caffeine fix, bad.'

'I was actually talking about the money you doled out for one of those walks you pick up men on. What are they called? Ghost walks. Those ones.'

'It's cheaper than spending money on some loser club full of drunken yobs or buying drinks in a pub until either a man or myself gets up the courage to make a move.'

'Granted. Though if only you had my demure charisma, you'd be snapped up before you laid your money on the bar, anyway. The minute you walked in the joint.' Saying so, Kitty began to sing, placing her joint between two fingers and 'walking' it across the kitchen table. *'Hey, big spender! Spe-e-nd a little time with me . . .'*

Tesser, who was by now slightly stoned, giggled at the idea of Kitty looking demure enough to be picked up by a guy at a bar. She was a stunner – a law student with a shaved head and bright-blue eyes – but demure and pliable wasn't the look she had. 'Listen, girl – I know all about saving money. When I was working at various temping McJobs back in Seattle, I specialised in employment-level time-crime: photocopying 'zines for my friends, searching the Net whenever the big boss had his back turned, writing poetry on the pink telephone memo pad doled out to all temporary receptionists.'

'Wooo. Watch out, WTO.'

'Come on. Hear me out. These liberties were just the tip of the iceberg: there was a whole set of antisocial behaviour that had kept me getting up in the morning.'

'Let me guess: many small, petty, insignificant crimes which you felt entirely justified and even socially victorious – as only the truly broke can feel – in committing.'

'Uh, yeah. Got it in one. I don't want to be rich, Kitty – truly, I don't. I don't want the lifestyle or the headaches that go with it. But it's catch-22, see, because without money I can't do art that's *anti*-money.'

'So why don't you check out the bulletin board at the university? They always have some sort of weird jobs going. Drug experiments, if nothing else. You did some last summer.'

'I'll think about it.' Tesser took a long, thoughtful drag of the spliff. Only as a last resort, she mentally added.

'The job board's right there in the lobby when you walk in, same place as always. I'm sure they have an online version, too.'

Tesser coughed, and it was necessary for Kitty to pound her back for a few seconds until she recovered. 'I said, I'll think about it.'

'Think about it all you want, but don't come whining to me about needing dosh if you're not going to do something about it. Listen, I've got to split. The honey pot is never empty.'

'Encouraging cockney rhyming slang on the subject of funds?'

'No, it's my own little idiolect. I have to take a slash. PG Tips goes right through me, at least by the third cup. Later, chica.'

Yuck.

* * *

Jamie had got hold of his muse, all right, and after an evening of posing and fucking and sucking and licking, the muse had tossed her short blonde hair, shoved her toes back into the kitten heels she'd come in, in both senses, and had taken off back to the inner recesses of his oversexed mind. He had wanked away an entire evening, but at last Jamie felt relaxed enough to paint. Satisfied. He'd got that crazy American girl off his mind at last.

This time he started on the cardboard he had prepped earlier, and was soon into painting a tangled dystopian forest of weird, sexually fruiting flowers and strangely menacing trees.

And the next day Tesser's not-so-naughty colour Super-8 film went off for professional processing. The boy-on-boy B/W porn she'd developed herself the night before had come out beautifully, as had the B/W Peeping Tom stuff from the folks opposite that she brought to life in her developing pan the following day. She decided to keep the neighbours to herself, and to splice a bit of the Eric–Alistair action into *The Passion Flowchart*. She wasn't sure how it would fit into the narrative, at least not yet. She'd figure something out, though. Something subversive and homoerotic.

And she had professional scruples, of course. She wasn't going to use their faces on film – just their sweaty, fucking bodies. *Voilà*. Ladies and gentlemen, I give you Mr X and Mr XXX. Just look at their cocks. Now that's a whole lotta love.

Chapter Four

Jamie was absent-mindedly stirring a cup of instant coffee when Trevor barged into the flat. Must start locking door, thought Jamie, must start locking door.

Trevor took one look at the brand of coffee on the table and snorted in disgust. 'That stuff is evil, mate; you shouldn't be drinking that shit. They force women to nurse their babies on chocolate milk formula instead of proper breast milk.'

'Huh?' Jamie was so distracted he barely heard Trevor. 'Get a job, trust-fund kid,' he reacted at last. Trevor gave him a reproving look and waited. 'Oh, right. I won't buy it next time, if it gets on your tits.'

Trevor smiled only very slightly at Jamie's joke and rolled his eyes. 'What's eating you?'

Suddenly Jamie lifted his head up. 'Hey. Have you ever heard of Geyser?'

'A club? A restaurant? An Icelandic fountain?'

Jamie gave him a look. He got up and returned with a piece of paper. 'How about this? Does this sound any good to you?'

They were both staring at a flyer that read:

GEYSER – AN EXPLOSION OF UNDERGROUND NO-BUDGET, LO-BUDGET CINEMA. OPENING NIGHT OF FESTIVAL FRIDAY 13 JULY.

'Hmm,' said Trevor. 'This has to do with that girl again, doesn't it? The one you were telling me about.'

'Look, the thirteenth of July is tomorrow night, OK?'

Trevor looked at Jamie suspiciously. 'Yeah . . .'

'Well, you're coming with me.'

'Christ, Jamie. I hate that kind of shit.'

'A housewide ban on evil coffee brands, that's what I offer you in return.'

'Well, OK . . .' said Trevor. 'Only for the eventual destruction of the multinationalist economic system, though.'

'I thought you'd see reason, at last.'

She went on two ghost walks in the fourteen days between seeing Jamie in Spitalfields and the start of the Geyser festival: *Boo! Battersea Boo!* and *Spirits of the Tower*. The second was a repeat – the grizzled old tour guide recognised her, and intimated that perhaps her presence meant she intended to *learn* something this time, as perhaps she hadn't been paying enough attention the last time she went on the Tower walk. Tesser could barely remember last time – a girlish boy called Flynn, she thought, but she sulked throughout *Spirits of the Tower* this time around and it ended up being a zero-action situation. During the former, which took place in Battersea Park, Tesser picked up a repressed librarian named Marlene. They had just started snogging behind one of the park statues when a park worker approached, thinking there was a mugging taking place. The librarian had fled, leaving Tesser to explain things to the embarrassed groundsman.

So, while she'd had some creative success with the film editing, it hadn't been a lucky fortnight in terms of nookie. And, because she had spent a sizable portion of her meagre funds on two unvictorious ghost walks, she now had only ten pounds left for the month of July, which meant she had to stay at home because she was too broke to go out. Thank God the festival started tomorrow night. It gave her something to look forward to – the world premiere of *The Passion Flowchart*: a touching story of lust in stop-frame animation and semi-photo-documentary style. Hell, yes!

And it gave her something to look forward to other than an empty larder. Maybe she should try to scavenge some breakfast. She rifled through the cupboard, finding nothing of her own to munch on. She took a quick look around and then reached up to the top shelf and retrieved one of Jana's huge unopened bags of cheese and onion crisps. Jana loved to purchase the type of food that really appealed when a person wanted a quick snack, and then would snap at you when she found out you had succumbed. Anyway, Tesser promised herself, she would repay her when she got the money.

She crunched away on Jana's tangy crisps as she considered her money problems. It was so difficult to live here when you weren't gainfully employed and weren't on unemployment benefit, either. She would look into whether – as a dual citizen – she was eligible for the dole, but even so they would probably insist that she work in some soulless McJob. At least Britain *had* a dole. Back in Seattle when she had been really broke she had donated blood – $25 every two weeks for plasma. That had been a regular source of bucks. An extra £50 a month and couple of crackers and herbal teas in the bargain. Now she was in a country where even 'herbal' itself was a foreign word with an extra H. A country where it was felt immoral to pay people for blood donations. For once, Tesser appreciated the in-your-face pragmatic capitalism of the United States.

She popped another crisp between her lips. What would be the next step in her downward slide? Waiting tables? Stripping? She didn't have the time to work nights nor the numbness to work 'nites'.

Damn. She just remembered it was her turn to buy the groceries.

Of course, if she got a job, she wouldn't be the only beneficiary. The revenue of local businesses would increase: fewer toilet-paper rolls missing from the loo at the historic Sutton House! Fewer empty toothpicks on the Hackney Tesco sample trays! Fewer barren-looking grape bunches in the Somerfield produce section. Less petty shoplifting altogether, if that was what you called such trespasses. Tesser didn't think it was, exactly – toilet paper and the odd grape were in the same category as ballpoint pens and umbrellas: communal ownership, essentially.

She figured she would have to take Kitty's drunken and stoned advice and pop along for a visit to the university bulletin board.

She didn't make it to the university in the a.m. as planned, though.

As she left the squat and headed off towards Lower Clapton Road, she grew aware that someone close behind her was keeping time with her steps. She whirled around. It was a young man in his early twenties, a few years younger than she. He was wearing grey trainers, army-green baggy trousers and a bright-red clubber T-shirt. His dark, straight hair was cut long in front and short in back, New Romantic style. Or is that nu-New Romantic? Tesser thought worriedly. Never mind. Doesn't matter. She slowed her pace and, sure enough, Mr Trendy hung back, too.

He smiled shyly. 'I'm Karan.'

'Tesser.' They shook hands.

'You live round here?'

'No,' Tesser lied. She never told a guy where she lived, usually, otherwise they would end up throwing pebbles at her windows all night or serenading her or something.

Well, that was that. They continued walking towards the bus stop for another minute, and then Karan reached for her hand. A half-minute more and they were kissing like teenagers, stalled on the pavement while tardy 10 a.m. commuters swarmed past on either side.

Karan came up for air for a few seconds, breathless. 'You want to come back to my place?' he asked. 'My flatmates are already gone. I had a late start.'

Why the hell not? Tesser's skin felt desirous, tingly under the hooded sweatshirt and denim skirt combo she had thrown on. And his body was firm and lean. So she went back with him and they giggled and got stoned, and he let her wear his walkman earphones, which pounded out, of all things, the cool-sweet melodies of the *Nutcracker* suite. All this while he pushed up her skirt and pushed down her tights and underwear and then buried his face between her legs and licked her until she screamed. Music blasted into her ears via the headphones as she came, which was a novel experience. Afterwards, she looked down and caught his eye; when she realised the little bugger had slyly turned the volume up, they both laughed. His face was slick with her wetness: his lips glistening wet-pink with her juices as he drew away from her sex and brought his face close to hers – then kissed her.

The taste of her pussy on his lips made Tesser horny all over again, his tongue gliding smoothly in, icy as a diamond in the raw red pink of her mouth, and they snogged deliciously for what seemed to her like a very long time. The classical music was beautiful, gorgeous, so she just listened and enjoyed the sensation of his lingering, sexy kisses. He was hard, but he didn't want to do anything about it.

69

'I'm saving myself for my girlfriend,' he explained, smiling at her as they lay side by side on his single bed, their heads sharing one pillow.

Oops.

'Got to go,' Tesser said hurriedly.

Karan, who was still completely clothed, turned his languid eyes to her and stretched out his arms. 'OK,' he said and grinned. 'Hope you make it into town eventually.'

Oops again.

'And that,' Tesser finished explaining to Kitty, 'is why I never ventured into town to check out the job bulletin board this morning.'

Kitty looked at her watch. 'It's just gone three p.m. You could still make it, you know.'

Tesser felt a sex-rush surge through her body, all the way down to her cunt, when she remembered how gorgeous Karan's tongue had felt tickling her clit. 'Sorry? Oh, yeah. You're right. I'll make a second attempt. I could ride my bike in, I guess, and save the bus fare. I'm so broke I stole three grapes from Tesco after the Karan episode. I popped them into my mouth right there in front of the supermarket security guard. If I don't get some money, I'm going to be forced into a life of full-scale crime.'

'Yeah – the moment Tesser Roget gets some money is the same moment there are happier proprieters in *all* of the local mega-supermarkets.'

'Despite the fact that most of my little peccadilloes occur mainly for the small and vacuous thrill of it all: the illegal copy-burning of CDs –'

'The stealing of sample lipsticks,' Kitty inserted.

'Yeah, that's pretty much as far as it goes for me,' admitted Tesser. 'Despite that fact, I do not steal in the big time. I guess I'm just not very hardcore.'

'Hardcore, schmardcore. Listen, after you had a

70

whinge the other day, I had a Robin Hood stab of guilt and when I found myself outside that posh and snotty electronics store up the road towards Islington, I even considered wandering in and shoving a digital film software package into my backpack.'

'Jesus! I'd never take that big of a risk.'

'Oh, don't worry. I'd never do it either, because I'd never get away with it. If I could, I would, though. On pure principle of distribution of wealth. But don't get me wrong: when people rob the little guy, I think it's bloody disgusting. People should take care not to screw over corner shops – though the capitalist pigs that own the mega-chains can take care of themselves, I figure. They wanted to book you for pilfering a grape, let them go right ahead. I'll defend you to the highest court. I'll take it *pro bono*. It'll be the case that makes my name.'

Tesser considered this for a second. 'Or how about exchanging a pair of Salvation Army charity shop shoes, if you leave your old pair in their place?'

Kitty didn't seem to have heard her, and she was on a roll now: 'Steal only from the rich! Even though the poor have fewer locks on the doors! You want to be able to hold your head high regarding these matters, Tesser, even if there is often no reward but virtue itself. And that is its own circular prize, and so on, and so on!' Kitty was positively flushed. Tesser hadn't seen her so riled up in a long time.

'Virtue,' she said carefully to Kitty, 'isn't a grace that I rate high up on the scale.'

'So what do you rate?'

'Avoidance of a long prison sentence, so therefore no computers. Like I said, no big-time theft.'

'No computers from small businesses, anyway,' Kitty said.

'Whereas second-hand charity shops,' Tesser pointed out, 'just don't have the resources to prosecute for an act of exchanged shoes.'

Kitty stared at her. 'That's really despicable, Tesser. I think it's high time you got a job.'

On the student noticeboard were several lucrative options. It wasn't the first time Kitty had nagged Tesser into picking up a few extra quid in psychology and cognitive-science experiments. Last summer, Tesser had exploited this option to the extent that even the Abnormal Psych research students ducked when they saw her coming. Though there had been that nice doctoral candidate with the trendy specs, the one that Tesser had winked at last August in the graduate student photocopying room. The really cute one. Simone, that had been her name. They had shagged in the women's loo on the second floor of the computer science building. Mmm . . . Afterwards, she had scribbled out her number and presented it to Tesser with a grin.

Tesser, of course, had lost the number on public transportation that very evening. Typical.

She keyed in a text message to Kitty – NOTHING HERE SO FAR! Then she didn't send it. Because it was 10 pence per message, after all. She had to think of her financial situation, didn't she, because that was why she was here in the first place?

She scanned the entire bulletin board, looking for something out of which she might make a few bob. There were the long-term drug trials, which were no good to her, as the cash came only after a year of jittering and drooling from side effects. Then there was a notice for brain-scan volunteers paid with gratuities, right-handed males only. Nope. In the liberal-arts section was an A4 page stating that French language tutors were needed. Unfortunately, Tesser Roget, French kisser extraordinaire, like many Americans spoke only English fluently. Shame, really. There were probably many dark-haired, bright-eyed young students, intense and eager, to whom she wouldn't mind teaching a thing or two.

Jeez. Slim pickings this week. She jotted down the number and details of the right-handed-males experiment. Maybe she'd give them a call and see whether they needed left-handed females as a control group. And then she noticed a card pinned in the corner, one she'd missed before.

There at last it was! Bingo! It was as if Kitty had somehow secretly known that the perfect advertisement was going to be up, although when Tesser looked closely, she realised that judging by the date it had been posted only since the morning.

STUDENT FILMMAKER NEEDED TO FILM CHARITY DOCUMENTARY & OTHER PHILAN-THROPIC ACTIVITIES.

Well, it would be easy for her to pretend she was a student. No problem.

WE NEED SOMEONE HARD-WORKING, EXPE-RIENCED AND IMAGINATIVE. GENEROUS COMPENSATION OF £250. EQUIPMENT AND EXPENSES PROVIDED. PROJECT IN COLLABO-RATION WITH HACKNEY CONGRESS POPU-LARITY TRUST. CONTACT THE BLAIRSTONE CHEMICALS DIVISION OF AMI INDUSTRIES ON 0208 328 3094 AND ASK TO SPEAK TO DR MIR-IAM SHARKEY, LABORATORY EXTENSION 552.

She quickly tore the entire notice down so that no one else could grab it. Two hundred and fifty quid would pay for her meagre living expenses, including groceries for everyone in the house – plus her film! Yep, if she put the money dutifully into her account, she'd be able to make *Chain of Lurve* a reality.

She went outside the building, where the reception was better, and dialled the number on her mobile.

'Hello, AMI Industries. May I help you?' said a receptionist with a frosty voice.

'Um, yes. My name is Tesser Roget.'

There was a pause.

'And?'

'And I'm trying to speak to Dr Sharkey regarding the charity documentary.'

'And do you have an appointment?'

'No, I'm ringing to get an appointment.' Tesser counted mentally to five in the ensuing pause. 'I'm a student of hers . . . uh, I've been doing work over at the, uh, the central lab. I consider Dr Sharkey's groundbreaking work of the utmost importance to my own studies.'

That was laying it on a bit thick, and the unfooled receptionist audibly sneered at Tesser. 'I'm sorry, you consider *what*? *What* do you do? *What* is your name?'

'Tesser Roget.'

'I'm sorry, Tesser *who*?'

She repeated her name to the receptionist several times, and in a moment of pure inspiration gave out Kitty's pager number for a reference. 'I really need to converse with Dr Sharkey. She called me, you know,' Tesser added for good measure, 'and it's been difficult for me to find time to meet up. Circumstances haven't been good.'

'Well, excuse *me*. I've never heard your name before. I'll just see if Dr Sharkey remembers you, shall I?' She put Tesser on hold. When she came back on the line, she wasn't able to mask her surprise. 'Dr Sharkey says to say that she remembers you very well, and wonders whether you might be able to make a five p.m. interview today.'

Tesser gulped. She wasn't used to her fibs working quite that well. She took down the address from the nasty receptionist. Ironically, AMI Industries was located all the way back in Hackney. Along the canals, quite

74

near to where she herself lived. If she started pedalling back now, she'd make it home in plenty of time.

She set off directly, so she had time to quickly stop by her place. When she got there, she paused to look lovingly at her messy room. She wasn't a self-hating slob. She rather liked living in semi-squalor and, by nature, distrusted people who could see their floors. But she didn't dawdle too long, because she had an appointment with destiny. She lugged her Super-8 projector plus the box holding the *The Passion Flowchart* reel on to the rack of her bike, in case she was asked to show anything to Dr Sharkey. She secured both tightly with a bungee cord.

Damn. She would have to cycle fast if she was planning to make it there by 5 p.m. Fog rose eerily from the canal as she glided past joggers along the south side of the canal system. She arrived breathlessly in front of an old brick building with a sign out front reading AMI INDUSTRIES. She took out her jackknife and tucked it into her bra – you never knew, did you, in these first-time situations? She locked up her bike as quickly as she was able in the parking lot round back, entered the back door and ran up a flight of stairs clutching her equipment, following a further series of signs labelled BLAIR-STONE LABORATORY RECEPTION. Apparently, the actual laboratory was one floor higher.

The reception area didn't look like a lab setting: it looked like any other reception room: bland, beige, boring. Tesser didn't know what she'd been expecting – lab coats, bubbling glass vials, flaming Bunsen burners . . .

'Can I help you?' asked the receptionist. Aha! That was the woman she had spoken to earlier. As well having a frosty voice, she also had frosted hair. And she was giving Tesser the once-over.

Yes, you can bloody well help me, you superficial bint. But she politely gave her name and vitals. Giving

Tesser a glare that made it clear that her time was too precious to be wasted on lowly students and chancers, the receptionist informed her in acid tones that, as her appointment had been made so late in the day, her chances of discussing anything with Dr Sharkey were nil, actually – better to make a new appointment now and show up tomorrow instead.

Tesser gave the woman what she hoped was a winning smile. 'I'm just trying to get my foot in the door.' Trying to get a foot in the door and moving more quickly towards the day on which her bank statement would detail the deposit of two hundred and fifty quid.

The receptionist ignored these friendly overtures, and instead punched in an extension number on her telephone. 'If you don't mind?' She raised a pointed eyebrow at Tesser and Tesser stepped away from the desk. The receptionist turned away so that her back was to Tesser and then whispered something in the phone receiver.

Tesser went and sat down. She took out her mobile and texted Kitty: IM HRE NOW. GIVE ME A GOOD REFERENCE IF CALLED. BUT R THINGS GNG WELL? I DUNNO.

The receptionist had that cloying loyalty to her employer that Tesser so despised. 'I can't seem to get through,' she informed Tesser. It was only too obvious she was lying.

'Look, I'm sure she wants to see me. I'm only five minutes late. She wouldn't have made an appointment if she didn't want to see me.'

Tesser's bravado did the trick, for with suspicious glances, the receptionist pushed in a telephone number and, after a conversation consisting of reverent, hushed tones into the receiver, sourly told Tesser that Dr Sharkey would see her in a quarter of an hour, if she would please wait. The triple-stuffed armchairs weren't as comfortable as they appeared. The minutes ticked by slowly. There was a chisel-jawed young man in cycling shorts, ones that revealed stalwart legs. He was only several seats away, probably waiting for an interview as well, but for once it was money, not sex, on Tesser's mind. She could pay for the groceries, pay off her overdraft, get a cat . . .

The receptionist was looking at her. She would have been so pretty – in a Sloaney way – if she hadn't been quite so . . . snarly. But why would an It girl take such a shIt job?

'I said,' the receptionist muttered through her teeth, 'Dr Sharkey will see you now.'

'Thank you *so* much,' Tesser said in an appropriately chilly manner, stumbling over the muscular and surely – if there is any god – genetically dominant young legs of the eye-candy to her left. She approached a room at the end of the reception chambers. The door was ajar and a waft of cigarette smoke was curling out into the greater reception area.

She hesitated.

'Come in.' The voice was low and resonant.

Tesser's first impression as she entered the room was of a lean figure with a large bun of grey hair lounging forward on one of those office chairs that look as if they actually do adhere to the principles of ergonomics.

'Close the door.' The voice continued to warble on with what Tesser had accurately pinpointed as an amazingly resonant quality – a voice that had experienced just a touch of whisky, or perhaps too many cigarettes. 'Please take a seat.' The hand holding the cigarette motioned to a seat perhaps five feet from its owner, an imposing and not precisely intimate distance. Tesser sat down, naturally, and waited for Dr Sharkey to speak first, for now it seemed as if it was she who had sought out Tesser, rather than the other way around.

'Tesser? Is that correct? Tesser Roget.' Tesser found herself dry-mouthed and unable to answer immediately. Damn. Dr Sharkey was a stunner.

'Uh, right. Most people don't pronounce it correctly.'

'Indeed. And such a charming transatlantic variation.' The tone of her voice made the word 'variation' imply unimaginably perverse pleasures.

Tesser felt ill at ease. The woman was gorgeous in the way a sleek, tawny lioness was gorgeous. She looked around forty and had dark, grey-streaked hair bound back in a tight bun, and huge grey-green eyes that were inquisitive, intelligent and dangerous. But certainly not kind. She wore a loose-fitting caramel-coloured wrap-around skirt and a long-sleeved apricot turtleneck, which was embarrassingly tight over her high, small breasts. Embarrassing for Tesser, anyway, who found herself trying desperately to look anywhere but at Dr Sharkey.

She suddenly realised that Dr Sharkey must have phoned Kitty in order to get a reference. Otherwise, she'd never have got the pronunciation right. Kitty must have given her a smashing recommendation for Tesser now to find herself in the cosy confines of Dr Sharkey's office.

It was not at all what she would have expected for an office along the Hackney canals. It didn't have the generic business feel that the reception area had. There were real velvet curtains at the window, amber-coloured ones, and the plush, leather-upholstered furniture was also the shade of warm, mellow whisky. The luxurious armchairs and the sofa and even the dark mahogany of the desk all looked brand-new.

'Doctor Ridley tells me you're an excellent worker.'

For a moment, Tesser was confused and fearful, until she caught up to speed. Trust Kitty Ridley to elaborate and award herself an honorary doctorate. At least she wouldn't say what any genuine former employer would have said: that Tesser was unfailingly late by twenty minutes every working day.

'I'm going to put my cards on the table.' The doctor

spoke in a rapid, tick-list manner as soon as Tesser sat down. The woman doesn't waste any time, Tesser thought admiringly, as the doctor leaned over the desk towards her, both her palms on the polished wood. 'Firstly, I want to find out more about you. I've already spoken extensively with your referee, so I'm anticipating most of the answers, but I just want to confirm some things. OK?'

'OK,' Tesser said.

'OK.'

The speed at which the doctor now talked and moved left Tesser feeling stunned. She was starting to have the sensation that her brain was being squeezed out through a garlic press.

'Well, let's first see what you have.'

Tesser looked wildly around for a socket, and, when she saw one, she plugged in the projector and screened *The Passion Flowchart* on to the wall. The feedback that followed would be her first. But Dr Sharkey, who was standing unnervingly close, said not one word through-out the entirety of the film, and, when Tesser sneaked a look at her elegant, fine-lined face, it was impassive. With a sick feeling in her gut, Tesser turned off the projector and relooped her film. She seemed not to have impressed.

'You're here regarding the filmmaking position,' Dr Sharkey said abruptly. No shit, Sherlock. But it was a statement and not intended as a question.

'I am, actually. Though it's video, really, isn't it? Instead of film, I mean.'

'That's splendid. Really. A *know-it-all*, are you? Charming. Yes, it is video, not film. I trust you know how to use a video camera.' Dr Sharkey tossed back her head and emitted a low, throaty chuckle. 'I also trust this . . . *video* camera won't skew your *oeuvre* to such an extent that you won't be able to participate, Ms Roget. We haven't had the response that we anticipated, and I

79

would hate to think that you turned down the opportunity because of snobbery over artistic medium. Lack of flexibility is a minus point, in my book.' She managed to sound both sarcastic and cajoling.

Yikes! She didn't want to lose the job now. 'To be honest,' Tesser replied, 'I think my *artistic* weakness would be, if anything, that I'm too focused on my work: too hard-working. Experienced and hard-working. That's me. And imaginative.' Tesser had a sudden fear that she might be quoting verbatim from the original noticeboard, but she wasn't sure.

At this last answer of Tesser's, Dr Sharkey slammed both of her palms down with a resounding thud. 'Your artistic weakness. Very droll, Ms Roget. All right, then – tell me more about yourself. And I don't want just standard interview patter. I want real information about yourself. I want flair. I want personal details that will convince me that you have the heart to take on such a project as this.'

Tesser stared at the doctor, open-mouthed. The grey-haired woman was openly toying with one of her nipples, stroking it through the thin, tight material of her turtleneck. Tesser was unsure whether this was conscious behaviour, so she averted her eyes and swallowed hard, looking at the floor. 'Um,' she mumbled, 'I'm Tesser Roget, single carnivorous biped of twenty-four years.'

'Oh, you're being flippant,' inserted Dr Sharkey. 'Cute. Please continue.'

Tesser was uncomfortably aware that Dr Sharkey was still rubbing the tip of her breast into a hard little point, so she spoke quickly, still staring at the floor. 'I live on the unfashionable end of London's East End, in a shabby top-floor room of a shabby squat. My room holds my camera, loads of funky clothes and shoes and a mattress surrounded by foil crisp bags, books and unfolded laundry. My line of expertise is Super-8 filmmaking, and the reason I stay in London despite my chronic skintness is because I have a – call it a feeling, a hunch –'

'Perhaps *prescience*?' Dr Sharkey suggested.

Tesser nodded, feeling like her mind was turning to mush. Now the good doctor was stroking her finger over the curve of her right breast, just inches below her throat, skimming over the material. Tesser imagined the creamy white flesh beneath –

'And this prescient feeling indicates . . .?' prompted Dr Sharkey, in a mock-encouraging tone.

'Um, that it's here in London that I'm finally going to finally make the thirty-minute Super-8 film I've been bragging to my friends about ever since I left film school. *The Passion Flowchart* is just a kind of warm-up.'

'Well, Ms Roget, I'm sorry to say that your experience is perfectly adequate. Or rather, merely adequate. And I was very kind to you, you know. I allowed you an interview when it was quite obvious that you had lied about knowing me personally. Though it must be said, I admire that type of initiative. Yet absolutely nothing you've said in person or that I've observed has suggested to me a collaboration that would show dazzle or extraordinary talent.'

For Chrissakes, Tesser thought – it's a goddamn charity video! Get real!

'Unless,' Dr Sharkey continued, 'you can convince me otherwise, I'm afraid my answer to you has to be "no".'

Tesser's mind was whirling as she thought madly, desperately, of diminishing hopes and dreams of *Chain of Lurve* – this was her one chance to get the money to make it; her one big break.

'Are you willing to convince me?'

Tesser wasn't sure that she'd heard the other woman correctly. God, she was a bitch but she was achingly beautiful, like a chillier Catherine Deneuve. Even the fabric draped so elegantly over her legs looked like it would be cool, sensual to the fingers –

'I'd love to be able to convince you,' Tesser assured Dr Sharkey. She imagined her spread over that fine, smooth, dark, wooden desk, her bare tits pressed up against its glossy surface, her yellow trousers at her knees, yelling for Tesser to stop fucking because she'd had enough. This was a technique Tesser often used when she felt unsure of a situation – imagining that person in her total sexual control, desperate for her favours . . .

'How do you intend to convince me?'

'Excuse me?' Tesser flushed, embarrassed to be caught thinking such dirty thoughts. Dr Sharkey meant convincing in terms of work, of course. 'I, uh, was a direct-action filmmaker once, so that we'd have visual evidence in case the police lied as they usually did, and maybe that street-look thing would be good for a populist video like you're doing, um, and I have a lot of experience shooting the canals, and I know the bad press Hackney Congress has been having lately, and I'd like to do my best to turn the tide of public opinion, and –'

'Ms Roget –' the doctor took out a clipboard from the desk and now pushed her wheeled chair closer to Tesser, so that she sat only inches away, '– do you really think that type of nonsense is what I meant by "convince"?'

'Isn't it?' Tesser could now feel that her face had become a searing, brilliant red.

Dr Sharkey didn't comment and her face betrayed none of her thoughts. It should be obvious to them both, Tesser thought, that what Tesser Roget wanted was money. Like a slow magnet, her eyes were drawn down to the doctor's chest. At least that was what she thought she wanted. The doctor's nipples were stiff under the fabric, her breasts like two golden peaches under the yellow material: firm and high. Tesser crossed her legs and concentrated on a small, dark mole on Dr Sharkey's face, a beauty spot placed just to the left of her lips. It seemed safer to look there, somehow.

'Is – isn't it?' she repeated. Jesus, she was even stuttering.

'If this is your persuasive argument –' now Dr Sharkey leaned forward and clasped her hands, and Tesser immediately knew how a mouse felt when being toyed with by a cat, because Dr Sharkey had obviously ingested all the information Tesser had fed her and was now going twist it somehow, wring Tesser's soul and body dry '– I'm not impressed. I *had* thought to offer you the position, but now I'm not so sure –' She broke off and hesitated momentarily, looking at Tesser appraisingly while she slowly tapped the peach-lacquered tips of her fingernails against her cheekbones. 'I thought artists would be more sensitive and perceptive,' she said abruptly. '*Are* you an artist, Ms Roget?'

Tesser's head was swimming. She didn't know whether she was coming or going. To make matters worse – oh, Jesus fucking Christ! – Dr Sharkey was opening her thighs, and the way that the wraparound skirt fell meant that Tesser could see all the way up her smooth, pale thighs. Damn, damn, damn her. 'Yeah, I am. Do artists get more money?' Maybe a commission was in order – perhaps even a patronage. Tesser leaned slightly forward, and looked down underneath the fringe of her eyelashes. Then she was nearly sorry she did so, because she could see every fucking gorgeous moist detail of the doctor's sex. Fragrant, lovely, obviously aroused.

Tesser was shaking with lust. She wanted to lick the woman's luscious pink cunt until she begged for mercy. Just look at it. A beautiful dripping wet pussy, all spread out there for Tesser to see. She squirmed in the chair, closed her eyes and prayed for the strength not to look down at Dr Sharkey's lap. She began to babble nonsensical lies: 'Oh, yes, I've been making art films for years, really.' But all she could think about was what the good doctor was showing her, albeit not on purpose, and desire was already pounding a rhythm in her own pussy.

I need to get fucked, thought Tesser. *I – need – to – get – fucked*. All she could think about was pussy. All she could smell was pussy. All she wanted to do was get down on her knees and ram her lips against Dr Sharkey's hot, wet snatch, rub her face against all that gorgeous juice . . .

She tore her gaze away from Dr Sharkey's crotch and smiled weakly. Dr Sharkey was smiling, too: a slight, rather cruel smile.

Was she doing it on purpose? No, thought Tesser, there's no way she could be. A woman like this doesn't go for an unpolished girl like myself. But then something went ping in her brain. Didn't all these high-society ladies have the Lady Chatterley complex? Didn't they all *really* long for a bit of rough? Tesser crossed her legs again and groaned, quietly.

'Excuse me?' Dr Sharkey looked up from her clipboard.

'Nothing,' said Tesser. Jesus! The woman was exposing even more, now. She made Sharon Stone look like a nun. Tesser gulped, and felt her face flush immediately bright red.

'You look quite warm, Ms Roget. Shall I open a –'

'No!' Tesser said. 'Don't open anything more. Just close – um . . . I don't know.'

'Just close what, Ms Roget?'

Tesser slumped back in her chair and closed her eyes. She felt like she was about to faint.

'You want me to close my legs?'

Tesser's eyes snapped back open. She gaped at the older woman. Dr Sharkey got up – she had the grace of a wild cat, as well – placed her clipboard carefully on her wide desk and then returned, moving so close that her crotch was at Tesser's eye level. The room was silent, but Tesser had the sensation that the whole office was dripping with moisture, as an apricot will do in hot weather, slowly sweating out its sweetness, liquid pearls of concentrated flavour. If Tesser were to stick out her tongue, she would taste the doctor's excitement. That was how close she was. She reverently lowered her lashes and moved her lips closer to the doctor's juicy, ripe pussy, soaking wet and so delicious ... Tesser breathed in the smell of cunt; the scent made her panties sopping wet –

Smack!

'Ow!' Tesser gave the doctor an injured look and put a hand up to her smarting cheek. 'You didn't have to do that. If you've got something on offer, you can't blame me for wanting to sample the goods.'

'You crude little bitch. Get down on your knees and apologise immediately.'

'What?' This wasn't how Tesser had envisioned things, at all. She had planned on going down on the doctor until the older woman weakened in glorious, delicious submission and sighed intimate things in Tesser's ear. Still, it wasn't often she was taught something herself, so p'raps she'd better bow to her betters. Besides, the thought of being ordered around by a strict doctor wasn't such a bad one after all. 'Can I be the sexy nurse?' she asked, impulsively. She envisioned herself in a tight blue cotton dress, with Dr Sharkey sticking a hand down her cleavage and rubbing hard and painfully on one of Tesser's nipples while Tesser squirmed up against the surgeon. Yes!

'I'm a PhD, you silly little girl, not a medical doctor. Now get down on your knees and give me a nice, long apology.'

Ah, now Tesser understood. She dutifully slid off the chair and began tentatively kissing the older woman's sex, slipping her tongue down into that gorgeous, moist cleft below the doctor's tiny, stiff clit. She began to lap rhythmically, flicking her tongue just a little bit. Oh, she tasted so good; Tesser's face was drenched with sweet juice; she felt like she could come from just licking her. Oh, yes, she wanted to come. Yes. The doctor was sighing. Tesser thrust a hand under the waistband of her own denim skirt, but couldn't reach all the way down. She was going to have to unzip it. She licked and licked, drinking in pussy juice, rubbing her face all over the doctor's snatch. It was warm and slippery and horny as fuck. She drew down the zipper and inched her hand south, south, south. Jesus, her fingers felt so good on her pussy. She groaned and began to rub, trying to keep up her mouth rhythm all the while. Fuck, yes. This was good. She pushed her middle finger into her cunt and ground her thumb against her clit. She felt hot pleasure: in her mouth, tasting the musk-sugar juice; in her cunt, as she wanked and wanked –

'No, you don't, my dear.'

'Wha –'

No! The doctor was gently but firmly pulling her hand up so that she couldn't touch herself. 'Please . . .' Tesser wailed, but the doctor's grasp was tight.

'The moment you start that you begin to lose concentration. It's rather selfish, Ms Roget. I'm afraid I can't trust you to go back to the business at hand.'

'You can trust me,' Tesser assured her. All she wanted was to lose herself in the doctor's pussy again. Or touch herself. Hell. She wanted both things. Or at least one of them. 'I'll be good,' she promised.

But the doctor advanced towards a wall cabinet. She was classy, but her figure was that of a sleazy showgirl's, especially her ass with its taut, high cheeks. She was just strutting around. Yet despite the fact that she was clad in only a tight turtleneck and a pair of expensive pumps she hadn't lost one shred of her dignity. Her ass swayed enticingly as she opened various drawers. Tesser felt her mouth water but, just as she started to rise from the floor and move towards the older woman, the doctor turned round, returning with what looked like a spool of silver thread.

'Sit on the floor in front of the chair,' she said to Tesser.

'Hey!' said Tesser. 'I hardly think that thread's going to hold me, right. And anyway, I'm not sure if I'm into all this bondage stuff, OK?'

'No, sorry, not OK,' Dr Sharkey replied. 'Unfortunately I'm going to have to insist that you're into all of it. If you want the job.'

Tesser thought rapidly of the thirty-minute film she dreamed of making. Then she looked up at Dr Sharkey and something loosened in her. Talk about dreaming. She just wanted to lie down in front of this woman and let her do whatever she wished. Oh, Tesser needed to taste her again; needed to have her hands against those strong, slim thighs again. She whimpered a little. She needed it. Fuck, yeah, she needed it. With a strange feeling of calm, like she was floating high on some cloud of sheer lust, she moved towards the chair and sat down in front of it, on the floor, legs folded underneath her.

She let the doctor push up the sleeves of her sweatshirt and then wrap the thin thread around her arms and fingers, binding her lightly to the arms of the chair with the silver thread. This will never hold, Tesser thought, but she kept silent. She was mesmerised by the sight of the doctor's crotch swaying back and forth, tantalisingly, as she moved from right arm to left arm and back again, tightening and adjusting the frail, glittering bonds. At last she seemed satisfied with her work and she stepped back, surveying Tesser. Tesser had that oddly reverent feeling again, like she ought to lower her eyes in respect. She amazed herself by doing exactly this.

'That's a good girl,' Dr Sharkey said softly. 'You look so lovely there, your legs demurely tucked away, your arms lifted up and your tits thrust out. Like a blonde statue, some sort of water nymph. No, that's the wrong allusion.' She paused and thought for a moment. 'Like Leda. I'm thinking of a particular surrealist painting, actually, where the cords hold both her and the swan in flight. Yes, that's right. And you're like a bound bird yourself, all tied up and nowhere to fly. Do you know the story?'

Tesser could only shake her head. She felt a heaviness overtaking her. The threads weren't tight at all, but her arms were weakening, since they were held up mainly by her own effort. She felt as if she were floating in some wicked, surreal dream.

'Now listen very carefully, Tesser –' it was the first time she had used Tesser's first name '– I don't want you to break a single shiny thread. Not one, do you understand?'

'Yes,' Tesser whispered.

'You're not being held by any cuffs or belts or ropes. You're held by silver thread, my dear, and by the strength of your own dirty mind. You break even one thread, just one, and I stop, and you're to leave immediately. No amount of begging will sway me, either. This is, after all, your second chance.'

'I know,' Tesser managed to say in a hoarse, low voice. She could feel the delicate thread biting into the soft skin of her forearms, but she knew that, if she were to shift, the thread would snap, and that would be the end.

'I'm glad you understand,' said Dr Sharkey, and with that she stepped in closer and lowered her wet pussy down on Tesser's face. 'Lick me, you smug little bitch.'

Oh, God! Tesser didn't realise how much she had been thirsting for just that taste, and she again started to lick between the doctor's legs, caressing with her tongue, all the while conscious that she was straining at the threads, threads that now bit like ice as she tried to move her head forward so she could lick one delicious swoop down to the older woman's anus. The threads felt like cold fire on her arms, from her wrists down to her elbows, but she couldn't break them, because then she would never get *Chain of Lurve* made; never get to taste this woman's pussy again . . .

She licked as skilfully and forcefully as she could, and her reward was Dr Sharkey shuddering and sighing above her. She knew when the doctor came because the woman shoved her pussy down on Tesser's face as hard as she could, her hips jerking back and forth as she rubbed her clit roughly against Tesser's proffered tongue. Dr Sharkey spat out the words, 'Fuck, fuck, fuck, fuck,' which startled Tesser, because every other word the doctor uttered seemed to be chosen with care.

Fuck *me*! Lick *me*! Tesser screamed mentally, but she didn't dare say a word out loud. She wanted to break the threads and thrust a hand up the woman's cunt, feel her and then fuck her. No, she wanted to be fucked herself; Dr Sharkey's fingers plunging into her; no, she wanted – she wanted –

'*Very* good,' Dr Sharkey said in an approving tone. Tesser hadn't even noticed that the doctor had stopped panting and was now standing over her, demeanour completely restored, examining the filaments that bound Tesser to the chair. 'This one's a bit frayed, but, overall, *very* well done. And such energetic licking, too. I'm really rather impressed.'

Tesser was so desperate to be fucked she felt like her whole being was on fire: from the roots of her hair to her toes to her arms, which were tingling from strain of position. 'You can touch me now, too,' she suggested in what she felt was quite a respectful manner.

Dr Sharkey gave a short laugh and ran her hand down underneath the neckline of Tesser's hooded sweatshirt. She must have felt the cool metal of the knife Tesser had stuffed down her bra, though, because she snatched her fingers away. She appeared to collect herself and slid a hand down Tesser's still unzipped skirt. 'My goodness, you look like a little tart with your skirt undone like this.'

'Please . . .' Tesser didn't even trust her voice. Please rub me and don't stop, she finished silently.

For a minute, it seemed as if Dr Sharkey was going to do exactly this. She skimmed her hand over Tesser's hard, aroused clit and dipped her fingers into the hot pool between the younger woman's legs. 'Oh . . .' Tesser sighed. That was perfect. That was wonderful. She had been waiting so long for it . . .

'No . . .' Dr Sharkey said. 'I believe you've convinced me already.' She drew her hand out and sucked on her moist fingers, flashing a bit of pink tongue. 'Mmm . . . Yes, I don't need any more convincing. Filmmaker, did you say? I'd like to have a look at your curriculum vitae, if you don't mind.' She walked over and deftly tied her skirt around her waist again – to all appearances completely at ease. Whereas Tesser was sprawled on the floor, bound to a chair, with her skirt unzipped like a cheap whore. And she was as desperate for it as a cheap whore, too! The doctor didn't fuck her! Tesser almost couldn't contain her fury. But she couldn't lose this job after she'd earned it so well – oh, Jesus!

'Don't move, dear.'

Tesser froze. Maybe now it would happen. If she kept very still and just let the lioness approach.

As if she were truly concerned over Tesser's pussy-anguish, Dr Sharkey now walked towards her with a sympathetic look on her face and, in a surprisingly quick motion, pushed her hand down Tesser's front, retrieved the knife, flicked it open and methodically cut through the bright strands. I could have broken them myself, thought Tesser – but she hadn't been quick enough and it was evident that the doctor wanted to do the releasing as well as the binding. For a moment she paused and looked down at Tesser and smiled. 'You were a lovely

Leda,' she said, placing a hand on Tesser's cheek for a fleeting second. She then carefully pushed the knife back between Tesser's breasts.

Screw Leda, whoever she was. Tesser wanted to get off! But it didn't look like it was going to happen.

'Curriculum vitae,' Dr Sharkey reminded. She was all business now.

'I'll email my CV to you tomorrow.' Tesser stood up. Her knees were trembling. She had to sit down soon or she was going to collapse in Dr Sharkey's arms, whether she wanted to or not. At the moment, she just wanted to go someplace private and shove a hand between her legs. She looked down at the floor of the office. The only indication that something untoward might have taken place were the slender threads of silver strewn across the floor like last year's holiday tinsel.

'I'd prefer it if you mailed it, actually. I'm an old Luddite in some ways.'

Shit. Tesser could have used the Internet service in the temporary Hackney library. Now she'd have to pay for postage. It was evident that she was now expected to leave. Unfulfilled fun aside, she hoped this had been a sound investment. Her stomach rumbled and reminded her that she hadn't had a proper meal all day. Perhaps some of her irritation and desperation for money showed, because, just before she stepped out of the office, Dr Sharkey called out her name. Tesser paused in the door-frame.

'Don't worry, Tesser,' Dr Sharkey said from the distance of her desk, 'you've got the job. If you need money badly, Fiona will give you a sub of fifty pounds. She has that much in the petty-cash box, so make an appointment for Wednesday morning at eleven on your way out and tell her I approved the sub. I won't need you the rest of the week, but Wednesdays are important.'

Money at last. Financial, if not physical, relief flooded

through Tesser. She said goodbye and carefully closed the door behind her.

But Fiona wasn't having any of it, and the surly receptionist made a point of calling Dr Sharkey's extension to confirm the sub. It was only afterwards that she suspiciously counted out fifty pounds in cash – thank you, Jesus – and noted down the 11 a.m. appointment next Wednesday.

Tesser had won the bid, so to speak.

She pocketed the money. It was only then, for the first time, that she felt a twinge of trepidation regarding her ability to perform the necessary work, all bullshitting aside. It wasn't that she was incapable, but there was such an air of an old-fashioned, mentorship style surrounding the doctor that Tesser worried that she might disappoint the woman. It was her teacher complex: a certain type of strict woman always had this effect on her. Deliciously strict. Yes, indeed.

Tesser felt a surge of self-esteem. She smiled to herself and then made sure Fiona saw the smirk – the dumb little rich bitch had been proved wrong after all. Tesser *did* belong here. She was a talented underground film-maker and they were lucky to make use of her skills. In the future, people like Dr Miriam Sharkey would be knocking down her door to work with her.

Oh, but Tesser was still horny. Maybe she should give Jamie a call. Yeah, right. And totally prove the three-shag rule. Nope. She'd go home and play with her favourite pearl vibrator. Yeah. And order some Chinese food for delivery. Now *that* sounded like a good idea. She eased her way across the floor, walking towards the door that led to the stairwell, and then suddenly she swayed, her brain caught in a net of vertigo. When she looked up, Fiona was sneering back at her; she must have staggered in the course of those few seconds.

'Do you need some assistance?' Fiona enquired nastily. Tesser didn't know how she managed to insinuate drunkenness, but she did. The door was still far away.

'No,' Tesser said. Her voice was thick. She felt weird. 'I'm fine.'

'You ought to sit down for a bit.' This was a new voice; it belonged to the handsome cyclist Tesser had marked on the way in. He was still sitting there, waiting. He had probably been waiting a long time. Tesser had no idea how long her interview had lasted.

'No, I'm fine, really.' Tesser had entirely recovered. Fucking lack of food, that was what it was. She tried to regain some dignity by attempting a swooping exit, but bumped her head on the door-frame instead.

Maybe it was the awkwardness of the moment, but their eyes met at exactly the right time.

'I need a fag,' said the fit young man, standing up and stretching his arms. He didn't look the type who smoked. Tesser grinned, suspecting a ruse. 'Will it still be a while?' he asked Fiona.

'I'm not a psychic,' Fiona snapped. 'If Dr Sharkey buzzes you in and you're not here waiting, you miss your appointment, simple as that. I'm not going to wander around London trying to track you down.'

'Then I guess I'll take that risk,' said the young man. 'Care to join me for a cigarette?' He gave Tesser a *look* as he addressed this question to her and she felt her heart begin to thump double-time.

'Sure,' she said, and she swayed her hips slightly as she headed out the glass doors of the reception. She'd gently break the news that she'd already acquired the job. Maybe not too gently. She looked sideways, checking out those firmly muscled legs. She had an itch, and, damn it, *this* time she was going to scratch it. Yowza! By the time they had made it down the staircase, she was blushing.

The young man wasn't blushing. 'My name's Andy,' he said, and then, getting right to the point, 'Why don't we go and smoke around the corner? There's some serious privacy there,' he added meaningfully.

Tesser followed him. Yes, yes, yes! He was well cute. A quick, satisfying shag was just what she needed. The Chinese food could wait a little bit. Sex before food. Good, her priorities were again in working order. Besides, this cyclist guy was nice and direct – in fact, he reminded her a little of Jamie. She fumbled for her cigarettes, just in the odd case that she was misreading his signals. She smoked only about three cigarettes a week usually, but a packet of ciggies was such a handy pick-up tool.

They were ghastly cheap menthols she'd bought from a man peddling them on the black market just around the corner from her local Lidl store, but their saving grace was that very few people tried to bum them off Tesser once she'd revealed their state of mintiness.

Chapter Five

*I*n a moment of idleness the next morning, she dyed her hair bright green. The rest of the morning she spent splicing and cutting and editing, putting final touches to the film. To hell with Dr Sharkey's initially lukewarm response to the preview. She knew it was good, and therefore she would get a second opinion. She worked like the devil and, when she was happy with the result, she gave Kitty a private screening in her bedroom. Personally, Tesser felt she had successfully enhanced her short film with the added scenes of boy love.

'Wow!' Kitty said when Tesser flicked the lights up after the ten-minute short. 'That's . . . pretty explicit.'

'You mean the sex bits? It's pretty horny, isn't it, if a bit hazy . . .? Yeah, well, if you think about it, everyone's fucked someone who's fucked someone else, pretty much, unless they were a virgin, then it doesn't work. Imagine if you could see all your lovers' ex-lovers, though! That's one of the points of the film, after all. If you think about it, everything's connected: we're all, like, sharing intimate physical pleasure with everyone on the planet, maaan.'

Tesser was suddenly worried. 'You weren't actually able to make out anybody's faces, were you?'

'No.'

'Good.'

But there had been something Tesser had discovered while doing last-minute editing on the short, something she hadn't noticed while developing or in compiling the first cut. She even went back to the stuff she had filmed of her neighbours to check. And it was a perfect match. Eric's tattoo was a twin to the shaven-headed guy's tattoo. How could she have missed it? But then again she had been fairly preoccupied at the time of both recordings. It was that heart-shaped pattern on the upper arm, like some kind of weird valentine. Must be a popular bit of 'flash'. Well, she wouldn't think much more on it: she wasn't planning on including the bald man and his lady friend in any of her final projects, anyway. She might indulge herself in a rewatch from time to time, though. Tesser felt pretty turned on just from scrolling the footage, but instead of playing it again she occupied herself with looping up the reel marked NEXT-DOOR NEIGHBOURS and then stored it away beneath her bed.

Well, who could blame her? You would have to be a saint not to go weak at the knees with a show like that. She had already watched NEXT-DOOR NEIGHBOURS four times. Yesterday, she had been so inspired by the couple's cinematic lovemaking that in a horny – or perhaps desperate – moment, she'd gone over to the house in question on the pretext of borrowing a cup of sugar, in the weak hope that they might invite her in for another session. She had rung the doorbell repeatedly until the elderly man gardening next door informed her that the house was deserted, and that no one had lived there in the past five years. There was an owner, worked locally, but he didn't come round too often.

'Are people squatting there, then?' Tesser had asked.

'We don't deal kindly with squatters round here,' the old man had answered, and had given Tesser such a dirty look that she had given up banging on the door and had hurried away, empty sugar bowl still in hand.

Today, the momentous day of the festival opening, she lay down on her mattress and closed her eyes and thought about what the couple had looked like. She had called up the cinema collective that ran the festival and volunteered to be there to help set things up before it all started at 8 p.m. She needed to relax, needed to get rid of her nervousness about the public screening. Lying in her bed and playing with herself was a sure-fire method of distraction. But, as inspirational as her neighbours had been, she wasn't getting the desired effect. So then she conjured up a vision of Dr Sharkey binding her with thread, gold this time, tying each finger separately, tying her legs as well. But even this vision, tempting as it was, wasn't working. And then, at last, she touched herself and thought of Jamie. It worked. Afterwards, she fell asleep, cheerful and satiated.

When she woke up several hours later, she felt strangely recovered. It was a beautiful day. She still had plenty of time, and rather than worry about editing the film further or wanking herself silly, she really ought to take a walk or something. Relax and look forward to the night. Chill out. So she packed up her reel in her backpack and began to cycle towards town, via London Fields and then on to the canal path that headed further westwards into the city. It was lovely to feel the sun on her bright green hair. When a small boy threw a rock at her bike and shouted, 'Oi! Greeny!' it didn't even annoy her. She cycled around London in a casual, haphazard kind of way until to her surprise she found herself in front of London Zoo.

As she locked her bike and took out her wallet, it hit her: she no longer had to worry about money. It was a damn relief. Yeah, yeah, yeah – usually if she could afford a packet of salt and vinegar crisps, she felt she was doing all right. But impending auteurhood was making her take things more seriously. Maybe she was growing up.

She paid her fee – posing as a student for reduced rates – and went in.

She wandered around the animal houses, feeling reflective. It would be good to be in the black again. Unfortunately, she hadn't lived in London long enough to have developed a steady friend base to see her non-judgmentally through any sort of personal crisis, financial or otherwise. She did have a couple of people she could talk to from the squat – Jake and Kitty. They were friends. It dawned on her suddenly that her sexual habits hadn't ensured anyone willing to listen to her as a friend in a time of need, out of all the people she had slept with. Except possibly her ex, Noriko, but Tesser hadn't called her up in a long time. And maybe Jamie, but she wasn't sure. That kind of threw her. She was lonelier than she thought.

She found herself standing outside the gorilla area, staring at a juvenile whom the other gorillas seemed to be avoiding. That must have been what put those lonely ideas in her head. Maybe the young gorilla had vast problems in her isolated gorilla world that Tesser couldn't even imagine. She sent a text message to Kitty: GORILLAZ R US. The gorilla began masturbating and Tesser changed her mind. Fuck that 'promiscuity is bad and the reason you're lonely is because you're not coupled up' bullshit – Tesser knew dozens of lonely, unhappy people who happened to be in relationships. Maybe the gorilla was even giving her a bit of inspiration: there are some things in life that actually are more pleasurable when you're alone. It was probably a very well-adjusted gorilla, content and really popular with its playmates. Tesser was the weird primate, standing numbly watching a gorilla masturbate. Tesser looked around. A non-giggling human crowd was gathering to watch; Tesser began to suspect the gorilla was showing off.

As she turned away from the enclosure, she saw a business card lying on the well-trodden, muddy ground. It was made of high-quality thin cardboard. Tesser knew it hadn't been there before, as she would have noticed it when she was the lone spectator, before the act got popular. The fancy card had to be from one of these ape-wank-watchers. A high-rent pervert's card, she thought, turning it over.

SOOTHSAYING AND CARD READING, FINNA, 18 WEY-PROPTH ROAD, the card read. Finna? That was an unusual name. An occult enthusiast in the crowd or the psychic herself? Or maybe it was a secret society. Tesser's eyes skimmed over the rather bland crowd only once before she grew uninterested. Then she freaked. What the fuck time was it? 'Excuse me!' She grabbed the arm of a man in a tweed jacket. 'What time is it?' He looked frightened. It was the hair.

'Quarter to six,' he answered.

'Thanks.' She gave him a meek smile, to reassure him that all green-haired types were mild-mannered sorts, really. The man didn't seem convinced and hurried away.

Damn it, she had to hurry and get back to Hackney, because she had to help set things up, as agreed. She tucked the card in her jacket pocket as a souvenir and headed east, speedily.

Jamie and Trevor arrived early on the night of the Geyser Underground Film Festival, but the place was already heaving. The festival was taking place in a huge warehouse near Stoke Newington, one that was often used for alternative arts events. Jamie had even been in a group show of crazy, wacko art here once himself.

There was quite a cool bunch of freaks here at present, but there was also a sizable pretentious Hoxtonite delegation milling about in the space, drinking the cheap, nasty wine on sale and talking loudly about how bad it was.

'You want a beer?'

'Yeah. Get me a Beck's.' Jamie handed a fiver over to Trevor, who took off to the makeshift bar.

No matter how hard Jamie tried to move over to a more interesting group, the voices of the Hoxtonites followed him like a bad smell, their snippets of conversation blending together in an insidious mass, the dialogue fading in and out. At last Jamie gave up avoiding them, stood still and merely watched and listened.

'Jesus Fuck, Tara, you didn't tell me it was going to be *this* underground,' said someone who looked like a critic to a blonde who was probably his PA.

'I'm so sorry, Frederick,' Jamie overheard Blondie say, 'it's embarrassing, isn't it? The second film screened is by the daughter of my dear friend Marie. I don't know *what* Marie expects me to say. Hideous. Just hideous.' She downed her glass swiftly. 'Red or white?'

'Red. Do you need to ask?'

To Jamie's left was a man in his forties blabbing on about Bill Viola. To his right was a slumming St Martin's student going on about how much he loved cheap wine and how he always shopped at Somerfield for their two-pound specials. Straight ahead – oh, horrors! – was a well-known 'conceptual artist'. The only relief was that no one recognised Jamie from the *Sentinel* article and asked him why he had never sold a painting.

'Well,' the conceptual artist was saying to a sycophantic male hanger-on, 'I had a show at the ICA – just a little one, mind you – because they're so up their own arses these days, aren't they? I think they've lost the plot … I think I'm going to go with a smaller space next time, really intimate – yeah, that's what I'm going to do.'

The sycophantic hanger-on was spluttering with over-eagerness. 'Hey, have you been to the Tate Modern yet?'

Jamie found himself sickly fascinated, knowing what was going to happen next. He had a queasy feeling of anticipation. Sure enough, it happened. The buzz of Hoxtonite conversation stopped and disparaging eye-brows were raised in the hanger-on's general direction. Then the mélange of conversation continued. And so on, ad fucking infinitum.

Trevor returned and handed Jamie his beer.

'I don't see her yet,' Jamie said.

'Well, I'm sure she'll turn up.'

'Yeah.'

'Do you have any fags?'

'No.'

'Roll-ups?' Trevor pursued.

'No.'

'Look, I know I said I'd come as a favour, but I'm dying for a smoke, so you'll have to manage by yourself for a while.'

Jamie suddenly felt frightened to be left on his own. 'Where are you going?'

'The off-licence down the road,' said Trevor, 'to buy some fags. It's only going to be about fifteen minutes. Hey, chill out. You'll be fine. And if she shows up, all the better.'

He clapped Jamie reassuringly on the shoulder and weaved his way through the crowd. Jamie watched him saunter past the drinks table on his way out, where a surly young woman with a commercial-art fringe was pouring white wine into plastic cups. Her scowl was not that of a poser, though. Except for the people surround-ing him, *no one* looked like a poser. Among the clear transparent white wines on the bar-cum-table was the one remaining cup of beautiful ruby-red. Trevor swooped in, slammed a pound down on the table and grabbed it for himself, earning a dirty look from the critic's PA, who had had designs on the treasure.

Jamie smiled. Now where in bloody hell was Tesser?

Jesus, but she was nervous. She couldn't even handle watching the whole film herself; it was too nerve-racking. Three minutes into *The Passion Flowchart*, she ducked out back for a beer and a sneaky fag. It was gratifying to see, however, that most people were still inside watching. At least there hadn't yet been a troop of people storming out and demanding refunds.

'There's supposed to be some sort of big agent here tonight,' said Kitty, sidling up to Tesser and whispering *sotto voce* in her ear while Tesser was still fumbling around in her bag trying to locate her cigarettes. 'Aim to impress, girlfriend.'

'I don't aim to impress.'

'Well, you ought to. Even if you've got the money, you can always use more – postproduction costs, you know.'

Tesser considered this. Kitty walked away again, swigging at her metal flask like some kind of alcoholic slacker law-student spy.

'Hey!' Tesser called after her. 'Why aren't you watching my triumph?'

Kitty turned around to answer. 'Same reason you're not watching. Seen it before. It ruins things if you experience them more than once. Kind of like your three-shag rule, actually.'

Tesser glanced nervously at her watch. It was a bright Casper the Friendly Ghost watch that she got free with a purchase of Ribena. 'I *knew* that guy wasn't going to show. See – you scoff, but it's the three-shag rule, Kitty, and I'm damn close to breaking it. Tonight would have been our third occasion of sin.'

Kitty rolled her eyes. 'Assuming you had shagged. You *are* cocky, aren't you? Look, he'll show up. He's probably making stretcher boards for canvases, or something.' She stopped, distracted by the lo-tech animation that was currently being screened in the corner across the room. Little pink pigs were grunting their way across a huge, bloated sausage. 'Hey – I want to check some of his stuff out. I'm going to take a little wander, OK?'

'Yeah, yeah, yeah. I'm going to wait here for a while. It's not as crowded and I need a breather. I'll probably hang out, chain-smoking on the fire escape. I can't handle watching my own stuff. I need to relax.'

'Absolutely you do,' said Kitty. She grinned. Her parting words were, 'Remember about the agent! Money, money, money!'

Augh! Just what Tesser needed – more pressure. There was a low rumble from the screening room and, judging by how long the film had been running, Tesser figured they had gotten to the bit where the blurred male bodies suddenly burst into a shower of bright-red hearts. She had taken the idea from the upside-down tattoo on Eric's arm, and thought of it as her little valentine to Eric and Alistair, as in, 'thanks for a good time, boys'. She had mastered this effect with stop-frame animation and had felt sure that it was successful, but it was still nice to have her hard work confirmed by the audience.

She went out on the fire escape to have a cigarette and came back just in time to the sweet sound – wow! – of tumultuous applause. She drew closer to the door. The MC was saying that there would be a short break, and then the audience would be treated to fire-eating performance poetry. People started to shift up from their folding-chair seats and make their way towards the door. The first person out was an older woman dressed in a business suit with straight dark hair cut in a bob. She had a young man in tow. Whoa, talk about May–December. And then, before she could move away from the door and let them pass, Tesser was collared.

'Darling! You must be Tesser Roget! I've heard about you.'

'You have?' Tesser felt confused. No one had ever heard about her. Was this what fame felt like? Was this what happened when your short film was a success?

'Of course I have. I'm Eve. I'm a friend of Miriam's.'

'Miriam?'

'Dr Miriam Sharkey. She said you had just taken a position with her –' I'll bet she said that, Tesser thought '– and that she could really recommend your talents. She described you quite well.' She gave Tesser's hair a once-over. 'Although I believe she said you were blonde. And here –' she dragged forward the young man, who was pretty and shy with soft strawberry-blond hair '– here is my son Kevin. He's interested in filmmaking, too, aren't you, Kevin? Perhaps you could show him about the venue, dear.'

She was looking at Tesser expectantly. Tesser sighed inwardly. She didn't want to piss off a friend of Dr Sharkey's and jeopardise her job. She forced a smile on her face. 'Sure thing.' She looked around the room for help with this task, but Kitty was long gone and Jamie was a no-show. 'Come on, Kevin. Let's make the rounds.'

She introduced Kevin to a couple of the Geyser festival people she'd met earlier in the evening but, as she didn't know them too well herself, the introductions were on the awkward side. That lot seemed like a fun crowd, though, cool and cynical. She looked forward to getting to know them on future occasions. She and Kevin stood around drinking beer – Tesser got two free beers for the evening because she'd helped out earlier – and listening to the Geyser filmmakers curse the more-pretentious-than-thou crowd that had shown up tonight. Someone said that *Break-Time* must have advertised the event as 'hip and trendy', and that was why it had pulled in people who were disgruntled when the projectors broke

own or who hushed people loudly for discussing the
lms in process. This artsy-fartsy crowd just didn't get
, the crowd of Geyser filmmakers agreed, and Tesser
ound herself nodding along with them, enjoying the
anter and digs at what they called culture tourists.
evin, on the other hand, seemed to be getting a bit
witchy. Tesser looked at him out of the corner of her
ye. She recognised the signs.

'You need a nicotine fix, dontcha?' she asked.

'Yeah! My mum doesn't know I smoke.'

Tesser looked right and left, but couldn't see his
other in sight. Anyway, what did she owe Dr Sharkey
r her friends? 'Come on,' she said, 'we can't smoke in
ere, but there's a fire exit out this way where we can.'

Once they were outside on the fire exit, the boy
eemed overly impressed with the fact that Tesser had
irected *The Passion Flowchart*.

'Wow! That was your film? That was so great. The
ay everyone could have made love to everyone else
nd stuff.'

'Yeah, yeah, yeah.' Tesser felt a bit embarrassed. 'Do
ou want a menthol?' She had only two cigarettes left.
he was a light smoker, but she had been nervous, what
ith the festival and all. And starting a new job. And
aybe even about Jamie. Where was he? It had been too
owded and dark to see whether he was in the audi-
nce, and she had been behind scenes trying to get a
ide projector working when the MC opened the eve-
ing to the crowd.

Kevin took a look at the cigarettes on offer. 'Nah, I
as sort of exaggerating about how much I needed a
g. I just wanted to get a chance to talk to you about
e films and stuff. You're filming stuff for Dr Sharkey,
ren't you?'

The way in which he spoke and the way in which he
as leaning forward into her personal body space sud-
enly struck Tesser as familiar. She narrowed her eyes.

'Hey,' she said, 'this cigarette thing wasn't a pick-up line, was it?'

'So what if it was?' Kevin was staring at her in open appreciation. 'I'm a young guy. I'm still polishing m' technique.'

Tesser burst out laughing. Oh, Jesus. Solitude, flatter and in for the kill. A method she used all the tim herself, and she didn't even recognise it when it wa used on her. Then she tried to muffle her laughter because Kevin was looking a little put out.

'Hey, I'm sorry,' she said. 'It's just that it was s transparent it wasn't transparent, you see. It caught m a little off guard.'

Kevin moved closer to her. 'So?'

A little surprised, Tesser took a step backwards though not too far backwards, else she would take topple three storeys below. 'Kid, you're a bit too young for me, I think. I'm twenty-four. How old are you?'

'Twenty-one.'

'How old are you really?'

Kevin looked down at his feet. 'Eighteen. But m birthday's in four months.'

Tesser took a good long look at him. He was a cut kid. He was very pale, with bright-green eyes. He had freckles, as she did herself. She had to admire his spirit she had been exactly the same at his age – cocky an very hot to trot. Tentatively, she kissed him lightly on the lips. But he was much quicker than she was an kissed her hard, his tongue pushing quickly into he mouth. He wasn't actually a bad kisser. She drew away

'I have to meet someone,' she told him.

'So where is he?'

Tesser had a sinking sensation. 'He hasn't shown up yet.' And wasn't fucking likely to, now. She didn't know why she had thought he would. He had just seemed s smitten, that was all. She stepped away from Kevin an turned around so that she faced outwards, leaning against the rail of the fire escape. The heavens had darkened and it was a warm July night, but there still weren't that many stars out. There was an odd, rather fluorescent glow to the sky; it was seldom completely dark in London unless you were in uninhabited areas like the canal system. There was a word for that – yeah, 'light pollution', that was what it was called. A city that never slept. A city whose lamps blazed at all hours. A city burning its candle at both ends. Tesser felt reckless suddenly.

'All right, Kevin,' she said and turned around. She put her beer down on the railing, near the wall. 'Let's see what you can do.'

'Fucking right, we'll see,' said Kevin, and with that he pulled Tesser towards him.

I need this, Tesser told herself, this is what I need right now. She needed to block things out, to let herself go, to forget and enjoy ... She found it quite easy to do this as they wrapped their arms round each other and snogged. He smelled good and tasted good, of fresh shampoo and peppermint toothpaste. Maybe that was just 'cos she had an ashtray mouth at the moment, though. He was kissing her ear. It felt good. He bent down lower and nibbled at her neck. It felt good. He inched his hand up her chequerboard-patterned stockings. It felt good.

It all felt good.

Damn, but it felt good. Tesser remembered how she let go with Dr Sharkey, released herself into pleasure. Didn't plan or calculate. Maybe she would try it now. She let young Kevin bend her back against the hard iron railing in a night sky glowing and beautiful with its own pollution and kissed him smoothly, swimmingly, their tongues erotic and tense in each other's mouths. She was aroused, really aroused, wet and ready and up for it. She wanted him to fuck her with his hard young cock.

She wanted to think only of sex. His hand was grinding against her ass.

'Come on, then, fuck me,' she whispered.

Kevin couldn't believe his luck. And he jumped to it, as if she might withdraw the offer if she thought about it too long, unbuttoning and unzipping his trousers, yanking them down to his hips, hands already poised on the waistband of his briefs. And the truth was she might withdraw the offer if she gave it more than a moment's consideration. So she didn't consider. She reached down and took out his thick, long cock, already stiff and moistened at the tip. He was trembling as he rumbled around in his pocket for a condom, and she found this strangely touching because his hard-ass act was so well executed. He was just young, that was all. Young and well hung to boot. She began to move her hand over his prick slowly, and was gratified to hear him moan and groan. Oh, Jesus, he was just so naïve. In a way, tender.

Tesser felt a softness spreading through her body as she lowered herself down on him, he leaning back against the railing now, she fucking him. She was sticky for him. She was wet for him. She slid on to him like a tight, sheer glove over the latex and – oh, Jesus – it felt fucking good. Christ, it felt good. She began to move on him, faster and faster, her skirt pushed up, the crotchless panties that she had worn in hope of seeing Jamie no impediment, just as advertised in the £1 sale at Anne Summers. A pulse was moving in her; she felt heavy and sensual, voluptuous, shifting on Kevin. His eyes were closed, thinking God knew what thoughts, and his mouth was open, vulnerable, sweet. His pale lips and his thick, pale lashes. Tesser felt like chocolate fudge to his citrus: her limbs were laden with heavy eroticism; her lust was dense, coffee-coloured, darkened, burned. She forced herself down on him, moaning once when his cock hit a tenderness deep inside her. She was experienced. Corrupted. He was like a tangy clear citrus fruit: transparent, innocent, virtuous.

But willing to be corrupted.

This was the quality that Tesser found so attractive in him: his unpolished lust. He grabbed at one of her tits, squeezing so hard the sensation grew painful. Tesser didn't tell him to stop, although she could feel his fingers bruising her through her T-shirt. He really did remind her so much of herself when she was his age. Desperate for experience, wanting all the Eden fruits that existed, all at once, all the intoxicating juices she could swallow. And she had gorged herself on them, too, until she grew jaded enough to resample, and the taint of knowledge gave all acts, especially those of sex, fresh tastes: the shifted, perverted qualities that experience brought to familiar pursuits. He had a lot to learn. Oh, she was so wet it was nearly indecent: too much, too wet, too juicy. She hadn't wanted this, and now look: she was rutting, sliding her split cunt down on this horny, stiff-hard boy. He was gliding into her; she was devilishly slick around his tight, thick length; she worked her pussy down and up, his latex-bound cock glossy with juice; ready to pump . . .

He groaned, jerked his hips upward and came.

Fuck. Well, that was that. That was the problem with younger men.

With as much decorum as she could muster, Tesser lifted herself off Kevin and stood back. She was breathing hard. With a contemporary, she would insist on personal fulfilment. She ought to now, too, rather than teach the boy bad habits. But there was the whole festival going on inside, and there was that money-bags agent there, and maybe Jamie, and maybe she ought to be there inside, too . . .

Kevin impressed her by suggesting a continuation all on his own. 'Um, you didn't, um . . . did you?'

109

'No.' Tesser looked at him wryly, as she was already starting to pull her stockings up.

'Well, don't you want to carry on, then?'

Tesser looked at her Casper watch. She was up for it, but if on the off chance Jamie had arrived by now . . .

'Come on,' he pleaded, 'get your knickers off.'

Then she looked Kevin in the eye and melted a little. It was pretty tempting. He did want to do the right thing. And she really did want to let him. At the moment, she couldn't think of anything saucier than getting licked out on a fire escape. Although she was pretty sure that she could under normal circumstances.

'OK . . .' she agreed tentatively.

'But I want you to get off,' he told her solemnly.

'OK,' she answered back, with as much seriousness. 'You'd better do what you have to do, then.' Anyway, her blood was still buzzing with lust.

'How do you want me to do it?'

'How do women get off? Is that what you're asking?'

'The clit – the clitoris, right?'

Tesser pointed downwards and then got down on her hands and knees so that her ass was in his face, so that he was confronted with the sight of her split, furry, wet sex – pink and moist and juicy. 'Get licking.'

It felt great to have wet friction against her pussy, and she squirmed down on his face, smearing her juices all over him. She knew he hadn't been a virgin, though she doubted he was very far from it, yet he was licking her so well she felt he ought to give courses on the subject.

'Lean against the wall of the building.'

Tesser did as he requested and put her hands up against the brick wall, like she was being frisked. She pulled her skirt up so that her bare buttocks were visible, and then he knelt underneath her, licking her pussy slowly and lovingly, and she started to tremble. The cool breeze blew across her ass. She felt so slutty doing this, and she risked her balance to take a sip from her bottle of beer while he continued to lick. Now he was getting excited, because his breath was coming quickly, and he grabbed his dick out from his trousers and was wanking, too, wanking while he licked her. The point of his tongue played over the bead of her sex; he was practically squatting underneath her, tasting her, making her shiver with need.

Yes. She rubbed her pussy over his mouth, his lips, his tongue, slathering his pale face with her sex juice, trembling with tight, coiled desire that started at last to unwind as she moved towards a delicious climax, hands flat against the bricks, his tongue tickling lightly and frustratingly at her clit until she jerked into orgasm, snarling like an animal. It felt so wicked. It felt so bad. It felt so good. For a moment she rested there in position, panting, her pussy still dripping and exposed to the elements.

His eyes were closed, and he looked like he was still concentrating, and, if his expression hadn't been so ecstatic, Tesser would have assumed he was praying. Or maybe his face looked so ecstatic because he *was* praying. She didn't know him. It was highly possible that he was a religious nut.

'OK, Kevin,' Tesser said, causing him to blink his eyes open, 'you're not bad – actually you're kind of charming – and you're not a selfish lover by any means, and I like you, so I'm going to let you in on a fail-safe way to get laid. It works pretty well for chicks, but I've heard it works equally well for guys, too.'

Kevin's green eyes were wide with anticipation. 'How?' he said.

'Keep your virtue intact,' Tesser advised.

'No way!' Kevin said, with obvious disappointment.

'No, really, here's how: you reclaim a virginal state for each new conquest. Most people love to be the first, as long as you're eager and not as passive as a rag doll.' She scrutinised him favourably. 'And you're not.'

111

'I thought birds wanted blokes with loads of experience.'

'True. And guys like girls who know what to do in bed, too. But, believe me, this one works, because most people have an authoritarian streak, too. You'll learn to savour the dominant look in a lady's eye each time you confess in a trembling voice that it's your first time. Just don't overuse it. You don't want to find yourself using the line a second time around. You're lucky, though – you live in a huge city and you're a tempting piece of ass, so it should work pretty well. That's my little gift to you, Kevin. Think of me as your one-occasion-only sexual mentor.'

'Cool.' Kevin looked grateful for the advice. 'I'll try it right away. There was a cute girl with a shaved head when I came in who smiled at me. She looked like she knew how to party, too, 'cos she was sneaking a drink from this little bottle. Maybe she'd be up for it.'

Kitty batted for the other side nearly exclusively, but Tesser only grinned and didn't say anything. Perhaps even Kitty would fall prey to the 'virgin' ruse.

Kitty went through several rooms, looking at combination poetry/slide shows and VCR-edited movies, found-footage videos and entire short films acted out under a security camera. There was a girl handing out flyers in front of this last room on which it stated that, under the Official Secrets Act, citizens had a legal right to request security-camera footage if they offered the company that had installed the camera ten pounds sterling. Eventually she came to a 3D room, where for two quid you rented a pair of red/blue glasses and watched a three-dimensional short film.

She stood outside for a moment hesitating and jingling the change in her pocket. She wondered whether she should try to chase down perpetually broke Tesser and offer to pay her way – the 3D element sounded like something she would really take to and Kitty wasn't above doing a favour for a friend. But she couldn't see Tesser anywhere, so she went in on her own. It turned out to be pretty cool, especially the sky-diving scenes, and afterwards she exited the small room with a feeling of sheer vertigo. She wandered around looking at a variety of rather blurry films until she bumped into someone she knew had to be Tesser's boy *du jour*, the artist formerly and presently known as Jamie Desmond. Malcom X does Jarvis Cocker. From Tesser's description, there was no way it couldn't be him. He was tapping his foot impatiently.

'Hi, are you Jamie?' Kitty asked. 'I heard you might show up.'

Jamie looked up. 'Oh, hey. Nice to see you, um . . .'

'Kitty.'

'Nice to see you, Kitty.'

His voice was overcasual, which made Kitty wonder whether perhaps Tesser was right in trying to preserve her emotional distance. He was also pretending that he remembered her, which was of course impossible since their paths had never crossed. This struck Kitty as slightly insincere. 'Yeah, you too. You waiting for someone in particular?'

'Not really. I'm waiting for a mate of mine. How about you?'

Kitty gave Jamie a look of sheer disbelief. Tesser had behaved as if this was a date by any other name – one she was inordinately nervous about – but this guy wasn't acting as if that was the case at all. What was he playing at? 'Been waiting long?'

Jamie looked suddenly very worried. Aha! Not so casual after all, Kitty thought. Her attitude towards him softened a little. 'About twenty minutes, actually. My – uh – friend went to get some smokes, but I think he might have got lost.'

'You seem a little tense.'

'Not at all,' said Jamie, 'just pissed off. He should have been back by now.'

'Oh, OK,' Kitty said. She paused. 'You should check out the 3D room upstairs; it's bloody good. Of course, my mate Tesser seemed to be a bit anxious that a certain someone hasn't shown up, too. So again, just on the off chance that you're waiting around to see her, I'd recommend that you check out the door that leads to the fire escape. That's where I saw her last. Well, see you around again, no doubt.' She smiled at him.

Jamie twinkled his eyes at her, but he didn't smile back. 'Thanks for the tip,' he said, earnestly.

Kitty headed off towards a different room. But she turned her head slightly as she swaggered across the floor and, out of the corner of one eye, she watched a smile cross Jamie's face. There was now an air of purpose around his whole being, as he set off nearly immediately for the fire escape.

As they finished pulling up their various underthings, Kevin tapped Tesser on the shoulder. 'Hey. Remember me?'

'Hey,' she answered politely, but she felt distracted.

'Are you OK?' asked Kevin. 'You seem sort of nervous. I notice you keep looking at your watch. Nice Casper motif, by the way. On the watch, I mean.'

'No, no, I'm fine,' said Tesser. They walked back into the warehouse. 'I was just sort of waiting for someone.'

'A friend? Dr Sharkey?'

'No. Sort of a friend. A tall guy, black, with thick black eyeglasses.'

'Well,' Kevin said, 'a whole group of new people just came in through the back door exit. I think they're milling around in the upstairs rooms. Maybe he's there?'

Tesser cheered up. 'Oh, you're probably right.' She planted an impulsive kiss on his cheek. 'I'll go check it out and see if he came in that way. Thanks a million.'

First she went to the main screening room and retrieved her film and her backpack and then she went up and visually scoured the upper rooms of the warehouse. She didn't see him anywhere. She was beginning to feel a little agitated. Maybe even worried. Which was stupid, because if he wasn't here now he wasn't coming, and that's all there was to it. Unfortunately, the people that were up here were precisely the crowd that the Geyser lot had been scoffing at earlier. Was he with that bunch? Well, he was a famous artist, wasn't he? Practically. Her eyes flicked over the throng, but she didn't see him. She was behaving casually, wasn't she? It would be pretty embarrassing if he actually was here and he saw her looking around for him like some desperate wife. She pretended to concentrate instead on a short film being projected on to the wall, one that involved a narrative about an aubergine. At any other point in time, the film would have been intriguing. Yet she was distracted. There was Kevin's mother speaking animatedly with the culture tourists. At one point their glances met and Eve gave her a polite nod, but nothing more. She obviously had found a more prestigious target for schmoozing. Hey, lady, Tesser thought, I've just fucked your son.

She made herself appear absorbed in the eggplant film, but kept peeping round to scan the room, clutching insecurely at the box that held the reel of *The Passion Flowchart*. She felt like she was about to cry. The artchatter was rising in volume, with certain words more audible than others:

'. . . post-post . . .' an older, elegantly dressed man elaborated.

'. . . red wine . . .' said a well-coiffed blonde woman hanging on to his arm.

'. . . really true-to-life . . .' the older man was now saying.

'. . . noodle-bar installation . . .' muttered an art-studenty-looking type.

Through this tangle of words and people and half-caught glimpses, Tesser thought she heard Jamie's voice for a moment, fading in with the pretentious chatter and then becoming clear once more. The effect was slightly sinister. She whirled around to look.

There he was! Way across the room, Jamie seemed to be drifting, slow-motion, towards her. But he wasn't making eye contact. 'Jamie!' she shouted, but he didn't hear her. The art-crowd voices rose up again through the layer of sound. Everything seemed surreally slowed down.

'I don't care if she *is* Marie's daughter. It's crap, and I told her so. How dare she drag us down to this hole and subject us to dingy little homemade films . . .?'

'Ah,' said a male voice this time, floating through the air, 'but will I be telling my readers the same thing, Tara? That's the question.'

'Indeed . . .' said Tara, behind Tesser's back.

To Tesser's right, the art student was still blabbering on: '. . . and the site got five hundred hits the first day, too. My end-of-year project's about the same thing, like how many *hits* do we get per person per day in real life, yeah . . . "The Multimedia Body", I think I'll call it, or maybe "Inter-Active Flesh". What do you think . . .?'

'Ooh, yes . . .' said a voice just behind Tesser's right ear.

Things solidified once more.

Jamie was there, right beside her. 'You OK, girl?' He appeared to be startled by her radiation-green hair, running his eyes over her head several times, but he didn't directly comment on it. 'You're looking good,' was all he said.

Tesser didn't answer. She wiped a tear from her eyes – Jamie had not yet noticed how close she was to weeping – and gave Jamie a big hug.

116

He seemed gratified by the attention. 'Hey, sorry I couldn't find you.'

Tesser smiled. ''S OK.'

I've been looking forward to seeing you for the last two weeks, she didn't say. I'm so glad you're here, she didn't say.

'Tesser Roget!' (*Rodget!* Tesser thought to herself.) A young woman with dark hair and rather trendy, street-fashion clothes was hurrying towards her, pushing her way past the bodies in her way. 'Tesser Roget! I've heard a lot about you and I just wanted to say, I *loved* your film. I've been trying to track you down all evening so I could get a private word with you. A friend recommended you and I just had to take a look for myself.'

'Uh, thanks.' Jesus! This was the second fan in a row that Dr Sharkey had let loose on Tesser. Tesser was flattered, and she could get used to it but it made her kind of nervous, OK.

'Just a second,' she told Jamie. 'I'll be right with you.'

'OK,' Jamie said, with a game smile. 'I'm not going anywhere.'

The woman hustled Tesser out into the hallway. 'Oh, it's impossible to think in that room,' she said.

'Uh, yeah.' Tesser was starting to feel a little put out. Still, she supposed this was how it was: making time for the fans, et cetera. She resolved to be gracious but firm about her limited interview time. Because she wanted to get back to Jamie.

'Listen, I had to ask you –'

'Yes?' Tesser interrupted, revelling in her role as *auteur* and in the admiring reception her film was garnering. It certainly had proved to be popular with the punters.

'I had to ask you,' her dark-haired female fan continued smoothly, 'whether or not one of the men in the clipped-in episodes of your film happened to be named Eric. And what was the other one named? Perhaps you could tell *me*.' Her tone was disingenuous.

At this, Tesser froze. She had assumed that no one would ever recognise the men in the clips – in fact, her camerawork was a little faulty, and the sex scene could only be described as being of the blurred, impressionistic ilk. She started to feel very guilty about filming the young men without their permission; she wasn't without a conscience, after all. 'Ummm . . .'

That was when the woman made a grab for the reel that Tesser was still gripping tight in her hand.

Jesus! The second time in a fortnight she was being chased for something having to do with those two closet cases! And at her own ball, so to speak! She couldn't even get to her jackknife if she needed it to threaten, because it was deep within her backpack. Tesser pushed her way back into the room and frantically through the crowd, back towards the way she had come in, faces blurring past as she rushed through, trying to put some space between her and the woman pursuing her. Tesser was dimly aware of passing by Kitty, then Kevin – who was chatting up a predatory-looking older woman – and then, of all people, Jamie, of whom her fleeting impression was that he was staring at her open-mouthed.

'I'll call you!' Tesser screamed to him and she plunged through the exit door, accidentally spilling red wine all over the suit of the older man who had looked suspiciously like an art critic, the one she'd been half listening to earlier. He had been chatting to the younger blonde woman, but now he simply looked outraged.

Past the wine table, through the foyer, out the door. Like a thrift-store Cinderella, Tesser bolted from the building, ran straight to the bus stop and flung herself on to a fortuitous No. 38 bus.

What was she doing? But Jamie knew exactly what she was doing. He had been looking for her the whole evening and now she was trying to ditch him. Jamie's eyes stung, but he looked quickly down at his feet and cleared his throat. Who was he kidding? A cheap trick like her was never going to change her spots. He needed to leave. As a matter of fact, he needed to leave right *now*. Unfortunately, the St Martin's student was blocking his exit.

'My whole third-year show is about The Body, actually . . .' the student was saying.

'So 1997, Michael,' a second studenty type chimed in.

'Excuse me,' Jamie said, 'can I get by?'

'Nineteen *eighty* seven, thank you very much, and I'm very much aware . . .'

From halfway across the room, the conceptual artist's voice carried. 'Oh, good for you, good for you . . .'

'Excuse me,' Jamie said politely a second time, and then in desperation he pushed his way through. Ahead of him was Trevor, who was looking at him apologetically, a rollie in his mouth.

'There was a helluva queue.' He looked closely at Jamie. 'So, where is she?' He seemed unusually nervous.

Jamie was well aware that his expression must look pretty peculiar. 'No, no, I don't know. Look, never mind. Let's get out of this place.'

There was a bloody big crowd to get through. Just his luck. Jamie tried to worm his way out, and Trevor followed him. But they found their way blocked by the blonde PA and the critic, who seemed to have spilled red wine all over himself.

'Oh, I love Hackney –' The blonde was gesturing vehemently. 'I love all of East London, actually – it's so *trashy*.'

Jamie was now starting to feel panicked. 'Oh, I really need to get out of here.'

At last the two of them made it outside, whereupon Jamie threw himself against the wall in relief.

'Give me a fag, eh?'

Trevor handed some tobacco and papers over to him.

'She wasn't there, then, was she? The girl you wanted to see.'

Jamie concentrated on rolling the cigarette. 'Oh, she was there, all right. It's just that the stars weren't favourable.'

'Huh?' Trevor was flummoxed.

'The circumstances weren't right.'

'Uh, OK,' said Trevor. 'Oh well, never mind. Fish in the sea and all that.' He paused, evidently trying to think of a safer subject. 'Are you painting this weekend?'

'Yeah.'

'Are you going back to your place now?'

'I think I'm going to take a walk,' said Jamie. 'Later.'

Chapter Six

*T*he first day of her new job! It was kind of cool, actually. Tesser jumped out of bed and rummaged around until she found a bright-blue T-shirt that wasn't too stained. She sprayed perfume all over it. The colour went nicely with her newly green tresses, she felt. Coupled with those leopardskin boots of hers, it made her one foxy mama.

Irresistible, in fact. She looked wildly around her room, desperate to find something to wear on her bottom half. There were no skirts or trousers in sight, but she found a blue-green kilt in her stockpile of £4 Primark skirts, and then rifled through the not-so-dirty clothes pile in the corner and found a pair of black tights and the jeans jacket that she had been wearing the week before.

As she pulled it on, she felt something in the pocket and drew out a crumpled card. For a second she went blank, then her memory kicked in. It would not be fair to suggest that she had forgotten about the card entirely. The jeans jacket had been there in the corner of the room where she had thrown it after getting home the night of the festival. The card had piqued her interest, because an occult-loving voyeur was just too weird. She supposed it was narcissism, because after all she was herself a sex-mad ghost-walker. Occult voyeur: ghost-walk nympho. Loads in common. Definitely interesting. She glanced at her watch. She had an hour to kill. Maybe she should see if she could fall in unnoticed on one of those weekday ghost walks; if the guide didn't see her, she wouldn't have to pay. Then she looked at the card in her palm. She could change her habits for once. Do something unexpected.

The address: Weypropth Road. It sounded oldey-worldey. She didn't own an A–Z, but she left her house with the card and cycled to the Homerton library, where she asked to borrow the phone. They knew her and would generally let her do this provided it was a local call. She dialled the London Transport information service, and eventually an operator provided Tesser with very specific travel instructions. And she saved the mobile phone charges, natch.

Again, the location was in Hackney near the canals. Hackney seemed to be the buzzing centre of everything: no-budget film festivals, the most desirable squat properties, chemical research laboratories ... Actually, Weypropth Road didn't lie that far from the canal system itself. Tesser looked at her Casper watch. The job didn't start until eleven o'clock. It was only a quarter to ten.

She got back on her bike.

She stood outside the house on Weypropth Road, which actually did turn out to be only a five-minute cycle ride away from AMI Industries. Weird. Whatever. The terraced Victorian house had been painted, strangely, a bright blue. It was surrounded by fast-food establishments. In a 180-degree swoop, Tesser counted sixteen people chomping down on Egg McMuffins, chips and Tennessee Fried Chicken – the cheaper, British version of KFC – even at this early hour. She turned round, composed herself and rang the small silver doorbell marked FINNA. No one answered. Maybe ten o'clock was too early in the morning. The fact that she was a morning person had never failed to get on the nerves of her many shags. She pressed the doorbell again. Off in the muffled distance of the house's interior, she could hear a chime playing 'The Yellow Rose of Texas'. It was not the first time Tesser had come across that particular doorbell melody. She found its prevalence rather frightening, especially when she thought of the recent US election, for which she'd sent in her absentee ballot, with the words YOU'RE ALL WANKERS scrawled across it. Now she regretted it, since the election had been so close. 'All Hail the Commander-In-Thief.' That was a hard tune to hum, as well.

The door was opened by a striking person of indistinguishable gender. Tesser liked to think of herself as quite discerning in these matters. She knew to look for little giveaways such as indentations behind the ears, but she was also quite well versed in nose-bridge analysis, forehead slope or lack of it and, most importantly, jaw musculature. She could usually tell the difference between a very masculine woman and a very feminine man. It was more often a combination of traits than an anomalous single occurrence. Most girls can, with proper encouragement, grow a beard. Many have extraordinarily large hands, even in combination with low voices. Few can dent their nose bridges.

Even so, Tesser had seen a couple of dented-nosed women in her time and, all in all, it was the combination of many factors that put people into one gender box or the other. The proof was in the pudding. Her interest was not purely academic. Having a fondness for the extremely pretty male face, she had found herself in some unusual dating situations in the past. Jeez. There had also been that girl on her first London ghost walk who had turned out to be a boy – at least five years ago, when she had been in town visiting her auntie and uncle. Which was not to suggest that a jolly time was not had by all parties, but she had since developed a keen sense of gender discernment.

This only underscored to Tesser that when *she* couldn't tell someone's gender, the gender of the person concerned was unquestionably ambiguous. Ms Finna, if it was she, was a thin person, delicate-boned and elegant. She had a draw to her, too, some magnetic quality that made Tesser stare at her until she was sure she was being impolite. She had the strangest feeling of *déjà vu*. Were those breasts there? Was she or wasn't he?

'May I help you?'

'Um,' Tesser began, feeling she was starting out on the wrong foot, 'I found your card.'

'It's a bit early, but you're welcome.'

'Well, I'm not sure I can afford . . . I was just curious, really . . .' Her explanation sounded stupid even to Tesser's own ears. She'd better go along with it, whatever 'it' was.

'Follow on up,' Finna said in an annoyingly indistinguishable mid-range voice, and so Tesser did. She had the oddest feeling that they had met before, but Tesser had a terrible memory for faces.

'I own the entire house,' Finna informed Tesser casually.

Jesus! How much money did a soothsayer make? She had a chance to further observe the clairvoyant as she walked behind her on the stairs. Finna had sleek light-brown hair done up in white-girl hair wraps, to use a New Age term Tesser had once picked up at Seattle's annual Bumbershoot music festival, before she had embarrassed her data-entry colleagues and they had asked her to leave. That had been a good night. A lanky hippy boy, sweet-natured and smelling of patchouli. He had been thrilled by her faked virginity, and very gentle.

Finna didn't smell of patchouli at all – in fact, Tesser

was convinced the seer smelled of a combination of hashish and rosemary. For some reason, the combination made her feel kind of horny – probably because pot always made her kind of horny.

They stopped before a silver-painted wooden door, whereupon Finna pushed it open and beckoned Tesser in, somewhat impatiently, as if Tesser had kept her waiting. Her body was lean but wiry and her movements were graceful and studied. The room was full of dangling crystals, wind chimes and what looked like braided bits of hair, all of these hanging from the ceiling. The glare from the crystals actually hurt Tesser's eyes. She looked at her watch. Well, she was still good for time, anyway. As Finna turned to open a window and light incense, Tesser's brain finally clicked on the category 'male'. But Finna's 'energy', to use another term Tesser had picked up from the Seattle music festival, was definitely female. Peculiar. So she persisted in thinking of Finna as a 'she', as she had been subconsciously doing ever since she entered the house. She really did look familiar. And, whatever memory she was stirring, it was a good one. Tesser crossed her legs.

Finna cleared her throat and motioned Tesser towards a small wooden table and a chair.

Tesser sat down. 'I've never really done anything like this before –' she began, sounding like she was going straight into her 'virgin' speech – before Finna hushed her.

'Shh . . . It will be all right. Be still.' The seer spread out a series of cards, from which Tesser was prodded to choose and discouraged to observe the undersides. She looked underneath her lashes at the way the androgyne bit her lip in concentration. She found herself fascinated by the curve of her thin, dark-red lips, though it did not look like she was wearing lip colour. She found herself calming, too, a stillness overtaking her body – she was aware of her heart pounding, though apart from this urgency she was enveloped in a lethargic, heavy calm.

Finna's eyes darted up, caught Tesser staring at her mouth and cleared her throat. Tesser flushed, as if she had said something improper, or been caught blaspheming on Holy Saturday Mass (this had happened once as a child). Finna graciously said nothing. She then looked at the selection for another long moment and sucked in her breath.

'You will undergo a great change, an enormous change –'

'I know that,' Tesser interrupted. 'You see, beginning today –'

'Hush!' Finna's eyes flashed. 'There is something you need to clarify with someone close to you, but you're not being candid. You should try again. Maybe there is a birth, a new beginning but –' she peered more closely at the cards '– no, there can be no birth, for there is no partner, and therefore no love. Hmm . . .' Mildly impressed but disappointed, Tesser sulked while Finna fixed her with a gaze worthy of the chairwoman of the Moral Majority Council against Promiscuous False Virgins. The clairvoyant continued: 'Then it is not a birth, exactly, at least not in the normal sense . . . hmm . . . This is so unusual . . . I have to think this through . . .' She turned over the last card, which gave Tesser a little frisson when she saw that its title was THE LOVERS. Finna gave a little chuckle and murmured to herself, 'But how unusual! How . . .' She turned her attention back to Tesser. She seemed very ill at ease. 'What did you say your name was, dear?'

'Tesser. Tesser Roget.' She found herself responding to the strict, softly dominant tone of the seer, and shivered. She knew it was Dr Sharkey who had attuned her senses to such matters.

'Don't worry about the card, dear – it's not what it seems. Actually, it –' She jumped up, very nervous suddenly. 'I'll be just a moment, dear.' She couldn't look Tesser straight in the face.

126

The soothsayer left Tesser at the table as she went to another room. Tesser watched her movements with admiration. She had the grace of a court eunuch, or so Tesser fancied: the languid locomotion of a finely tuned castrato . . . Tesser let her imagination run rampant.

But her mildly lascivious fantasies dwindled after a while when Finna still didn't return. Tired, eventually, from twiddling her thumbs, Tesser got up and walked over to the window. On the sill was yet another silver object, which Tesser picked up. It was a tiny Russian church made of pewter or some such metallic medium. She put it back on the sill, went back to her appointed chair and continued to wait. Almost a quarter of an hour had passed and Tesser could no longer hear her voice. She began to worry that perhaps Finna had completely forgotten about her.

She got up and walked to the door that Finna had shut behind her. She opened it. The room she saw appeared to be an antechamber; the door that opened on to the outside was open. Tesser peered beyond that and there was a wooden staircase leading to the ground and a well-kept if eccentrically arranged garden. It was growing chilly in the room with the door wide open. Tesser glanced at her watch. 10.45 a.m. Shit – she had only a quarter of an hour before she was supposed to start filming.

Whatever the case, she couldn't afford to wait for Madame Finna to come back from wherever she was – an outdoor toilet? round the corner for a pack of fags? – no matter how intriguing the undisclosed fortune-card reading had been. She borrowed a purple-ink pen from the counter, pulled out an old grocery receipt from her pocket and jotted down a brief note: 'Sorry, you weren't here and I had to go. Thanks anyway.' She rifled through the cash she had remaining from the sub she had been given last week and added a ten-pound note, before she thought better of it and put the money back in her jacket breast pocket. She had to remember: she hadn't been paid in full, not yet. Then – she was ashamed to admit, but she was hardly shocked by the confirmation of her own habits – she headed back to the main room, ventured to the window, put the small silver church in her jeans jacket pocket and walked out the way she had walked in.

When she exited the house she felt guilty.

Maybe she ought to join Shoplifters Anonymous or something.

She patted the bump in her jeans jacket pocket that the trinket made. She had the address; she could always send it back. She took it out and looked at it longingly. Then, before she could change her mind, she slipped it through the letter slot, and it clunked on the floor inside the house. Finna, whenever she returned, would see it whenever she next used the front door. Rather than sneaking out the back door. Tesser was mildly insulted.

She showed up at AMI Industries five minutes early, feeling nervous and also feeling like a fraud in terms of her falsified video experience. But she still knew how to video, and she'd done some editing in the past, too. It would be OK, she assured herself. It would be fine.

Maybe Finna had been right. Maybe she'd feel better if she cleared things up. She took out her mobile, rummaged through her backpack and found the travelcard on which Jamie had written his telephone number – weeks ago, now. There was chemistry between them. If she called him, she'd be playing with the fire. There was that whole three-shag thing. But, to be fair, she owed him an apology for running off the night of the festival. She punched in his mobile number and then her finger hovered over the number pad. She hoped he'd be cool.

The phone rang.

'Hello?'

'Jamie, it's Tesser.'

'Oh. Hi.'

He sounded pissed off.

'Look, I wanted to explain what happened the other night.'

'Explain.'

No, he wasn't being cool. He was being plain cold. 'It's sort of *hard* to explain. There was a lady who was chasing me, and I don't know why. She tried to grab my film.'

'Yeah, I didn't get the chance to offer my congratulations on your fine film.'

'Just listen. Something to do with the guys I filmed on the ghost walk, you know, the ones I told you about.'

'The ones on the film. That was them, wasn't it? I could tell it was them from your description of the room. That was sort of unprofessional, wasn't it? Though I guess you couldn't see their faces. Probably serves you right, though.'

'Thanks for the sympathy. I'm being chased by some female hit man because of a serious case of homosexual panic and you're taking it very, very lightly.'

'Listen, Tesser, you stood me up, and then legged it. Sorry if I'm not coming over all sensitive New Age guy.'

Tesser paused a few seconds to consider this. 'Yeah. Except I didn't stand you up. Sorry about taking off, though. I'm really, really, really sorry.' She took a breath. She was about to break the three-shag rule. Assuming they'd shag. 'Maybe you might want to meet up again?'

He didn't seem particularly warm. 'Maybe.'

'Maybe I could come over tomorrow or something? To your place?'

'Well, I've got no idea where you live, so that would probably work out better.'

She let that pass. 'Tomorrow at ten in the morning? Too early?'

He sighed, and she imagined him smiling with resignation on the other side of the phone. 'Yeah, it is, but come on over anyway.'

And she was grinning too when she hung up the phone. Things were squared with Jamie and within a few months she would be editing *Chain of Lurve*. She gripped her backpack as she strode up the stairs; inside it was her Super-8 camera. She knew she didn't need it, but for some reason she had the feeling that all of a sudden someone was going to scream 'fake!' and then she could reach in her bag and pull out the camera, present it to them like some frigging FBI identity card, as if to say, 'Here, look, I really am a filmmaker.'

Fiona the receptionist was as nasty as ever. 'Your equipment is over there,' she snapped, nodding towards a lousy-looking video camera and a stack of blank VHS tapes on a table to the right of her desk. Jesus, what a bunch of cheapskates. A joint like this and they couldn't even run to a decent digital camera.

'Old format?' said Tesser, in the most disparaging tone she could muster.

'Yes. Old format,' Fiona threw back. 'Perhaps you were assuming we'd trust a student with our state-of-the-art digicam? I don't think so. That equipment is for Dr Sharkey's personal use only.'

Fiona made the word 'personal' sound sleazy and Tesser blushed, despite the implicaton that she was untrustworthy and technically incompetent. OK, old-format video it would have to be.

Tesser walked quickly over, trying to look as confident as possible while under Fiona's withering gaze. Fiona cleared her throat ostentatiously, as if she were trying to stifle a guffaw. She probably had Tesser totally figured out; probably knew very well that Tesser was just a broke ex-student and was just in this whole gig for the money.

Tesser looked hopefully around for Dr Sharkey, but she was nowhere to be seen. Damn.

Instead Dr Sharkey had left behind the key to the building and a set of specific instructions on what exactly Tesser was expected to be filming that day. AMI Industries had booked a canal boat and was sponsoring Hackney schoolchildren for a ride down the canals. Fucking A-OK great.

She hated kids.

The boat full of schoolchildren, several teachers and one grumpy filmmaker coasted slowly down the canal. There was a huge banner on the side that read SPONSORED BY BLAIRSTONE CHEMICALS, A DIVISION OF AMI INDUSTRIES and Tesser made sure she got a nice clear shot of that, figuring that was the kind of thing her employers would like to see a lot of in the final product. She wasn't really sure what she was supposed to be doing in terms of filming – was she supposed to be going for cool, experimental shots, or was she just supposed to be doing some straightforward mainstream filming? She had a strong feeling that it was the latter.

She dutifully filmed the little brats until she had used up an entire tape. One of the charming youngsters, a sweet-faced little girl with curly red hair, even tried to push her into the canal, so by the time Tesser reached for a second tape she figured she was lucky to have gotten away with the filming with nary a soak in the water.

After lunch, the teachers tried to interest the children in the various species of waterfowl along the Hackney Marshes. One of the adults kindly offered Tesser a tuna sandwich and an apple on which she munched away obediently. With nothing to film, she grew bored, and when the chaperone wasn't looking she filmed some nice shots of the sun coming through the tree branches, and some of the canal itself, and reflections of the industry buildings and factories that flanked the water on either side. Then on the return trip, just to ensure she had an establishing shot for the eventual finished product, she filmed the side of AMI Industries. The brick building looked interesting in a Victorian sweatshop kind of way. There was faded lettering on the side that she couldn't make out – only an 'of' and an '&' – words attesting to the building's antiquity, and two Gothic cupolas flanking the top that were onion-shaped, nearly Byzantine. The building seemed a bit of a hybrid in architectural terms, although Tesser was no expert.

She found herself looking forward to the next day. She hadn't slept with someone more than twice since she had got her fingers burned with Noriko. She hadn't even wanted to. Until she met Jamie. She usually got bored with the idea of rehashing – let's face it – an ultimately finite number of sexual positions. Until she met Jamie. She aimed her camera at a swan gliding down the canal, a smear of white against the muddy brown of the water. She tucked the second, unfinished tape into her backpack, reckoning she would fill it up on her next assignment. Things were looking up. She hadn't felt this way for a while.

Until she met Jamie.

'Hey! So this is your place in daylight!' She looked around the upmarket flat. She had bicycled over as planned and rung repeatedly on the intercom button until she'd woken him up. She felt disgruntled that he had forgotten she was coming over. He was still sleepy and wasn't giving her his full attention. The flat was wall-to-wall floorboards and it was a spacious apartment when you considered that it was placed slam-bang in the middle of Islington. It was classy-minimalist, complete with a single clear vase on the windowsill crammed full of blue daisies and small red roses.

'Yeah. You've only seen it through drunken, three a.m. eyes, haven't you? And then of course you took off pretty early in the morning.'

She was nervous. Was Jamie going to kiss her or not? Should she try to kiss him? Why was she nervous? 'Aren't you going to offer me a cup of coffee?'

'Last time you were here you didn't even stay for breakfast. I was just about to offer you a cup of *tea*, actually, but, being as you're a Yank, I'll bring forth the coffee. Is instant OK?'

'As long as it's not Nescafé. You know what they –'

'Yeah, yeah, I know.' Jamie's voice was muffled as he rumbled through the cupboard. 'Um . . . I seem to be out of instant, after all. Tea, then?'

'Earl Grey, thanks. I'll just make myself comfortable, shall I?'

What the hell was she doing? She was at least an hour early and he wasn't even properly awake yet. And there Tesser was, lying down on the chaise longue, her kilt riding up so that her underwear was visible through her tights. It was transparent and Jamie was aware that his eyes kept darting back and forth to her crotch while he tried to concentrate on making the tea. He knew quite well she was doing it on purpose. She was a little minx, and he wasn't sure he'd forgiven her yet for the festival fiasco, though she had apologised profusely. Looking at her now, though, so brazen and flirty, made him realise that she was easy to forgive. Well, at least his cock seemed to be forgiving her. He turned away to hide his erection, inexplicably embarrassed.

'I've only got tea bags, I'm afraid,' he told Tesser. Damn, she was still in the same position, looking up at him expectantly: half innocent, half knowing. What was her game?

'What else would you use?'

She looked perplexed for a moment, then an expression crossed over her face and she managed to hide whatever had flickered over her mind during that moment. Jamie had seen that look before with other

133

people – the realisation that his background was different, that realisation that their worlds were different. He sighed to himself and poured milk into Tesser's mug. So far, the fact that he was well off had not seemed to be an issue with Tesser. He thought it maybe had been because she was American, and they couldn't dissect British class signifiers the way his own countrymen and countrywomen did.

He brought the mug over to her, along with his own. 'Here's your tea. I know that Americans like it with lemon instead of milk, but I don't have any lemons.' Well, maybe he could impress her with his sensitivity to cultural mores, at least.

Tesser took the tea gladly and gave him a bright smile. 'Thanks.' But no, there was something different about her, as if the realisation of their inequalities had shifted something in her manner – tainted it, maybe. She looked a little sneaky. The change was not necessarily bad. Sneaky might even be good. Yes, damn it, she looked hot and sneaky lying there on the couch.

He sat down on the hardwood floor in front of the chaise longue and gazed at her, watching her sip the tea in silence. There was that lingerie advertisement a couple years ago – it was probably Agent Provocateur or something. A blonde in sheer black nylon panties, quite pornographic, so you could almost see everything, and a caption that read, EVERY LADY DESERVES A PEARL NECKLACE. Something like that. It was just ambiguous enough to escape the wrath of the Advertising Standards Authority, but to anyone in the know – and surely that had to be 99.9 per cent of the adult population – the inference was clear. He thought of it now, and his cock tightened. The way the picture had looked, with the woman lying back, her legs spread like Tesser's were now. The see-thru sleazy/classy black nylon just opaque enough to make the viewer guess at what the crotch was or wasn't showing. Just like Tesser's. The flesh around the model's throat and upper chest already blushing with a sex-flush. No doubt applied by skilful stylists, but effective nevertheless.

The first time he had seen it, it had made Jamie want to wank all over the model's chest and spray her throat and wet pink lips with hot come, which had surely been the advertisement's desired effect. The model had looked like she wanted it. She *had* wanted it. The thought made him firm and stiff as rock even now, just thinking about. It made him want to re-create the image and then degrade it, wanking over sexy, sleazy Tesser and shooting out all over her pale, innocent-looking neck. Maybe he could get her to wear a long blonde wig, for pure trashy porn appeal. He had one here in the flat; Trevor had left it behind after a modelling session with him and his lover. Jamie placed his tea down on the floor.

'Just a moment,' he said, and stood up.

'Where you going?'

'Just to get something.' He exited to his bedroom and rummaged around until he found the shopping bag that Trevor's boyfriend had left behind, the one filled with clothes, lingerie and a wig. Trevor's longtime boyf was a drag artiste, but when in mufti he was alarmingly butch. He pulled out the hairpiece and carried it back into the main room.

'Can you put this on for me?' he asked, his tongue dry with nervousness. What if she said no?

Tesser gave the long blonde wig a good hard stare. 'OK,' she said at last. 'I'll wear the wig if you wear it for me first.'

'OK . . .'

That was simple enough, although he found it hard to guess what Tesser might have in mind. She definitely had *something* in mind, though, because she was fumbling through her large backpack, taking out heaps of make-up, even nail polish. Then she walked over to his own worktable and started piling up in her arms a heap of various acrylic paints. She had some cheek. She picked through the brushes he had soaking in jars. 'Don't use those,' Jamie warned, suddenly anxious. 'Those are the boar's-hair ones. Use the cheaper ones, with the beige handles.'

Tesser turned around and gave him funny look. 'I'm not willing to use cheap brushes. Deal with it.'

'Uh, OK.' What the hell was she planning on doing? Jamie ran his fingers through the wig that he still held in his hand, feeling the strands of plastic flaxen hair. He didn't want to let go of the image of the pearl-necklace girl. 'You're not touching my paintings now, are you? I can't handle it when people join in on a painting; I broke up with my first girlfriend because she did just that.'

Tesser headed back across the floor towards him, her arms heaped with various tubes of paint and with the expensive brushes.

'What did she do?' She smiled, rather wickedly. 'So I know to avoid it, of course.'

Jamie looked nervously around at the plain pale wood of his floorboards and the cool melon green of his bare walls. He wanted his flat to remain the way it was. There was no way he was going to let her slap paint on either the walls or the floor. 'I had done some paintings where people had no eyeballs, like their eyes were blank. One day I came home and found out that she had painted in eyeballs on every painting. We split up the next day.'

'That was very naughty of her,' Tesser agreed. She looked him directly in the eye, the fingers of her left hand on her throat, obviously lost in thought. Jamie swallowed at the sight of her vulnerable, milk-pale neck. There was a light sprinkling of freckles there, too, not just on her face. 'Very naughty.'

Against his will, Jamie's cock twitched a little at the word 'naughty'.

'Strip, OK?'

'Now?' Jamie looked at the door. They really ought to

lock it. Trevor could do his usual thing and walk in at any minute.

'It's not locked. So leave it that way. And strip, as I said.'

He stripped, holding her gaze as he took off first his shirt and then his trousers, his underwear and socks, his trainers.

'And your watch. I want you mother-naked.'

'Shouldn't that be father-naked?'

She gave him a rather odd smile. 'Oh, I don't think so.'

Though he did as she asked, at the same time he was tempted to say something cheeky and flippant; wanted to regain some semblance of control here in his own flat. But it was difficult when he was standing nude and shivering. She spread out a couple of sheets of newspaper.

'Sit down on the floor,' she commanded.

Meeting Finna had put an interesting idea in Tesser's mind. The image of the soothsayer had been nagging at her all last night. She couldn't figure out why, but there had been some residual inspiration due to her faulty memory. Now if only she could follow through with it . . .

She hovered over Jamie, who was sitting cross-legged there in front of her. She felt potent, adrenaline pumping through her veins. She suspected this was how Dr Sharkey felt with her: the hesitating moment when the pussy grows even wetter, when you wonder whether you have the guts to actually make the fantasy come true.

Tesser bent down to try, her hand trembling. She reached ceremoniously for her palette of eyeshadows and a foam eyeshadow applicator. Then she lavished his eyelids with colour: yellow at the tips, gold lines just underneath his brows, detailed with liquid eyeliner. A shimmering streak of matte blackberry powder over his heavy lids, so that the eye make-up shone purple-gold on top of his dark brown skin.

'Look.' She showed Jamie the rhinestone-and-feather necklace she had unearthed from her bag, and then in front of his eyes she took the pocket knife out from behind her breasts and cut the string that linked the beads and feathers. The baubles rolled across the floor, the movement a nice complement to the sway of green feathers, which were slowly, slowly floating down to the floor. Then, making ingenious use of her little glass tube of false eyelash adhesive, she pressed his lids down lightly with the tips of her fingers and began to glue a series of the small teal feathers across his cheekbones in a descending angle, which just heightened the severity of his square jaw. The effect was not feminising. She felt uncertain, and not exactly pleased.

He looked less like a drag queen and more like some highly decorated god or icon.

This had not been her intention.

Jamie was breathing lightly, sitting on the floor with his legs crossed like a guru. He seemed to be caught in some unreal, otherworldly space. She painted his mouth with a gilded shade of dark cranberry and, as she stroked the waxen colour on to his full, beautiful lips with a tiny brush, their natural beauty and shape was clear. As if on cue, he licked these lips, his tongue darting out quickly like some raw, red, ripe animal thing among the artifice of wax, and she crouched there, transfixed above him. Just as the make-up had accentuated his masculinity, so did the pantomime of cosmetics only serve to emphasise his vitality and life force. Tesser admired her handiwork before she attended to him once again. He looked beautiful, no less masculine but just possibly more androgynous. Tesser's sex became moist in anticipation when she grew aware that she was realising the image she had planned, after all.

This was the secret. She'd worn make-up since she

was fourteen, but this truth had somehow eluded her. As she fetishised and decorated Jamie's particularly male beauty in the same way, she understood at last that women clothed themselves with cosmetic masks: not to hide, but to accentuate. If only more modern human males wore make-up. They should take inspiration from the peacock. She knew for a fact that Viking men frequently wore both mascara and eyeliner.

She covered him with acrylic paint and watercolours, painting his toes orange with silver lashings and then drawing long blue stripes all the way up his thighs. He had gone strangely quiet and submissive for a moment and he spread his thighs for her carefully, so that the taut limber muscles of them showed and Tesser's mouth went dry with desire. Anyway, neither acrylic nor watercolour was toxic unless it was ingested in great quantities. On the blue length of his legs she glued the tiny rhinestones, picking them up like pearls from the floor where she had spilled them. Once adhered, they looked encrusted in his skin and when he shifted the paste gems glittered in the overhead light. Then she painted each of his fingernails with radiation-green nail polish.

Then at last she crowned him with the blonde wig.

'Wait a moment,' she whispered. It wasn't quite right. She searched through her bag until she removed a can of hairspray. She twirled the artificial flaxen hair in her palms in an imitation of his jet-dark dreads beneath, spraying it with a soft little hiss from the can and rolling each bunch of pale hair in her palms so that it too dreaded. And while her palms grew sticky with the residue of spritzer, so did her panties moisten between her legs. When she finished styling, she walked over to the window and took the glass vase that stood there on the sill into the kitchen and drained it over the sink. She took her time, knowing that with each delayed moment Jamie was growing more and more impatient.

She returned carrying a bouquet, and then twisted

flowers throughout the wig. The tints of the blooms were red and blue, each shade the other's opposite. The petals were not pastels but pure unsaturated colour; the starlike heads of the artificial blue daisies were lake-blue, eyeball-blue, berry-blue and the venous bright-red roses were also blindingly untainted: Beaujolais-red, lipstick-red. She wrapped these contrasting flowers round each dread in turn. When she finished he still did not look effeminate, as surely most men would have done in a similar situation. Instead, he looked pagan and earthy as he sat there half smirking, his body language still cocky. She had the feeling that he was waiting for her to falter; waiting for her to lose her nerve. Still, this was certainly what Pan himself would have looked like: decadent, pagan, decorated. She wished she could film him outside in some green glade.

'Let's see your handiwork.' Jamie's voice startled her, then she felt confident again. He had no idea what he had coming to him. She stared him out. Her clit grew stiff with power.

'All right, then,' she said lightly, handing him a small mirror from her purse so that he could see clearly and specifically exactly what she had done to him.

'Not bad,' he admitted. 'You're not a bad painter at all.'

'Thanks very much,' Tesser told him. 'Now I'm going to paint you a pussy.'

'You *what*?' Jamie nearly choked with surprise. He seemed shocked at last.

Aha, got to you, didn't I, Mr Outsider Artist?

She took the mirror away from him. He didn't seem so cocksure now and Tesser relished his uncertainty. Then she took out her cosmetics set and his watercolours and painted a dark-brown-and-purple cunt along his prick and balls, one adorned with hot-pink lipstick detailing and a clitoral hood crafted of silver lipstick .

'This is fucking perverse, Tesser, I hope you know

that,' Jamie said, but he let her stroke and touch and polish him with colour. She was generous with his new genitalia, extending his artificial labia below his shaft, all the way back to his asshole, which would serve as pussy. It was only at this point that he gave any indication that he was enjoying her attentions, and a small moan escaped his lips. Tesser smiled and with her fingers kept massaging the paint into the sensitive flesh between his balls and asshole. She was getting hot too. She had created her own androgyne. Her pussy grew creamy as she endowed him with this second sex, this sex-on-top-of-a-sex. Jamie groaned softly and his cock, which had previously been flaccid, began to stiffen a little, and by the time she was curling the paintbrush around his asshole he was shivering and his cock was thickening, stretching its coat of colour.

It was necessary for her to add a second coat of purple watercolour to his prick, because his erection was spoiling the clit she'd given him.

Breathing more and more quickly, she tickled the dark fur around his anus, and then daubed it with red and purple paint so that it too became a pussy hole: a vivid blood-purple, the same neon-purple as his eyeshadow. Lovely. Lovely. Lovely.

'Take a look now, you little tart.' She loved speaking to him this way, hissing the words into his ear. He wouldn't look at first, but she thrust the mirror into his hand and made him lower his eyes to look at himself, to look at the beautiful cunt she'd painted on to his genitals: glowing purple-pink, lurid, pornographic. He grabbed his cock, his Day-Glo green nail varnish in contrast to its stiff painted beauty, and kissed Tesser deeply, shocking her with the sudden movement, his tongue thick in her mouth. She moaned, and moved towards him, feeling an itch to have that violet-stained cock inside her.

'Fuck me,' he moaned. 'Fuck my pink cunt.'

She was immediately horny, and felt such intense desire that for a moment she thought she was going to faint. Fuck, no – not if she missed all the fun. She wanted to plunder him, fill him. She shoved her hand deep down between his legs, down under his shaft and balls, all along his newly painted pussy, her short fingernails skimming against the heavily laden colour. The lower she moved her hand, the more he leaned into her.

'I'm running my hand all over your wet pussy,' she whispered in his ear. 'How does it feel, Jamie? How does it feel?'

'Good,' he managed to say, and he loosened his own grip on his cock, and submitted himself to her perverse caresses. Her hand went lower and her fingers found his asshole, his asshole that she had painted like a dark-red, wet vagina, like a wet, tight fuck hole – purple-red, creamy, empty. She rubbed at it. 'Ohhh . . .' he managed to moan.

'You like your pussy rubbed?' Tesser asked.

'Yes! Rub my pussy, touch my clit, wank my cock, I don't care.' He was spreading his thighs wide now, the muscles and sinews of his inner thighs as taut as a dancer's, and his hips were starting to move in rhythm to Tesser's insistent hand.

'You little slut. You've got one pretty snatch, I'll tell you that,' Tesser informed him. 'I'm going to fuck your cunt and fuck it good.'

Jamie squirmed under Tesser's touch, and then began to slide his crotch closer to her fingers. She took a bottle of lube from her bag and squirted it all over his cock, balls and asshole.

'You're all wet now, now aren't you?' She ground her hand against the lube, smashing the gel into his stiff cock and his balls. He groaned. He *was* wet. He was all wet and sticky for her. His cunt was wet. She kept stroking back and forth over his sex, long movements all

he way down to his arse. This felt so good he broke out
nto a sweat, could feel perspiration beading on his
row, making the make-up start to run. 'Ahh,' he
noaned, jerking his groin closer, closer to Tesser's hand,
o she could touch more of him; he wanted everything
uched, everything fucked at once.

'Fuck me,' he whispered. He felt vulnerable, open. It
as wonderful.

She slid a finger deep into him. Her finger was a hot
hread of pain, but then it turned sweet, so sweet,
rawing lust out from his gut, and Jamie wanted more.
e found himself trying to grind down against the digit,
hich was slippery with lube. She added another finger,
nd began to fuck him slowly, and all he felt was a great
irty relief. He lay flat back on the floor, raised his hips
nd let Tesser fuck him that way. Her hand moved more
nd more quickly, and he could only lie there and pant
nd groan. It was too intense.

'You want more, you little slut?'

Yes. He wanted more.

'Answer me.'

He couldn't.

'More?'

'Yes!' he screamed at last. And she gave him more,
ith four fingers thrusting into his arse and her other
and gripping his stiff prick. The wig scratched against
e bare floor, the paste jewels fell off his face, the
athers fluttered down to the floor. He wanted to shoot
ll over his painted cunt, spray out over Tesser's neck
st as he had originally desired. And she bent there,
tense and dominant, her hand in his arse, her tits
waying each time she pushed into him; each time her
st jerked his cock. Oh, fuck, he was going to come. He
as going to come. He let go, spraying all over her
roat. It felt so fucking good. It reminded him of the
dvertisement. It reminded him of when he'd come over
er cleavage in the men's washroom at Liverpool Street

Station. He didn't care what it reminded him of. He jus'
shot his come out, white and creamy over her tits and
throat. Fuck, yeah, it felt so good, so good . . .

He groaned as he spent the last of his come and lay
on his back, empty, trying to catch his breath. And
slowly, slowly, Tesser glided her fingers out of his arse
He felt bereft for a moment. She was saying something
to him. He ought to be listening.

'What?'

'And is that all?' Tesser was saying.

'Course not. I'm a millennial guy, you know. I'll take
care of you. Just give me a second here.'

'That's not what I mean.' She had the strange smile on
her face again. 'I'm talking about you. If you're a chick
you ought to be able to keep going, even after you've
come. That's the way we're designed. Lucky, huh?'

'Yeah, but I'm a bloke,' Jamie explained in a patien
voice.

'No, you're not,' she said stubbornly, 'not with this
still here.' She ran her fingers over the painted design
between his legs. He felt vulnerable again, and he shiv
ered. Maybe he ought to play along. She began to stroke
him firmly again, a long caress that ran from the head o
his cock, down to his balls, over his perineum, smudging
the tip of her finger just outside the rim of his anus. He
looked down and saw that her hand was wet with juice
and paint. Her finger was hovering at his arsehole. From
nowhere, he felt a spark of desire again. Impossible. He
was planning on going down on her or fingering her
not fucking her. It usually took him good half-hour to
recover from coming – at least.

'There we go,' Tesser said, keeping a tight grip on his
prick, and even he was surprised as it firmed in her we
palm, the moisture rubbing against his cockhead, mak
ing it suddenly sensitive. 'Now shove that gorgeous
painted pussy of yours into mine, and let's get started.
For a moment, her words echoed his, and Jamie fel

blood rush to his face as he recalled screaming out the words, 'fuck my pink cunt!'

Now he wanted her. Wanted to shove it into her. He got to his knees, was momentarily shocked by all the mixed colour on him, everywhere – they were both dripping with paint and semen – and then pulled Tesser towards him, pushing up her kilt, rolling down her tights. She stepped out of those tights and also her underwear and then he tackled her, went directly on top of her, pushing his cock into her pussy, which felt as hot and smooth as melted butter but much, much more tight. The friction made his cock pulse with lust. She let him sink down into her, and he put his mouth to one of her nipples and sucked and bit and licked, his dark-red lipstick staining her nipple. This seemed wickedly perverted and made him fuck her all the harder.

Yes. Jamie was good. She let him plunge into her and she leaned back, put a hand down on herself, rubbing, enjoying the plundering. No one could fuck like he could. No one could – wait! What was she saying? Many people could fuck like he could. There were many, *many* fine fish in the sea. Jesus fucking Christ! Here it was happening. This was their third shag, and now it would all come to no good end.

Then she stopped thinking that and moaned aloud while he pumped into her, screwing hard and fast and dirty, because the truth was this particular shag was coming to a very good end indeed.

Afterwards they took a shower together, and snogged while the water washed the paint and come from their bodies. Once while kissing Tesser opened her eyes and watched as the colour on Jamie's body swirled down the drain. For a moment, they both stood there with their arms around each other. Her own hair was still dripping green liquid, too, because, although the dye was permanent, she knew from experience it would take a few more washes until it 'settled'. As she had been the one who had decorated him so elaborately, she took it upon herself to make sure she scrubbed him clean, and he yelped good-naturedly as she washed his groin. He in turn soaped up her hair and made her giggle as he worked it into a froth. He was so much taller than she was that she reached out her tongue and licked at his dark, small nipple. He was just as beautiful without paint, too.

He was beautiful, period.

'Here you go.' He handed her a fluffy white Egyptian cotton towel as she stepped out of the shower after him. Jeez. There were some advantages to dating a rich guy. Um, not that they were really dating, right ... He dried himself quickly and stepped out into the main room. Tesser, who was never one for prolonged drying, swiftly followed afterwards, dripping on the floor. She hoped he wouldn't notice. He stood there stretching out his lanky body in the sunlight in the middle of his floor. At first, Tesser's eyes were drawn to him. But then she noticed a painting stacked against the far wall that she hadn't seen before, because her back had been to them the entire time. She stopped stock-still, feeling with sudden clarity how naked and exposed she was. She felt like she couldn't breathe.

The painting was of Eric, from the ghost walk two weeks ago. He was painted from the back, his head turned round to face the viewer. The fronts of his upper arms weren't visible, so for a moment she wasn't sure. The tattoo would have been the clincher, since she was so bad with faces. She walked closer, confirming that it was actually him. And it was.

'Jamie,' Tesser said slowly, her brain completely numb, 'please tell me why you have a naked painting of this man in your apartment.'

'Hey.' Jamie came up to her and snuggled her from behind. 'So I paint nudes. You're not jealous, are you?'

Chapter Seven

*F*reaky.

The guy in the painting – Eric – was Jamie's stepbrother's boyfriend. Tesser thought about it while she bicycled home later that afternoon: her life had been full of some weird coincidences lately. Stuff was getting complicated.

She skidded through a rain puddle, splashing water on a woman with a baby carriage walking nearby.

'Sorry!' she hollered back, but the woman only cursed at her.

Jamie had promised that he would tactfully ask his stepbrother about the ghost walk, but he would do it subtly; he didn't want to stir too much, as it looked like bi-try Eric was cheating with guys and girls alike. (Tesser had been somewhat relieved that Jamie's brother hadn't been named Alistair.)

She whizzed past home on Chatsworth Road and on towards Hackney Central to buy the groceries. At last. She could get a lot of food on her remaining fifteen pounds – as long as she bought Tesco's 'value' brand. There were savings to be had.

This was the case. After shopping, her backpack was

full of peanut butter, pasta, 49p day-old bread, 5p economy cans of tinned tomatoes and a huge, heavy sack of potatoes. She walked her bike back, worried that she would drop the lot if she simply cycled home as usual. Along with the replenished food supply, she still had the VCR tape from yesterday in her backpack, having forgotten to take it out and hand it back to Fiona. She was, all in all, cheery: a latter-day Saint Ms Nicholas with a sack full of nutritional treats for the deserving good little boys and girls of the squat. But when she got back home, there was a sombre, tense meeting around the kitchen table. Her first thought was that she was going to be kicked out; that she had delayed too many days in making this grocery run.

'What's up?' she asked nervously, removing the plastic bags and plonking them down on the counter. She slid into the seat next to Kitty. Even Kitty didn't meet her gaze. Oh, Jesus, this was bad.

'We've had stuff stolen,' Jana said accusingly. She glared at Tesser. 'I hope you've been locking up properly. Someone's come in through a back window in the basement and gone through all the rooms.'

'Shit! What's gone?' She thought immediately of her extensive collection of 1970s platform heels.

'Weird stuff. Some of Kitty's law books. My hairdryer. Jake's CD player. Mmoluke's mobile phone. You'll have to look for yourself to see what's gone.'

Kitty gave Tesser a stricken look. 'Take it easy –'

But Tesser was already running up the stairs to her room. The shoes were all there. Good. Then she looked near the window, where she always kept her Super-8 camera. No way! It was fucking gone. She looked under the bed – all her VCR tapes, homemade or originals: gone. She raced to the darkroom/closet, where she stored film reels – nothing! Nothing! *The Passion Flowchart* was lost for ever. She sank down to the floor, her head in her hands.

'Hey,' Kitty was standing in the doorway, 'I thought that might be the case. Look, we'll figure out what –'

'This is shit!' Tesser wailed. 'What the fuck am I going to do without my film?' That bitch Jana, for having suggested that she might not have been locking up properly.

She trudged back down to the kitchen slowly, feeling totally defeated. Kitty trailed silently behind her, obviously having deduced that this wasn't a good time to speak. Tesser fought the urge to burst out in tears. Recently, things had seemed to be working out so well, what with the job and possibly even with Jamie. This sucked. This totally sucked.

Since she had finally replenished the communal supply, she distracted herself by making a round of peppermint tea for the depressed masses. Kitty passed around a nice fat spliff and pretty soon things started to feel a bit better.

'We've had a lock put on all the windows downstairs,' Jana said. 'I went and bought some today. The price tag was hefty and, believe me, it's coming out of the communal household supply funds, 'cos I'm sure not paying out of my own pocket. I've had enough irritation today with my hairdryer going missing. At first I thought it was you –' she turned to Tesser, '– since you like to borrow things like crisps without asking first, but then I realised that your hair's too short and you like to drip-dry, anyway, judging from the state of the bathroom after you use it.'

Tesser was fuming, but she bit her tongue. 'Sugar?' she asked Jana sweetly, stirring the tea with unnecessary violence.

'Hey, now,' Jake interjected, 'let's keep it calm.'

Jana was smirking, happy she had got in a dig at Tesser. 'One, please. And I don't like it too strong, as well you know.'

'Listen, you,' Tesser said, half-threateningly, 'you may have lost your bloody hairdryer, but I have lost *art*.'

'That's what you call your little slide shows? You should get a new camera, sweetie. You're using the same make my uncle used back in the seventies. There's been this thing called technology since then, you know.'

Tesser simmered, but didn't say anything. She sat down next to Jake and tried to let the joint work its magic and calm her, relax her, chill her out . . .

At least one of the tapes was already with AMI Industries and the other one was still safe in her bag. Jesus! Think if she had taken all that equipment home, and the thieves had taken those tapes, too. She would have been sacked: no money. She might have lost her beloved short, but this way she could still afford to make the thirty-minute movie. It could be worse: those sicko crims also could have stolen the left-foot shoe of every shoe pair – this had once happened to an unfortunate former roommate of Tesser's. Thank God she'd left both the equipment and tape number one at AMI, because she knew Dr Sharkey would have fired her on the second. There was no way the company would pay for new equipment and there was no way they would even sponsor a second boat trip for those underprivileged schoolchildren just because Tesser had lost a tape. Tesser could have ended up owing *them* money.

'You seen this?' Trevor threw a magazine over at Jamie. 'Look on page fourteen.'

UNDERSTATED® JURIED ART SHOW. **UNDER-STATED**® IS THE MOST PRESTIGIOUS EXHIBITION AROUND, SPONSORED BY THE LEAGUE OF UPWARDLY MOBILE LIBERAL BROADSHEETS, BRITISH OIL RESERVES, INC., BRITISH TELEPHONE MONOPOLIES LTD AND THE HAPPILY SOON-TO-BE-PRIVATISED LONDON SUB-

TERRESTRIAL TRANSPORTATION SYSTEM®. BROUGHT TO YOU BY THE PEOPLE WHO INTRODUCED SUCH SUCCESSES AS THE MAKE-YOUR-OWN-MILLENNIUM PUBLIC CONCEPTUAL ART RAVE. £10,000 CASH PRIZE AND UNDREAMED-OF PERSONAL FAME. SHOE-IN FOR THE GUINEVERE PRIZE – HEY, WE'VE FIXED IT, YOU KNOW – AND ANY OTHER BRIT-ART® ACCOLADES OR PRIZES AWARDED FOR THE NEXT THREE CALENDAR YEARS. CONFIRMED DEAL WITH ALL THE CUTTING-EDGE STYLE MAGS. TURNING-IN DATE 30 JULY. INSTA-RESULTS POSTED THE NEXT DAY ON OUR WEBSITE. QUICKEST ART JURY IN TOWN.

'Better get a-painting, bro. This could be your big shot at fame.'

'Hey, shut up.' But Jamie read through the contest details. OK. It was intriguing. The problem was, he didn't have a bloody clue what he ought to submit.

'Eric asked me to pick up his stuff, by the way,' Trevor told his stepbrother. 'Where have you hidden it?'

'The bag's in my room,' Jamie said. 'Tell him to remember it next time he models for me. Hey, that reminds me, about Eric . . .'

'Yeah?' Trevor called from the bedroom. 'What is it?'

Oh, hell, he couldn't break his brother's heart and tell him that Eric was cheating on him, according to Tesser. 'Never mind. Um. Just tell him, sorry about the flowers in the wig.'

'You're a weird one, bro.'

'So they say. So they say.' Jamie went back to scanning the call for submissions. But talk of the wig had reminded him of Tesser. He was going to give her a call.

He was going to ask her out on a proper date.

* * *

Tesser, meanwhile, was having a bit of a personal crisis. Her entire short film had vanished. Now she was desperately scribbling down ideas and images from *The Passion Flowchart*, so that the ideas behind the short weren't lost for ever too. The film had been a rough draft for the thirty-minute movie, so the more she remembered, the less she would have lost.

She was surprised when Jamie rang. Surprised as well at how her heart beat faster; how she smiled when she held the phone to her ear. He wanted to go to a movie, and that sounded all right to her. They agreed to meet at the Rio Cinema, halfway for both of them: in Dalston, between Islington and central Hackney. When nighttime rolled round, she found some cleanish clothes: a pair of bright-blue combat trousers and a swirly, 70s-ish long-sleeved psychedelic shirt. She pulled out a pair of motorcycle boots and her outfit was complete (though she was too much of a chickenshit to ever really climb up on a motorcycle, even to ride pillion).

The whole bus ride in, she found herself unaccountably grinning. But then, as surely as if someone was fine-tuning the dial on her emotions, her initial bright giddiness swerved, and she felt uneasy. There was something, some reason why she shouldn't trust him, not just yet, and it had nothing to do with the three-shag rule. Some memory, or even foresight, hinted at this – but she couldn't figure out why.

When she got there, the place was heaving. She didn't see Jamie at first. But the Rio was a cool old cinema, one that had been recently refurbished. She bought herself some popcorn and waited. She had been happier earlier, but now she felt a kind of icy chill at the thought of seeing him. She didn't know whether her suspicions were even fair. But her gut feeling was screaming 'Red alert! Red alert!' Would she pay attention? Or was she going to follow her clit? She ate the salty popcorn, and tried to concentrate on her most base, obvious feelings towards Jamie: she liked him; she wanted to shag him; he made her laugh.

'There you are! I didn't see you round the corner.' Jamie's voice was as friendly as it usually was, but this only made Tesser more nervous. She was glad she hadn't said anything to him back at his apartment about the psycho lady who attacked her at the film festival. The psycho lady who had known Eric by name.

Jesus. She didn't know who to trust; it was terrifying.

But in a way, it was also kind of a turn-on.

Romantic, sweet Jamie. Evil, calculating, man-with-possibly-psycho-friends, great-shag Jamie. She didn't know which one she preferred. But she kissed him on the cheek and tried to act as normally as possible.

He seemed to sense that there was something on her mind and didn't prod. They sat there uncomfortably watching the film for a while; Tesser munched away on her popcorn. She was aware of Jamie inching his hand closer to her lap. Did he want popcorn or a sly grope? She tried to concentrate on the film, which turned out to be a trite romantic comedy. Jamie cleared his throat self-consciously, and she could tell he was bored, too. This whole situation reminded her of Mickey Rourke in *Diner*, where his character eventually resorted to sticking his cock up through the popcorn so the 'nice' girl he was on a date with would touch it. This scene had always half horrified and half fascinated Tesser, since it seemed to be such a desperate act: inevitably unsuccessful, and yet Rourke's character was obviously so driven by lust and longing that he no longer could correctly gauge what was correct sexual behaviour. He was controlled by his crotch. Tesser could relate.

Jamie at last made his move, by reaching over and running a hand up Tesser's leg, then resting it lightly on her thigh, on the fabric of her blue trousers.

'Look,' he whispered in her ear, 'this film is boring.'

'Do you want to go to the arcade and play Ms Pac-

Man? Best two out of three?' She remembered that he too was into lo-fi arcade games. In fact, she dimly recalled his saying that he was a great fan of Pong. Surely not.

'No, let's go somewhere a bit more dangerous.'

'I am putty in your hands.'

They walked back along Kingsland High Street. As usual, the mood was charged. Clubbing people were excited; skinny intense people were high on crack; teenage people were giggling and shrieking, happy on a night out. She let Jamie guide her: he had said, intriguingly, that they were going somewhere 'dangerous', but there was a little danger in the air here too. They dodged broken glass. A superannuated skinhead spat on them for being a mixed-race couple. Yep, you could say Dalston was dodgy after dark. But as long as you kept your head down, knew where you were going and kept on going there, you were usually OK. Still, the moment Jamie and Tesser stepped off the high street on to Amhurst Road, things began to feel more unsafe. The pavement was emptied of pedestrians and all along the road were quick cars manned by people eager to emigrate to more salubrious areas, even if just for the night; buses that roared as fast as they could towards the centre of London, away from the places where London life was really visceral – places like Hackney, Brixton, Peckham. Unlike the vehicles, Jamie and Tesser weren't headed towards town: they were going deeper into Hackney. Adrenaline made Tesser cocky and she kept pace with Jamie despite the fact that he was so much taller.

They didn't hold hands. It didn't seem right tonight: there was no romance between them and this was a relief. In an angry little spot in the back of her head, Tesser was still full of rage about the stolen film, so angry about it that she wasn't capable of bitching about it. Instead she let herself float on her anger and permitted Jamie to lead her in this nontactile manner back towards Hackney Central, down Graham Road, down Lower Clapton and then Millfields Road, submitting to the silent journey right up until the moment she realised he was leading her towards the canals.

Her mouth went dry with fear, for just a second, and she hung back. But Jamie kept walking like someone who was driven, and she had to run to catch up with him.

'Where exactly are we heading, mate?' The British vernacular tasted sour in her mouth, for once. She usually liked to mix 'n' match her slang expressions.

He gave her an odd look. 'Never you mind. Just keep up.'

It was creepy. It made her nervous. Jamie was dead-set on heading down to the deserted, spooky canals at night, a time that facilitated so many rapes, so many murders down in gritty, scary places like the canal system. But she wasn't going to bring that up. That sleazy, gloomy feeling she had had back at the Rio Cinema began to slither around in the back of her mind. Jamie was trustworthy, wasn't he?

She did her best to keep up. They now were crossing a park. The night was as dark and heavy as a pint of Guinness and the fact that the marshes lay on the other side of the canal made light pollution a moot point. Was he trustworthy? Why was something itching at the back of her head, some memory that she couldn't grasp?

It was the Jamie–Eric connection, wasn't it? Jamie's stepbrother's boyfriend. Tesser's feet sank into the damp grass as she followed Jamie further and further down towards the water. What Jamie had told her about his 'stepbrother's boyfriend' was starting to sound pretty lame. What about that woman chasing her the night of the film festival, trying to grab hold of her film? The film that had now been stolen from her house. Christ. She looked quickly behind her, over the breadth of desolate Millfields Park. It was too late to turn around and go back on her own now. She was following Jamie towards the canals not because she trusted him, but because she was near certain she would be attacked if she went back alone. Better the devil you know than the devil you don't.

They were down by the water, staring into the mist. Some swans floated by, brief smudges of white, and then disappeared in the mist again. It had never occurred to Tesser to wonder whether they might be nocturnal and she wasn't about to start worrying about it now.

'Beautiful, isn't it? Really eerie.' Jamie looked down at Tesser and smiled. She tried to stop herself from flinching. Better the devil you know. 'You want to walk along the path alongside the water?'

'I'm not sure.' She was stalling, trying to put pieces of the puzzle together in her head. But the jigsaw she came up with was a jumble; nothing made sense. Jamie put a hand on her shoulder and she jumped.

'Hey, steady on, now. I'm not going to hurt you.'

Even his words sounded false. There were other things she was remembering now, too, things she had dismissed as coincidence that couldn't possibly be: Dr Sharkey sending a friend along to the festival – just genuine artistic admiration? It hadn't seemed like it. The soothsayer's card that she found on the ground near the zoo; the soothsayer who lived practically next door to AMI Industries. And oh, Christ, there was that tattoo on the couple next door, the one that had been on Eric's arm as well. The heart shape. Where had she seen it before, aside from being inked into flesh? Where had she seen it? It hadn't been a love context and she wasn't a Valentine type of gal. She couldn't for the life of her remember where. She couldn't for the life of her . . . She shivered; Jamie was staring down at her. He looked bemused, but he could be faking that, too.

'Sounds great to me,' she said in an overbright voice.

'Let's get walking.' She thought – and she knew Jamie thought so too – that her voice sounded very artificial.

She had her knife in her jacket pocket, the one she had kept with her ever since she had been set upon by a gang of frat boys in Seattle when walking out of a gay bar. After two black eyes and a bleeding lip, she knew that she was never again going anywhere without protection. She wasn't sure she could bring herself to use it, but just its presence made her feel more secure. The *fact* that she had a knife.

Of course, Jamie knew about the knife, because she had cut both their underwear off with it at Liverpool Street Station.

As they walked, he took up her hand for the first time that evening and, instead of feeling comfort, Tesser felt peril. Her hand was clammy in his. Fear made her stomach ache, but she forced herself to babble on about maybe redying her hair; she was getting tired of green already. It was so hard to wash out, didn't he think?

'Might want to keep it down,' Jamie suggested in a low voice. 'I don't think we want to draw attention to ourselves round here. It's kind of dodgy, don't you think?' He squeezed her hand tightly for an instant and Tesser's heart started to pound.

Did he want her to keep it down because he was afraid someone would attack them, or because he wanted to make sure no one overheard them?

'OK,' Tesser said in a light tone. She grinned and her teeth ached with the effort.

Better the devil you know.

They came to an underpass – a dark alcove formed by a footbridge that spanned over the canal – and she hesitated.

'What's the matter?' It was so dark she couldn't see his face. 'I thought you liked risk.'

'I do.' The dark recesses of the underpass were impenetrable; there could be rats in there or maybe rapists or even murderers: beings that could cause her harm. Maybe Jamie wanted to cause her harm. She looked at him and remembered his sweetness, his nice laugh and the twinkle in his eye. She didn't want to let him know that at the moment she was afraid of him. He would probably be hurt. She recalled his kiss when he said goodbye to her yesterday afternoon. She was drawn to him despite the fact that her life might be in danger. And after the shower yesterday, after he had cooked breakfast for her. His kiss had been tender and rather lovely. She would take a leap of faith. She would trust him. She held on to his hand and took a step into the murky area underneath the footbridge. In that kind of space, no one could hear you scream – at all. We're not talking taglines here.

All of sudden they were there, underneath the bridge, and Jamie pulled her close into him. Then she did try to scream, but her voice had dried up and she could manage only a rasp. Jamie pulled her tighter. Maybe she could grab for her knife now; maybe if she shifted her elbow just a little . . .

'Shh!' Jamie hissed violently in her ear. 'Stop rustling. There's someone following us.'

She tried to switch gears, tried to think of Jamie as her sudden ally – and found it difficult. Yet she let him hold her tightly, and she could hear *his* heart racing too. Maybe he was frightened. Maybe he was excited.

But no, he was right: there was someone up above, walking across the footbridge. Tesser forced herself not to breathe, not to fidget or blink. Jamie stood stock-still, his arms frozen round her like the encircling arms of a statue. The footsteps above them paused and Tesser tried her very best to stifle the high-pitched scream that threatened to spill from her dry lips. Then the footsteps faded away, walking back in the direction from which Tesser and Jamie had first come. As if they knew her detective trailing trick and were trying to go one better on it. Still Tesser and Jamie didn't move, scarcely daring to breathe. Certainly not daring to speak.

From a long distance off, Tesser could hear a discussion, but the unknown speakers weren't close enough to determine age, gender or subject of conversation.

All of a sudden she felt very grateful that Jamie was there holding her in his arms, even if he had got her into this dodgy state in the first place. He was a tall guy. Maybe if he took off his glasses, fluffed up his feathers a bit and bared his teeth he would look intimidating as any other tall bloke. Of course, then he wouldn't be able to see for toffee.

She pressed her head to his chest, listening to his heartbeat. Then, as if they had planned it all along and this whole episode had been kinky foreplay, Jamie bent down his head, their mouths met and they kissed deeply, tongues wet and searching, all the fear alchemised into pure, magic lust. Tesser wanted to fuck. Here in this black, hidden cranny that smelled of piss and mildew and the dank watery scent of the canals; here with someone stalking them out there along the canal. She wanted to fuck; wanted to feel the warmth length of his cock shoved into her. She was horny as if he'd been working her up for hours. She didn't want to think. She didn't want to talk. She wanted to fuck, fuck, fuck, fuck, fuck.

She grabbed his hand and shoved it between her thighs, so that he could feel her bush through the cotton fabric of the combat pants. She rubbed his hand back and forth, and he took the hint and grabbed hard at her crotch, twisting it towards him, her knees buckling as her crotch slammed against his legs. He unbuttoned and then unzipped her trousers. He fingered her roughly. His hands were cold in her pussy. She liked rough. Rough was good. She seized his crotch and he was so hard, the outline of his stiff cock pushing up thick and desperate beneath his jeans. She squeezed and he winced. Then he thrust his tongue in her ear in a sleazy, perverted way, like he wasn't doing it for her pleasure but for his own; like his motive was lust and the only thing in which he was interested was relieving what was pent up and burning in his rigid cock. He wanted to shock, to lick and plunder. His tongue in her ear made her squirm, half in dirty pleasure, half in disgust. His intent was selfish. She liked it.

She unzipped his jeans.

But just as her fingers slipped beneath his underwear and touched his hard, hot flesh, she heard something.

'Be quiet, yeah?' she whispered. 'There's still someone out there.' Yes, there were footsteps walking towards them again. They both froze, and Tesser realised something. She was turned on by the scent of fear in the air. This was genuine teeth-rattling, pants-shitting fear. They could actually get killed in a place like this. What if whoever was out there had a knife and they actually knew how to use it, unlike her? What if they had a gun? Jamie's hand stopped moving in her pussy, his limbs as frozen as her mind, which admittedly was full of icy dread.

In the middle of this nightmarish situation, she sank to her knees. It was instinct, it was something; she didn't know what it was. The sound of her fingernails scratching against the denim seemed to reverberate around them. She pulled out his prick. She could still hear footsteps. And she began to suck his cock, which had been softening with fear. She was so wet she was dripping. Her clit was hard. She wanted to rub it against him as if she had a dick of her own.

Someone cracked a stick or a stone, perhaps ten feet from where they stood. Maybe it was the click of a switchblade. Thankfully, they couldn't be seen within the shadows underneath the footbridge, not without near proximity of no more than six inches. Right then Tesser learned something: fear didn't have only a softening effect. Jamie's prick was growing fat, filling her mouth. Jesus. She began to really suck, rolling her tongue over him. *Crack*. It was impossible now to tell how far away the footsteps were. If he began to make his usual groans and moans, they were done for. But Jesus, his cock was so hard and so tempting. She knew he was afraid, too. This was exciting. He was shaking, but his cock kept growing harder, thick and tight, like he couldn't control it. Which he probably couldn't. She wanted to stop licking him, wanted to tear her lips away and keep perfectly, perfectly silent. But she didn't have a choice. With a lust that felt like a gun held to the back of her neck, she worked her mouth down on him. The tip of his cock was juicy. He was nervous.

Closer, the footsteps came. Closer.

She had his cock at the back of her throat; it was swelling, bursting in her mouth; she was so wet. What the hell was she doing? Panic made her squeeze her thighs shut; her cunt was aching with need. There was another *crack*! – above their heads, this time. They were in the middle of the Hackney Marshes canal system in the middle of the night. Hackney, a borough strewn with yellow MURDER: WITNESSES APPEAL signs on nearly every corner. Yesterday when she had cycled back from AMI Industries, her bike had crunched over a bone that looked suspiciously like human vertebrae. She had kept on cycling. There were some things in Hackney you just didn't push your nose into. So what in hell's saints was she doing here?

Jamie leaned back against the damp wall and let out a breath of a sigh, a faint whisper of an exhalation. It could have been the wind, but Tesser knew that it was degraded pleasure: fear that had flowed into bliss. Fuck, yes. She blew him hard – almost wanting him to react, wanting a gritty, lustful groan. Maybe it would be worth it. She didn't care. If this cost her her life, then so be it.

She drew back and she could sense his disappointment, maybe even bitterness, but he made no sound.

She was as quiet as she could be. There was a cry from far off, somewhere on the other side of the park. She stood up, felt her hand up to the bristle on his chin: raspy, sexy. For a second, her fingers touched his lips in the dark. He kissed them, so lightly. She pulled down her already unzipped combats and panties to her knees, and then placed herself next to him. Except she was facing the wall – as if she was being frisked, or maybe like she was a cheap, desperate rent boy. Her palms were wet from the moist, dank wall.

She didn't need to say anything. He was behind her. There was a rustle of a condom and she froze, terrified that this would be overheard. And he shoved his prick into her from behind, shoved it into her slippery, trembling pussy. Her fear was balanced with her lust. And, oh, God, she needed it so much. She wanted him to pound into her, just pound and fuck and screw, and he did this. She was shivering with cold. Fuck me. Yes. His cock was thick in her hole, too thick, and she winced a little. But then she ground the sliding lips of her pussy back on him and took him deeper inside her, deeper and deeper. Yeah. It was a cold night. There might still be someone above them on the footbridge. But he was forcing his cock into her; the sensation was so sheer, so pure. Sleazy and delicious. She was drifting on top of her fear now, uncaring, just wanting her body to hum along with this pleasure – away from the rank, clammy Hackney canals, away from risk. He drove his cock into her, screwing her hard. How did it look for him? Could he see flashes of her rounded, pale ass in the moonlight as he thrust back and forth like a bloody jackrabbit? Was he dreading that she was going to sigh and moan, make a sound?

Dread was so sweet. She twisted her pussy down on him, wetting his pubic hair, and she felt him come inside her, an explosion of power in her cunt. In her mind, she became her pussy: sugary-soft, tender and yearning for steely solid thickness. It might be dark outside, but her whole body felt hot-pink. Then he brought a hand round and rubbed her until she came too, his still-hard cock inside her; she could feel herself clenching around him. Fucking beautiful. At last, when his cock began to yield into her smoothness, he withdrew.

They still hadn't spoken out loud.

It was quiet in the darkness that surrounded their hidden alcove beneath the footbridge. There were no footsteps.

Jamie turned her round and held her close to him. 'You'd have preferred a movie, maybe?'

She wished she could see his face clearly. She stood up on tiptoes to kiss him. 'Nah.'

When Tesser woke up the following Tuesday, she lay in bed for a while, which was unusual for a morning gal like herself. She frowned up at a crack in the ceiling until she realised what was bothering her.

It felt weird to be sleeping on her own.

It was already happening. She was getting hooked. She needed to get him out of her solar system – like, way the fuck out in outer space.

Maybe it was time for a ghost walk.

No fortune-tellers, no paranormal shit. A plain old-fashioned pick-up. A ghost walk it was, then. She would walk up Chatsworth Road and purchase a copy of *Break-Time*. She'd been slacking on the cruising lately: she couldn't even remember exactly which historical walks took place on Tuesdays.

On the way to the news shop, she was suddenly struck with an image of Jamie's brown eyes. It hit her there like a film flashing into her mind, and she stopped right in front of the swinging door. His long lashes, the warm brown of his irises. Yeah? So? She got hold of herself and stalked into the shop. It didn't need to mean she'd lost her libido, did it? There was even a pro-promiscuity

163

theory – she had once read about it in *Scientific Layman* in the dentist's waiting room – that stated that a multitude of sexual partners with the usual precautions minimises the risks of both disease and pregnancy. Tesser felt better remembering this, picked up her copy of *Break-Time* and headed towards the counter. She could recall the argument in crystal-clear detail: the female body treats the beau in question as a very foreign body indeed and retains a strong immune system. See? There was scientific backup that promiscuity was good for you.

She purchased the magazine and marched home. She even scribbled her mobile number on the receipt and left it for the cute till attendant, unsolicited as it was. He looked shocked and Tesser knew he wouldn't call, but at least it kept her in good form.

Yet then when she got home and was poring over the list of historical walks over a politically correct cup of Fair Trade coffee – snitched from Jana's supply, but she'd been such a bitch lately that it served her right – none of the walks detailed looked appealing. They looked boring and touristy. Oh, this was pathetic. The last thing she wanted was to be so hung up on her current shag that all she did was whine around the house thinking about him. She was no 'stand by your man' type. Romantic love meant settling down to have sex with only one person for the rest of her life. That was how she read it.

She was having none of it. She circled the first walk on the list and reached for her mobile.

Chapter Eight

Time was ripe for change. Yep. She rubbed the black-berry-coloured dye into her hair, until it foamed up like purple whipped cream. Purple-black hair was the way to go, she thought. Gonna wash that man right out of my hair. Bye-bye, Jamie. You are history, my friend.

Forty-five minutes later, the bath water turned a beautiful violet. She soaked happily. It had been a satisfying day. Such a pretty young man, a wispy speccy type with Jude Law-like good looks. Eyes like stars, hung like a horse – who could ask for more? Her pussy still ached, but it was a pleasurable ache.

She scrubbed her hair one more time for luck and lingering thoughts of Jamie were rinsed off as thoroughly as the hair dye. It had been a damn good day.

Next morning. It was Kitty's turn to buy food, thank God. Since Tesser was in a caring, sharing mood, she offered to help lug the bags home from Tesco.

'I'm getting sick of Jana,' Kitty confided to Tesser as they walked back, each with a bag in each hand. 'She's really getting on my nerves. She's always been a pain in the arse. Ever since the break-in she's been worse.'

'This is news?'

'Yeah, she even accused me of snitching her crisps, can you believe –' But whatever Kitty found unbelievable suddenly became a very low priority in Tesser's mind, because there was a black Ford Mondeo heading straight for them, up off the kerb. It swerved round Kitty, and, if Tesser hadn't at that very moment jumped up off the pavement into a shop doorway, she would have been run down.

'Bloody hell!' Kitty screamed and then, 'Tesser? You all right?'

Tesser was standing in the shop doorway, nearly catatonic with fright. That car had its windows all blacked up with one-way screens. That car had no discernible licence plate and even now was already speeding off into the distance. That car had tried to hit her. She was sure of it.

'Very odd.' Kitty was visibly trembling.

'So freaky. There's so much freaky shit going on around me at the moment that I wouldn't know where to start telling you about it. That Jamie guy is bad news.' Tesser was shaking, too, but she tried to mask it with bravado. She picked up the shopping bags she had dropped earlier and started walking quickly up the Narrowway, Kitty trailing behind.

'There's something I forgot to mention about "that Jamie guy", by the way. How long have you been seeing him, anyway?' Kitty said finally when she caught up with Tesser.

'I am not "seeing" anybody.'

'Suit yourself. Anyway, he called your mobile while you were upstairs dying your hair yesterday. Jana had a fit about you leaving it in the kitchen again and "disturbing" her with calls, by the way.'

'And?'

'She picked it up and answered. She was pretty pissed off. And he's a charmer, I'll grant him that, because he

166

sweet-talked her into giving him the address here and he's coming round at eleven o'clock in the morning on Sunday to see you. I'm sorry – I would have told you sooner. You were so long in the bathroom that by the time you got out, I'd forgotten all about it.'

'Thanks a million.'

'Don't shoot the messenger, yeah?'

Tesser couldn't be bothered to ring him back to cancel, so she let it lie. But she knew she needed a diversion. She thought immediately of her ex, Noriko, who never said no to casual sex. Tesser hadn't yet exploited this quality because of all the emotional entanglements their break-up had caused, but if anyone could get her to shake off the fakery of romance, it would be Noriko. Noriko would shag her wonderfully and then she would talk some sense into her.

She called. 'Hey, Noriko – it's Tesser. You want to meet up?'

'Tesser, *baby*. Long time no hear from – what's the matter, you hard up for a shag?'

Her ears turned red with embarrassment. 'No,' she lied. 'Just wanted to meet up and catch up.'

'I know what you want. You're not fooling me, honey. But listen, I have a *very* full slate at the moment, if you know what I mean. The soonest we can meet up is the afternoon of the twentieth.'

'Uh, OK.' That seemed a long way off. But at least Noriko would shake some reason into her.

'Meet me at the greenhouses on Springhill Park at four thirty p.m. on the twentieth, then. Look, I'm writing this down, so you had better do, too. You remember where. I know you remember where.'

Indeed. As she hung up the phone, Tesser's whole face was flaming from the memory.

When Sunday rolled round he was there on the doorstep knocking away, promptly at 11 a.m.

She opened the door with a smile on her face, determined to be friendly but distant.

'Hey!' Jamie said. 'What the hell have you done to your hair? It looks great. Surprised to see me, by the way?' He was grinning cheekily, and Tesser knew it was because he had tracked her down.

Tesser smiled a small, smug smile despite herself. She knew her hair looked great, but it was nice to have it confirmed. 'Nice detective work. Cute. Don't you have to go to church on Sunday mornings like this one?'

'Aren't you going to let me in?'

They went up to the kitchen. No one else was up and about, as they were sleeping off drink- and drug-addled hangovers from the free party up Lea Bridge Road the night before, which Tesser had bowed out of, pleading exhaustion. Tesser checked the hallway quickly and then made a hasty cafetière of Fair Trade coffee from Jana's supply. Jamie dawdled around the kitchen while she did this and then absent-mindedly turned on the radio. Embarrassingly, it was still tuned to that dorky teeny-bopper station.

Jamie started to laugh. 'This is why you're always humming those lame boy-band tunes.'

'I am not always humming lame boy-band tunes. I'm just easily influenced by my surroundings, and my dear squatmate Jana likes to listen to that crap, OK?'

'Maybe you need more salubrious surroundings for once.'

'This from the guy who endangers my life down in the canal system on a movie date? Thanks, but no, thanks.'

Jamie got up and put a hand on Tesser's shoulder. 'What's with you? You're so touchy. I knew you liked risk. I thought you enjoyed that as much as I did.' Tesser didn't answer. 'Oh, I get it. You're getting cold feet. Why don't you chill and hang out with me today, in a no-pressure, unheavy kind of way. I'll show you a good time, I promise.'

'Nothing heavy?'

'Nothing heavy.'

They walked through Columbia Road Flower Market together, jostled by other people frantic to spend their wages on flowers, trees, herbs and shrubbery. Tesser was at heart a wilderness girl, and felt uneasy in gardens that were too carefully weeded, too carefully controlled. It had always struck her as horticultural fascism. Yet it was fun in a way when you had no impulse to buy. Like window shopping, except here the goods were out in the open, much more varied in shade and type, and they smelled a lot better. The flower vendors screamed out the attractions of their wares in voices hoarse and gravelly from years spent along the whole of Columbia Road hawking plants to *nouveau riche* yuppies.

'Hey, you have to do the traditional shrimp-bucket thing,' Jamie told Tesser. 'None of those upwardly mobile designer bagels. I can't believe you've never been here before, not when you live so close. And you call yourself an East London girl.'

'A transplanted East End girl,' Tesser corrected him good-naturedly, getting into the gardeny spirit of things with a harmless pun.

Actually, the whole place was pretty upwardly mobile, but in a nice way. It was good to get away from the gritty area of the borough and walk around and listen to the buskers playing classical music. Tesser mentioned this to Jamie, and then mentally berated herself for her champagne socialist tendencies. Well, maybe her Aste Spumanti socialist tendencies.

'Yep, even the buskers in Colombia Road Market are up-*market*.' He emphasised the last word and waited for her to giggle in the expected way people do when they have made a very, very, very bad pun. There are harmless puns and there are harmless puns. This particular 'wordplay' was so bad it didn't even deserve a grimace, so Tesser pretended she hadn't heard him. It was by far the most polite thing she could do.

He didn't repeat the joke.

She thought she had offended him because all of a sudden he turned to her and asked whether they could meet up later in the day.

'Sure . . .' she said, a little put out. Just when the no-pressure afternoon was going so nicely. She actually had been lulled into really enjoying herself. 'You just want to take off here and now? Right now?'

'Yeah. I'll explain later. Don't be mad. Just promise me you'll meet me at my place at three o'clock.'

Well, she supposed she could. 'No pressure?'

'No pressure.'

So she agreed half reluctantly. They headed off in opposite directions of the crowded flower market. She was tempted to sneak around and follow him, but then decided she couldn't be bothered. She was becoming far too paranoid these days.

She walked back, distracted, picking up discarded stray flowers on the way back until she had compiled a bona fide bouquet to bring home. She put them in a water-filled jam jar and placed the makeshift vase in the centre of the table. Kitty and Jana had dragged them-selves from their respective mattresses and were making politely uncomfortable chat over toast and tea. But even Jana was pleased that Tesser had made an effort towards communal beautification.

Jamie's building. She locked her bike up outside and then pressed the button that read DESMOND.

'Come on up,' Jamie said via the intercom and buzzed her in. 'The door to my flat is unlocked.'

Tesser took the elevator up, feeling out of place in such a ritzy place with her scruffy backpack. She was clutching a newspaper plus a takeaway coffee from a 'caff' down the road – she had peeked into his cupboard on the previous occasion and seen only Nescafé.

But when she pushed open the door to his apartment and saw how he had transformed it, she was so flabbergasted that she nearly dropped both the broadsheet and the Styrofoam cup of coffee.

There were flowers and petals everywhere, huge summer bouquets: violets, roses, hyacinths, daisies. Everywhere. He must have purchased them at the market. How much did they fucking cost? He was a rich boy, but come on: it took a bit of dosh to spread this wealth of blooming flowers all over the floor, the chaise longue, the armchairs. For a moment she winced at the idea of his stripping such gorgeous ruby-red roses of their petals, but with white tapered candles flickering all over the room and Moby playing softly on the CD, the effect was nearly religious. The windows were open but the shades were drawn, which darkened the room while maintaining the glow of afternoon. It was bloody beautiful, that was what it was.

She ventured into the room somewhat nervously, still holding tight to coffee and paper, afraid to tread on the delicate petals, afraid to set the coffee down and spoil the magic atmosphere.

'You done with the coffee?' Jamie asked. His voice was gentle. She nodded. She didn't want to drink it now: swilling coffee seemed such a mundane thing to do suddenly. 'I'll take that stuff, then.' She handed him her backpack plus what she was carrying. He retreated to the kitchen and came back with empty hands.

Tesser bent down and took off her socks and trainers, which were second-hand blue-green Nikes from which she had cut the logo. Then she stepped upon the rose petals, which were so soft against her bare soles. It was a pretty romantic setup. Hmm. It was sweet and all, but it didn't exactly fit her definition of 'no pressure'.

Jamie must have detected something in her expression, because he said, hurriedly, 'It was just that this morning – you know, when you said you were influenced by your surroundings – I wondered whether you'd feel differently in a really heightened, romantic setting. Like a stage, you know, for ...'

Well, Tesser's heart was not made of stone. But neither was it made of Silly Putty.

'I know it's corny,' he continued, 'but I thought you might sort of like it.'

She did sort of like it. That was the problem. The twinkle-tremble of the candlelight was reflected in his eyes. She looked down at her bare feet, a half-inch deep in crimson rose petals.

Jamie saw her looking at the petals, and he picked one up and offered it to Tesser, the velvety rouge of it glowing against the pale skin of his palm. 'She loves me,' he said.

Aha, that old chestnut. She didn't even know British people played the flower game. She stared at him, extracted another petal from the layer and placed it in his hand. 'She loves you not.' Then she paused, looking around at the expense and time and effort he had gone to. He was looking stricken – crushed. Slowly, she plucked off another skin-soft petal and gently offered it to him. 'She loves you. She loves you –'

'Let's leave it at that for the time being,' he interrupted. She didn't say more and let the subject lie. He exhaled a breath of relief.

Heavy, too heavy! She wasn't ready for any kind of lovey-dovey stuff. Jamie was too romantic. On the other hand, he was a bloody good shag – so she'd keep her mouth shut.

She shut her eyes for a second and tried to think, but then Jamie was kissing her, before she even had a chance to raise her lashes again. When she did, his face was right before her. His bee-stung pout was as red as the rose petals themselves, red as fever; his hand on her ass sexy but not adamant; his tongue hot, warm, cold. It was all temperatures as he flickered it past her teeth and the sensual pull in her mouth was echoed, faintly, by a tug of need in her sex. She was aware of every curve and plane of her body, and every plane and slope of his, as well. Her nipples, tight now against her bra, tingled as if he had been stroking them. But he hadn't. He had only kissed her.

She put her hands to his waist and moved them upwards, feeling the hard arcs of his ribs beneath his dark beautiful flesh. She ran her hands upwards this way, up over his chest, up to his armpits, and she felt how his skin grew sensitive, electric from her touch; savoured the goose bumps that tickled over his skin where she had laid her hands.

'Just a moment,' he said, and he got up and locked the door to the flat, the first time she had seen him do that. 'I don't want Trevor walking in,' he said.

Tesser smiled back at him, weakly. She watched him walk back towards her. That a guy could make himself vulnerable in this way made her suddenly feel a flush of shame, and she paused just before she lifted his shirt over his head. She was a coward not to allow herself a smidgen of vulnerability. He hadn't knifed her in the canals; he hadn't chased her in a Ford Mondeo. His body was so gorgeous, as if one of Michelangelo's sterile, clinical, marble-pale statues had been painted the colour of life. Jamie was all right. He was all right.

He helped her draw the shirt over his head and then they both sank down together in the petals, kissing hungrily, every kiss a slippery and perfect one, no matter how they varied. She was growing smooth and moist between her legs and longed for him to stroke her there slowly, in time to the rapturous music: long cool strokes. Tesser's head was buzzing. His arms were toned, graceful. His torso slim and elegant; his ass and cock earthy, even vulgar – like her own sex, like all genitalia. She put all of these parts of Jamie together in her head and came up with the whole, neither angel nor animal but an interesting combo. Probably like herself.

'Tesser, come closer to me. Come and lie in my arms and relax for once,' Jamie said in a low, surprisingly hoarse voice. She wanted to. She wasn't sure if she could. It was one thing surrendering herself to someone like Dr Sharkey, when there was no emotion or tenderness. This was much scarier: opening herself up and exposing her insides to someone who – well, goddamn it, someone who she might *care* a little about it. Totally different.

He was sexy. Damn sexy. Maybe she should let him hold her.

He lounged back on one hand, shirtless, blue jeans, barefoot. His dreads stood out from his scalp like sun rays. The candles sparkled all over the apartment, their shine demanding attention, but she found herself powerless to look anywhere else but into his eyes. He was radiant. Petals were everywhere. Their fragrance was heady: rich and sweet. *Loves you. Loves you not. Better the devil you know.*

She knew she was safe with him. She sank to the floor, let him wrap his strong, tight arms around her and she laid her head back against his chest and shut her eyes. Even with her lids lowered, there was a dance of candlelight outside them. She smelled cinnamon, which was Jamie, and an opulent perfume, which was the blend of different flowers. She heard the soar of the music and she also heard and felt the rhythm of his breathing.

She rested there, melting into him until she grew so conscious of his lanky body that her flesh grew separate from his by virtue of desire. By the time they kissed again she was wet for him, wet as a river, a stream, a brook – anything active and wild. He pushed a hand between her legs, felt her juices. He laid her down on

174

the petals and kissed her shoulder blades, her elbows, the spot halfway down her throat – intimate, neglected areas. Each kiss was a cool brand; each kiss froze her into immobility just as it aroused her. Snow-kisses, snow-scars that chilled her and made her flow, made her clit stiffen and her flesh react with such extremity that she felt embarrassed.

She was chilled through with the weight of this intimacy, but she did not ask him to stop. He bent his head to her lap; he kissed and then licked at her clit and she moaned for him; gave herself up for him, pushing her groin into his face with each pulse of her climax. When he brought his face up to hers, his lips tasted of roses, sharp cinnamon, but they also tasted of her. She hugged him close to her, as hard as she could, and realised that there was a thaw loosening in her. Tesser brushed her lips against his closed eyes, and for a moment she felt a heat as sheer and piercing as the flames that glittered on the wicks around the room.

That evening, Tesser found herself at a loss for what to do. Jamie had left her on her own for twenty minutes while he went to pick up some Vietnamese takeaway for the two of them. Eventually her eyes lit upon the VCR, and then on the VHS adaptor that would allow her to view the Blairstone footage. Yes, Jamie had mentioned that he owned an old-format camera for making records of his painting work. She went over to her backpack and removed the cassette she had shot for Dr Sharkey. She might as well ensure her work was good before she turned it in, and, since there was no VCR at her place, this time was as good as any.

She scanned through the VHS footage once on Jamie's VCR, hoping to get through it by the time he returned home. They were bonding. They had even made plans for a picnic tomorrow. All systems go. But it just wasn't the done thing to make liberal use of a brand-new quasi-

175

boyfriend's video recorder the minute he wasn't present. He had a DVD player as well, she noticed, but hadn't yet managed to amass many DVD films. Tesser peered at the footage. There were the brats on the boat, and the trees and the water, and the front side of AMI Industries. So far, so good.

Hey! What was that? Just for a moment, she caught a flicker of movement in the tape. Someone was doing something by the side of the canal, just outside the building. But the movement was so quick, she couldn't make head or tail of it and, when she finally managed to pause the tape in the right place, it only showed a man in a bright-green hooded sweatshirt bending over the canal with a large plastic jerry can. Still, it looked pretty weird. She wished she could zoom in on the scene, like they always do in Hollywood hi-tech thrillers. But she didn't have the necessary gizmos.

She knew who did have the proper technology, though.

She rustled through the backpack until she found the programme she had kept as a souvenir from the night of the festival and then called up the Geyser Collective mobile phone number. A girl with a slight Australian accent answered.

'Hey,' Tesser began, 'I was the one at the festival who did *The Passion Flowchart*.'

For a moment there was a pause and then the girl's memory obviously clicked in. 'Oh, *right*. That was great.'

'You guys have some various video techno stuff, dontcha?'

'Well, we have some stuff we rented that I've not yet returned –'

'Great. Do you mind if I come over – tomorrow afternoon, maybe around four – and use it?'

'Well . . . I live on one of the houseboats and it's kind of awkward –'

'Wonderful, thanks. 'Cos it's really urgent.'

'Oh, all right.' The girl sounded defeated, but slightly amused. She gave Tesser the boat mooring number. It was hitched up on the leftward-running canals, by Springhill Park.

In the sunlight, they doled out their picnic treats on top of last week's *Sentinel* sports section, which neither of them ever read. Tesser had bicycled home in the morning in order to stop by the Turkish shop up Chatsworth Road. She had picked up hummus, *pide* bread and proper kalamata dark-purple olives, too, so lush and plump and swollen that they made your mouth water just to look at them. And then there were the pickled sweet red peppers in garlic olive oil, moist and succulent. They nearly melted on the tongue.

'That's a nice little spread,' Jamie said in an approving tone.

'Yeah, well, I'm not a very good cook, you know. My repertoire only extends to spring rolls and pasta. I thought it might be nice to treat you for a change. Thanks for last night's Vietnamese food and the flowers and all that.'

'You're very welcome. How much did this all cost you? I know you're skint. I can pay for half.'

'Don't bother. It came in at under four pounds.'

'No kidding!' He looked impressed.

'See? Deals to be had along Ye Olde Chatsworth Road.'

'I'll say.' He lavished hummus over an open piece of the soft Turkish bread and bit deeply into it. 'Mmm.'

Tesser did the same and took a big bite of the chickpea, garlic and tahini spread. She licked her fingers. Yep. It was good, all right.

'What kind of bread is that?'

'*Pide.*'

'You mean pitta bread.'

'No,' Tesser said in slight irritation. She didn't like

177

being corrected. 'I mean *pide*. It's completely different stuff. You should listen to me, you know.'

'Let me have one of those olives.'

She leaned forward and pushed one into Jamie's mouth. He sucked on it sensually, and then spat the stone out on the grass. He reached for Tesser and pulled her towards him, kissing her ear, pulling her on top of him so that they were giggling there in the middle of Victoria Park.

'You're crazy,' Tesser told him, laughing in spite of herself.

'Crazy like a fox.' He wiggled a piece of pickled red pepper several inches from her mouth. 'Say it and you get it.'

'Say what?'

'Say the tongue twister.'

'Peter Piper picked a puck – oh, fuck it!' Tesser lunged out and bit at the pepper anyway. Victory was sweet, even though it was not a fair one.

It was a glorious day. It was pretty near perfect. The sun was tremendously hot. They ate up everything Tesser had brought and then Jamie brought out the dessert – starfruit, kiwi, strawberries, bananas and plums.

'You went all out on the posh Islington fruit, I see,' Tesser teased.

'Well, I better show you the Islington way, then.' He grabbed at her ass.

'Hey!' But she was still laughing when he managed to get one hand down her pants. All of a sudden Tesser began to blush, as he rubbed briskly on her anus, his fingers skimming over the crinkly little star. Jesus! 'This is a bit public, don't you think?' It wouldn't be the first time she had messed around in the middle of a park, but even so.

'Maybe not public enough. Have a strawberry.' And Jamie pierced her asshole smoothly with the tip of his finger, just as he crushed a shiny red fruit in her mouth. Then he withdrew the probing digit. 'Not like this.' He peeled a banana, took a bite of the soft flesh and then rolled the rest between his palms so it was sweet mush.

'Oh, no, Jamie. You've got to be kidding.'

'Just give it a chance, yeah?'

Tesser looked down at his messy hands. She looked up at the blue sky and the sunlight filtering through the tree branches. It was hot, even for July, and she was getting sticky. She felt reckless. 'All right, then.'

He rubbed some of the banana against her ass. It felt vulgar and crude but it felt good, too – exciting. He began to move his finger in and out, inserting and then withdrawing it. She noticed he was getting hard. She groaned at the penetration and slid down on his creamy digit.

'You love it, don't you? Do you like me fucking you in the arse like this?'

'Yes,' sighed Tesser.

She wanted more, more in her ass. He pushed another tangy strawberry between her lips and the juice ran down her chin. The strawberry was tart in her mouth. He fucked her with his hand for a while, beating out a rhythm in her anus, oozing his finger into her, such sweet pain. It was one of those sensations that are so familiar each time you feel them, like you never should have forgotten how good it felt. She panted. Her pussy was getting so wet, but she didn't want to touch herself yet.

So sweet. She looked up at the sun again, past Jamie's somehow reverent face – eyes closed, concentrating on fingering her. She had soaked through her panties, she was sure of it. Maybe it was time to touch herself now, at last. She put a hand lightly inside her cunt. She was so wet and slippery that her fingers slid in immediately. His fingers were still in her ass, his own breath coming fast. And she was panting more and more quickly as she

179

played with herself, and then eventually she came: a drawn-out orgasm that made her grunt with pleasure and slide up and down on his finger like it was a slick cock, working her ass down on his hand. She was surprised at how crude she could be when she needed satisfaction. She didn't give a damn how it looked, however. Jamie gently glided his finger out of her ass and wiped it off with one of the picnic serviettes.

He handed her a two-litre plastic bottle of mineral water and she drank a long cool swallow of it. She kept catching glimpses of his face through the bottle, distorted and magnified by both plastic and water. She liked this way of looking at him – like a funhouse mirror. Which face was his real one? Was he looking through the bottle and wondering the same thing?

She suddenly slammed the bottle down on the grass and jumped to her feet.

'Hey, what's up?'

She was beginning to recognise his 'disappointed' look. 'No, don't worry. It's not what you think. I'm not freaking out. It's just that I've got an appointment on a houseboat at four. Look, I'll call you,' she added, noting that he didn't look merely disappointed, but genuinely upset. 'I mean that. I promise. And believe me: I don't say that to all the boys and girls.'

'You gotta do what you gotta do.'

She gave him a long kiss for good measure. Then she raced her bike to Springhill Park, where the boats were moored – though not before first cycling home for a quick shower so she could wash the banana off her backside.

'Dr Sharkey?' Tesser hesitated outside the door.

'Come in, Ms Roget. I can hear you lurking around out there. Don't be shy.'

Despite her resolutions not to, Tesser felt herself blushing as she entered the room.

'And what can I do for you *today*?'

Tesser was sure she wasn't imagining the emphasis. 'Well, I just thought you should know that I saw something kind of weird on the VHS tape stuff I shot for you.'

'You did? Whatever might that be?'

'Well, it looked like someone was dumping something in the water. Right outside this building, in fact. Right outside AMI Industries.'

'Really, dear? It was probably someone emptying a vase after the flowers faded, don't you think?'

'Yeah, that's what I thought at first, but you know what? I checked it out this morning and it wasn't any old manual dumping: it was from this kind of pipe network. I guess you probably know about the pipes already. I took the liberty just now of seeing where they lead to, and they led me all the way back to the left side of the building, where there's another metal tube coming straight from the brick, you know, like a gutter offspill. I hadn't noticed any of this before, but then as I looked a little more closely at the pipe – and it had WASTE on it – the only thing I could come up with was chemical waste, you know, this being Blairstone Chemicals and all. I just thought you should know.'

'Really? And this is on the tape you filmed, dear?'

Tesser suddenly had a very ominous feeling over the back of her neck, like she was being warned. She made a split-second decision not to tell Dr Sharkey about the second tape with the image that the Geyser Cinema girl had blown up for her on Monday. 'That's right.' She could feel her face go bright red, as it always did when she was nervous or when she was telling a lie. 'It was on the tape I handed over to Fiona after the boat trip.'

'I'll certainly look into it. Thank you so much for the tip, Ms Roget. Was there anything else?'

'Uh, no.'

Dr Sharkey was giving her a pointed look, so Tesser got the hint.

'Bye,' she said, and clicked the door behind her. As she walked through the reception area to the stairwell, she couldn't help but have the feeling that Fiona's eyes were boring into her. It was creepy. The whole situation was creepy. Tesser dashed out the door and nearly ran down the flight of stairs, eager to get out of the building.

The whole time she cycled back home, she had the feeling she was being followed. It wasn't *that* paranoid when you considered that within the last couple of weeks she'd been attacked by three total strangers – once on a ghost walk, once at a film festival, once with a car – and had had her place ransacked. Yikes. Maybe someone was following her up Chatsworth Road even now. She considered trying to take a detour, but then reasoned that if it was the same people who had broken into the squat, then they already knew very well where she lived.

By the time she cycled up to the squat doorstep, she was breathing hard from both effort and panic. Her T-shirt was soaked straight through.

Man! She was going to do something about this toxic-dumping business. If possible, she wanted to get paid by AMI Industries first, for the sake of *Chain of Lurve*. Eventually she would call Greenpeace and Friends of the Earth and get them to start some serious lawsuits. But first she had to get some real proof. She didn't think a fuzzy videotape would be good enough. Also, maybe AMI Industries could claim the tape was their property, too, since they had commissioned her to film. She needed more proof. She needed help. Kitty was in the middle of summer exams, and therefore Tesser didn't think it was fair to ask her. But she knew someone she could trust. Someone who had earned her trust the hard way.

She dug out her mobile from her backpack and rang Jamie.

As the number rang out, she happened to glance in the cracked full-length mirror she kept leaning against the wall in her room. Wow. Her new hair colour really did look groovy. Magnificent. She ran a finger through her short, punky style, mighty pleased with the dye job she'd done. Brunettes were going to have more fun, at least in her own personal world. She was La Femme Tesserkita.

And now it was time to go kick some corporate, Earth-destroying, toxic-dumping, capitalist pig ass.

Chapter Nine

*I*t took a while to get him up to speed. She met him in the Chaucery Museum café the next afternoon on Kingsland Road and spilled the beans. She told him about everything she hadn't mentioned before: the toxic dumping as evidenced on the VCR tape, the tattoo on his stepbrother's boyfriend and even the tarot-card reader called Finna.

He seemed sort of quiet.

'What's the matter?'

'It's just that – hell, never mind; forget it. I'll help you. I think the canal dumping is the big thing, though, not the tattoos or the clairvoyant. If you don't mind me saying.'

'Don't go cold on me, Jamie Desmond.'

'If you don't go cold on me, Ms Tesser Roget.' He tried to plant a kiss on her lips, but she dodged him.

'It's getting late. Jake's already let us stay and chatter longer than we should have. We have to get out of here before they lock up.'

Her squatmate Jake worked on some dole training scheme for the Chaucery furnishing museum and loved it. He was the one who had let Tesser in on the secret that there was actually a wonderful café to be found in Dalston and, if she wanted to impress the rich-boy totty she was dating, then the museum café was the place to take him. Jake's only caveat was that Tesser promise not to nick anything from the museum. Promise given, Tesser and Jamie had already spent three hours looking through the rooms, each of which was kitted out according to the home-decorations taste of a middle-class family from the 1520s to the 1990s.

There was a voyeuristic appeal about this museum, more so than with other museums, and Tesser had been pleased that Jamie had been entranced: cooing over the spinet in the Regency room; making scathing remarks about the blandness of the 'tasteful' 1990s loft room. As far as date venues went, it was an unusual one, but then so were the Hackney canals. She had tried to make a crack at choosing unusual meeting places, considering the effort that Jamie had gone to with those flowers. She didn't want to be outdone in the imagination stakes. Besides, he might even be worth the trouble.

'It's seven o'clock, you know,' Tesser informed Jamie.

Their cups and saucers had been gathered up about a half-hour earlier and the café kitchen had closed down; the lights were dimmed. They had been talking in hushed, furtive voices, sure, but certainly someone ought to have overheard them. Tesser had been waiting for Jake to come back, tap them on the shoulder and boot them out. Now, though, as they stood up and looked around with dawning alarm, it became clear to them that they were locked in.

'We'll just have to go back to the main door and try to break *out*,' Jamie suggested.

'We can't! They know we're Jake's friends. He's put in an application for a curator assistant education scheme. If they find out that he let us stay a few minutes extra – or even that we got locked in and he knows us – then it'll fuck everything up for him. He should never have given us carte blanche to stay late. We should have left when everyone else did.'

'How are they going to know we're friends of Jake? We could just be *any* dumb couple that found themselves locked in after hours.'

'You remember that nice old man that Jake introduced us to when we first got here, the one that was speaking at length about Elizabethan stairway styles? That was Jake's boss. They know we know him, all right.'

Jamie was looking nervous.

'What's the matter? You scared of the dark?'

'Not at all, in case you've forgotten our midnight canal excursion. I'm scared of getting arrested.'

'It's not so bad. They mumble something at you, book you, throw you in a room –'

'If you don't mind, I'd rather not think about it. What time does this place open in the morning, anyway?'

'Ten thirty, I think.'

'Great. We have to avoid capture from overzealous security guards for an entire night. I thought we were just coming here to canoodle and discuss illegal toxic dumping. I have to say, this wasn't on my plans for the night.'

'So deal with it.' Suddenly she saw a different side to Jamie: the person who was put out, slightly, when things didn't go exactly his way. It surprised her, but it didn't make her dislike him. It was just something she noticed: a glimmer of another facet of his personality.

'We ought to hide,' Tesser said. From far off, she thought she heard someone walking towards them. She really didn't want to screw things up for Jake, not when he had been so forthcoming with the date venue recommendation and all. They quickly left the high-ceilinged café area and took a right into a hallway that functioned as a type of walk-by channel that allowed the museum visitor to peer in on chronologically ordered living rooms. In this case, of course, they were heading back in time: past the Edwardian room, past the Victorian room. They had to dodge the blue-light stream of laser sensors at foot level; Tesser felt grateful that Jake had once mentioned these, so at least she was aware of their existence.

There were noises now around the café area, where they had just been. Any moment now the security guard was going to take a look down the hallway and see them frozen there, right in front of the Regency room. There was only one place to go. Tesser pulled Jamie forward with her, into the museum exhibit itself.

There was nowhere to hide in the room, so when the security guard drew closer, they froze in position, like sculptures. The guard seemed to suspect something in the more recently dated Victorian room – because there was a great shuffling around in there, and they could hear it through the thin walls. Tesser knew the guards weren't really supposed to touch the furnishing or ornaments, because Jake had told her, but it sounded like this particular guard was having a right good old search. Hold on. That was where the blue laser sensors had been, just outside the Victorian room – she or Jamie must have missed one of them and then tripped it off.

'Bloody mouse,' Tesser heard the guard mutter to himself. She nearly wilted with relief. 'I thought we'd taken care of you, my little friend. We've only had one mouse complaint in twenty-five years and traps are going out tomorrow, you little bugger. That'll show you.'

Tesser was a little surprised at the long speech, but then figured that security guards really didn't have that many people to talk to all night, now did they?

The security guard stalked past the Regency room without a glance to the right, in which case he would have seen a very anxious and wide-eyed Tesser and Jamie staring out at him from the exhibition space. Once they heard his footsteps at the end of the hallway, all the way back in the 1520s, they both exhaled. Tesser looked up at Jamie from the upholstered sofa on which she had flung herself. The July night was dark and warm.

The moonlight that was sieved through windows further along the corridor threw some light on the proceedings, but not much.

'Come here,' she whispered. It was happening again. Danger was turning her on. And this time, after the canal episode, she had the advantage of Jamie. Because she knew it turned him on, too. She bet his pulse was racing.

'Pull down your trousers,' she said in a low, very soft tone. 'Push your cock into me. Come on, do it. I'm already wet.'

'What if the guard returns?' he whispered back.

'So? We freeze in place again. Simple.'

He inched forward. Tesser reminded herself to be patient with him, because he was a goody-two-shoes nice boy who had never even got a slap on the wrist for being drunk and disorderly. He needed to live a little.

She lay back on the blue Regency sofa, pulled up her T-shirt, worked her skirt up over her hips, stepped out of her panties and then let him stick his hot cock in her. She felt full to bursting, and she imagined herself in a Jane Austen setting, a parlour maid ravished by the lord of the house. If she closed her eyes and concentrated hard while Jamie sucked at one of her breasts, she could just hear the spinet tinkling. Spinet. That was a good word. She felt no responsibility, just sensation. Feigning coyness, she put both hands on either side of Jamie's hips and pulled him towards her, plunging him so deeply into her pussy that she gasped. They moved back and forth on each other like this in the silent room, like one of the clockwork automatons in the Victorian room, ears attuned to the hallway in case the security guard made another round. Then Tesser pushed Jamie off, gliding his thickened cock out of her. At first she felt empty. Then she felt thirsty. She pulled his trousers down and knelt on the delicate tapestry work of the rug. The sound of the zipper was anachronistic in this prim environment. She couldn't wait to give him a nice, long suck.

She licked her lips and thought of all the parlour maids encouraged to suck at their masters' cocks in much the same way. They would have been timid and urgent, eager to get the job over before the mistress of the house returned, else they'd be revealed for the sluttish, wanton whores they really were, at heart. OK, maybe most of them were forced, but there had to have been some of them who looked upon it as just another job in hand. And maybe there were some who even would have enjoyed it. That was the kind of parlour maid she would have been.

'I'm going to suck you so sweetly you'll feel like you dipped your cock in a bowl of warm honey,' she whisper-promised Jamie. Perhaps a delicate china bowl of warm honey, brought in fresh from the hives by the tender young hands of the new parlour maid, unused and unwarned regarding the lord's attentions.

Jamie groaned softly. 'Then get down to it,' he said. 'Because afterwards I'm going to put my hand up your skirt and play with you for a long, long time.'

'I'm playing parlour maid. Who are you playing?'

'I'm not playing at all. Listen,' said Jamie, 'smug bastards like the rich men that owned these places were slave profiteers who made their money off human lives. It's a pleasure to degrade their false gentility by shagging on their sofas and coming all over their lily-white doilies.'

'Amen.'

'Hold on a sec.' Jamie pulled away and climbed up on to the old couch with Tesser. Then he lay down so that his face met her pussy. She took him in her lips again, just as he began to lick down between her legs. Oh, it did feel good. She felt pleasure spilling out from her, from her bursting head to her tingly toes.

She pulled his cock down into her mouth, wet with saliva. At the same time Jamie's tongue began diving in and out of her pussy.

Then it happened, what they had been dreading would happen. They both heard the guard coming towards them and they both froze like rabbits in headlights.

No, no, no! thought Tesser. Not now, not being caught in classic 69 flagrante on a spindly Regency sofa. So much for Jake's museum career as well. God, and Jamie's cock in her mouth, his balls by her lips every time she sucked him all the way down; his ass in her face like a J-O film. His pubic fur so close; the soft down between the cleft of his ass cheeks. He smelled good: ripe, earthy, of shower gel. Her mouth was watering all over him. He hovered there, splayed open in this pornographic position, his own mouth poised above her pussy.

She couldn't hear the guard now. She tried not to suck on Jamie's cock, just to let it rest there in her mouth. But it was like putting a lollipop between her lips and telling her not to enjoy the taste. Her mouth began to salivate for the candy; she began to get desperate. She wanted to savour his cock; to stroke her tongue along it. But like her limbs, she kept her mouth and her lips perfectly, perfectly still.

There was a bump in the room next to theirs, the Jacobean room. Jesus. The guard was right there. She wanted to feel Jamie pulse in her mouth. She wanted to taste him. Tesser sent him a telepathic message: Move your cock in closer. But he didn't shift forward, not even slightly.

The guard came out of the Jacobean room. He walked by the Regency room and they both held their breath. He must have passed even the Victorian room by now. Oh, Jesus, Jamie's thick dark cock was there like a fat stick in her mouth and she couldn't risk even a little suck. It wasn't fair.

She licked the velvety head and moved her lips down just a tiny bit on his cock, an intense little suck, teasing his prick with her tongue. It was wicked. She just couldn't help it.

A groan escaped Jamie's lips and his hips twitched, like he wanted to drive his cock further and further into her warm, wet mouth, drive it down her throat.

No! Don't groan!

But it was too late, because the security guard was coming back now; Tesser could hear his footsteps retreading the paces.

This was it, then.

He stopped before the Victorian room again. 'I mean it, Mickey,' Tesser heard him say, as clearly as if he was standing next to her, 'you'll be dead by this time tomorrow, you little bugger.'

Jesus. He was still talking to the mouse. She and Jamie held themselves silent and immobile until the guard walked away again into the future, towards the rooms of the twentieth century.

Tesser reached a hand out to fondle her hot, wet pussy, but Jamie stopped her. Then he drew back and bit her gently on one tender thigh.

'No,' he said. Granted, his voice was a bit muffled – because by that time he had bent his head down to her warm moist hole, his teeth briefly teasing her hardened clit, and had begun to lick at her.

Tesser loved sucking his cock, but feeling Jamie lapping and sucking at her pussy made her even hotter. She shuddered with delight as his beautiful lips nibbled at her, as his tongue licked and stroked. She spread her legs open and captured his head between her thighs in a firm vice. She wanted to tell him to lick harder, but her mouth was full of his slick, wet cock; she was gagging on him. So she let him know she wanted the direct

191

pressure of his lips round her clit by sucking harder herself. She could hear herself groaning, deep within her throat. She shoved her pussy in his face. Yeah, babe, lap it up. Lap it up, honey. It worked. The harder and more forcefully she sucked, the harder he licked. The more gentle and subtle her mouth was, the more tender his ministrations became.

Telepathy hadn't worked when she had tried it only minutes before. But this was better than telepathy.

She was frantic with need, but tried to be quiet as she pushed her pussy into his lips. Then she gave out mixed messages. She sucked up his cock desperately, but wanted him to lick her clit, gently, just gently. When he did just what she wanted she nearly screamed with pleasure, but thought better of it and instead swallowed his glistening cock. She was still going to scream. She would have to face charges tomorrow and she would be a little embarrassed, but so what? It was worth it. Need blocked out everything else in her life.

Oh, she was going to come, going to climax right on Jamie's mouth. She began to speed up her sucking movements and took out her hand so that she was masturbating him at the same time as she sucked him, up and down along his wonderful cock; oh, she wanted to come, she wanted to come. The taste of cock in her mouth. The taste of the juice from the slit in the head of his cock. She came. And so did he and she swallowed his hot juice down her throat. He kept his tongue to her clit, prolonging the agony of the pleasure. She might still scream from pure shagging satisfaction. She didn't know if she would scream or not.

Thankfully, he raised his head from her lap.

'I changed my mind,' Jamie whispered. 'I don't want to play with you after all.'

'What?' Tesser felt sudden shock. She vaguely remembered him saying something about wanting to play with her, but we're talking minutes ago. What the fuck had she done wrong?

'Don't look so worried. It'd turn me on more if you sat there on that nice couch and played with yourself.'

'Um, I've kind of already come. Be a little quieter, yeah? We've got no clue when that guard's going to be sniffing around again.'

'I know you're so hot for it that you just have to wank off whenever you can. Like you get so stirred up that even in a museum all you can do is lie back and wank, 'cos your pussy's so wet and swollen and hot. You don't give a good goddamn, as you might put it, who sees you fingering yourself here because you just need to come. You just need it so bad.'

Tesser's face was bright red. Did she want to play this game or not? She found his words strangely stirring.

'You just need to touch yourself so badly, don't you? Admit it.'

Oh, yes. She did. All she wanted to do now was lie back on the sofa and rub herself frantically, rub at the burning desire between her legs, rub at her stiff clit and wet her fingers in her slippery, juiced-up pink pussy . . .

But for some reason she held back. 'I want to be close to you,' she whispered. 'I want to touch you.' I want to fuck you. She didn't say it. 'I want you to fuck me.' I want to be back in that shower in your apartment, kissing you nice and romantic.

I want to fuck only you. I want to fuck everyone else.

'Come on, Tesser,' he coaxed, 'put your fingers on your pussy, right there on your clit, so I can see you touch yourself. Don't be embarrassed, just wank a little for me . . .'

'If you fuck me at the same time.'

With his cock pumping into her and her fingers working her clit, Tesser began to worry about the precious antique sofa giving way, but she was in sheer, sensual, slut heaven. Jamie placed a finger down on her asshole, rubbing at it back and forth, small careful circles. It reminded her of the picnic in the park and she felt a little embarrassed as he stroked her so carefully that her pleasure centred on her asshole.

She'd never admit it to him, but it still embarrassed her when people touched her there, even after the picnic. The thought that she was hidden away in a museum room, that Jamie's cock was gliding into her wet pussy so roughly it made her catch her breath in near pain, that her own silky gorgeous wet pussy was drinking him in, that her fingers were eliciting gorgeous twinges of pleasure every time she stroked her clit, that Jamie's fingers were obscenely coaxing out pure dirty sweetness on her asshole – well, it was enough to make a girl come all over again. So she did.

They eventually fell asleep. At 10.35 a.m. the next morning, they slunk out of the museum, much to the surprise of the morning security guard, who for the life of her couldn't remember letting them in five minutes before.

'Photography. No. Landscapes. No. Sculpture. No.' Jamie crumpled up the call for submissions and threw it across his flat. 'I want to be in *Understated* so much I can taste it, but in order to be in the show you have to submit a work of art,' he told Trevor.

'You'll come up with something. Take 'art, young man, take 'art.'

'Fuck off, young man, fuck off.' Jamie made his voice funny to let Trevor know he was kidding. He didn't even have the 'art to make a feeble pun straight back at him.

Wednesday again. Her task this time was to show how AMI Industries was sponsoring the Hackney Litter Control Club – a volunteer group that picked rubbish out of Hackney's major parks. It was mainly the newly retired,

194

but some older pensioners were there as well. Dr Shar-key hadn't said anything about Tesser's new dye job – she had bleached out the purple-black and dyed it bright blue this time, lava-lamp blue. Dr Sharkey had merely blinked and chosen to ignore it.

The only thing she told Tesser was that she had an extra filming job set up for her today, away from the AMI Industries building. This had bugged Tesser. A half-hearted pass would have been nice. But it seemed like previous conquests did not retain the doctor's interest. Nor had Dr Sharkey mentioned the dumping footage to Tesser, which was even weirder. But Tesser felt sure the doctor was on to it – probably in the process of gathering evidence, actually.

Tesser ran through the grass in her green sneakers and bright-blue hair, trying to get satisfactory angles on the senior citizens nobly picking up the trash. She hoped the rain wouldn't damage the inner workings of the expensive camera or anything like that.

Dr Sharkey had said to get right in close for a good shot. Tesser's feet were going to be as dyed green as her hair was last week if her shoes got any more soaked. But she held the camera steady and began to film the close-ups. There was a bunch of people moving in and out of frame, but Tesser reckoned she had enough good foot-age to edit, so it would probably be all right. Then she'd give Dr Sharkey the footage, and Dr Sharkey would be pleased. And – who knew? – maybe Tesser would even get a little carnal reward out of the whole thing. That would be good.

This was one of the things she hadn't confessed to Jamie at the Chaucery Museum: Dr Sharkey. But come on, she and Jamie weren't married; she didn't have to answer to him. She felt weird about it, though: not exactly guilt, but discomfort associated with the idea that she was withholding evidence, so to speak.

Now, this was why she didn't like relationships.

She was an honest person – except for the odd shoplifting incident. She didn't like lying to people and telling them that she wasn't seeing anyone else, even when it was what they wanted to hear. She knew that this fidelity was what Jamie wanted. She knew it, knew it, knew it, sure as she knew her green left foot. She also knew she couldn't give it.

By the time she had finished filming, her feet weren't the only thing dyed. The blue dye was more temporary than she had supposed; the rain that dripped down her face and neck was more indigo than transparent. Great – green feet, blue neck. Charming.

She put the tape into a plastic Somerfield's bag where it would be safe, put that back into her backpack and, like a wet bedraggled puppy, trudged back through the park, hopped on her bike and headed off to AMI Industries. The sun was finally making an appearance. Too late.

It was a clear sunny day by the time she made it back to the employers.

'What have you got there? You're not supposed to be filming today, as far as I know,' Fiona snapped, as Tesser took pains to ignore her and politely placed the camera out along the table in the reception. Then she took the plastic bag out of her backpack and removed the dry videotape. Fiona's eyes crackled with interest, but Tesser still didn't enlighten the sneaky, two-faced receptionist from hell.

She stepped into Dr Sharkey's room without Fiona phoning through first; without even knocking.

Dr Sharkey beamed, insofar as Dr Sharkey could be said to beam. She patted Tesser on the shoulder. 'Very well, that went very well. That's probably the last filming job we'll have for you; I think you've done quite well and earned your keep. We'll probably need you for one week or so of work when it comes to editing, but I'll let you know when that comes up. As discussed, that work is included in the basic two-hundred-and-fifty-pound fee, as I'd like to remind you. But you get the money first, so that's an advantage, anyway. There's a nice fat cheque waiting for you with Fiona on the way out. Minus the fifty-pound sub you already had.'

Oh, please notice me, Dr Sharkey. Please, please notice me.

But Tesser received only a courteous handshake. She sighed inwardly. She would have to face up to the fact that the Dr Sharkey episode had been a one-off. She looked longingly at the woman's strong, capable hands and thought of that happy moment when she had been tied up so successfully by them. Then she finally processed what Dr Sharkey had just said to her.

Money!

That put a spring in Tesser's step and she bounced towards the door as fast as she could. She noticed the doctor's lips twitch into an ever-so-slight curl as she murmured goodbye. What, had she never been broke?

Tesser picked up her cheque for two hundred big ones from the hateful Fiona. Her only regret was that now she wouldn't be able to get on Fiona's nerves any more. She had got to the point where she was getting a bit of a thrill from winding up the stuck-up receptionist. She'd miss her in a way. But she'd live.

She'd live very well indeed on two hundred fucking pounds. Yes! Assuming the cheque cleared, and she had no reason to suspect it might not, she could start story-boarding *Chain of Lurve* probably as early as next week.

She swung out the door with a jaunty air, but immediately upon exiting she felt groggy and rather sick. Over-excited. She decided to cycle to the bank to deposit her windfall – she still had time before they closed at five. It might clear her head a bit, too. She might be able to draw some money on her cheque in her account right away. And, even if it didn't clear immediately, the bank

197

might give her an advance, the cheque having the respectable source that it did.

The cool air did help. Tesser cycled towards her branch, which was all the way in Old Street. The traffic whizzed by her, but for once she didn't have a care in the world; she was jubilant. For the first time in many years she had a lot of money. She reached the Old Street roundabout, and, just as she steeled herself to negotiate the warrens of exits beneath, a passing van caught her eye. It was slowing down to let a guy out, but Tesser wasn't looking at him. She was looking at the van instead. BLAIRSTONE CHEMICALS, its multicoloured, wavy lettering read. She peered at the logo underneath the lettering: an upside-down heart. A hell of a coincidence, wouldn't you say?

She let it go, 'cos she had things to do. Like deposit the cheque.

Tesser entered into the labyrinth of tunnels below the Old Street roundabout, skidding her bike around corners and pissing off the pedestrians. She was happy she had the cheque – *Chain of Lurve* was as good as in the can – but she felt strangely empty. Her life ambition was about to be fulfilled as soon as she had a chance to shoot her screenplay, but something was stopping her from appreciating it.

She slowed down and idly wheeled around the corner of Exit 8. Then, to her shock, she saw the man from the lab, the one who wore the bright-green hooded sweatshirt, pushing his bike along. In flashback, it dawned on her that this was also the guy that the van had slowed down to let out. Then things happened quickly, nearly too quickly for it all to register at once. Tesser rushed towards the figure on the bike, pedalling as fast as she could. She thought that, if she got close enough, she'd be able to see him properly. But he saw her first, before she got to him, and he jumped on his own bike and pedalled furiously.

She had no choice but to follow. Up through Exit 8, up the ramp to the street, straight into the street towards Hackney, which was where he was heading, dodging a No. 55 Bus. Beeeeeeep! The driver slammed his brakes and pressed his hand down on the horn, but Tesser was already several streets away, pursuing the man in the green-hooded sweatshirt, wind whistling past her ears, her pulse thumping, Jesus fucking, Jesus fucking bloody Christ . . .

All the way down Kingsland Road she chased him. He was always several streets ahead, cycling with one hand, until he darted out in front of a lorry and swerved abruptly to the right, towards London Fields. This time, Tesser had to let the lorry pass or she knew she would be hit, and, when she finally turned down the same road, the green-hooded man was gone. So she cut across another block to the right to see if he had tried to shake her that way and indeed he had, for there he was, just a tiny green speck in the distance, heading towards London Fields Park.

She sped on to the park herself and straight on to the grass, which was sparkling with water from the previous rain. It made her bike skid across the grass and mud. She had to see who it was. She had to see. She put her head down and charged forward on her bicycle like a Tour de France racer, like a riled-up bull, like Evil Knievel before the biggest jump of his career. Swish! through the grass, swish! across the muddy football pitch, swish! on to the asphalt path. She was in luck! Far, far ahead, the man in his haste had run into someone and crashed his bicycle. And now at last she was gaining on him. She was able to make out more of his person with each second that passed. Green hood pulled up around his head, wearing gloves and sweatpants, running for his life. In a few moments she'd be on top of him and then she would get to the bottom of this whole mess. She was still in luck if she just kept pumping as hard as she could, if she just kept pedalling –

Smash! She ran into the same pedestrian that the green sweatshirt man had struck down, who had only just managed to struggle his way up and now was cursing like a sailor.

Fucking Jamie! 'What the *fuck* are you doing here?' Tesser screamed. 'Are you stalking me again!'

'Yes! I just stopped by your place to see if you were in after work! What the *fuck* are you doing trying to run me over? Like that bloke just did?' Jamie screamed in return.

But just then she fell off her bike and knocked Jamie over too, again. For a moment they lay there in a tangled mess of legs and fury. It was all so stupid that there was nothing to do but to laugh about it.

They rolled around on the grass, kissing and laughing. Tesser could smell him, that beautiful cinnamon musk scent. He pulled her up close to the black woollen jacket he was wearing and then she could smell it too: old cigarettes. On his jacket it didn't seem stale or sleazy; this scent too was beautiful. She was hoping, willing he would kiss her, but instead he just put both his hands up to her face and held it and she was unable to look anywhere else but in his eyes. She was unnerved, but Jamie's eyes were kind and his pupils were huge and dreamy and she let him hold her face like this – like lovers. She supposed they were lovers. It was intense. He trusted her.

She could tell that he trusted her. Trusted her with his heart and love and failings. Not trust that had to do with monogamy: not that kind of trust. A different sort altogether. This trust in his eyes was his gift to her and she wasn't sure if she was going to be able to accept it. But she still didn't turn her head. Their faces were an eyelash away from each other; their breath mingling;

surely their auras mixing there too on the green damp grass, mixing in glorious cinnamon cigarette scents, in shades of green grass and faded black woollen jackets and dark chocolate-brown and freckled, dappled pink. She wanted to turn away. She wanted to slip closer, into his skin, deep down into his veins and tissue and bones.

She believed the word was ambivalent.

Above them, the sun was hot-hot-hot, bursting heat down on her neck, on their faces, warming the dampness already on their clothes, the residue of rain. The trees were shifting and through their branches the sun was filtered: half-shadows, half-rays, neither/nor. Her head was thudding with emotion. She didn't know if they were in sun or shade. The wind rattled these branches so far above them, and they lay there, squinting, shivering. From above, their bodies would look mingled. His woollen jacket overlapping the green fur of a coat. To a bird, would they look like one grouping or two?

Her eyes began to sting.

Until this point, they did not kiss. And then they did, and his mouth was sweeter than the sun itself, sweeter than the painful light that made her blink away the sudden tears, and they kissed and kept kissing as the sun rolled over their faces and bodies and back again, when the trees moved above them. Their tongues were slow together and his lips were as soft as a girl's and still his hands were at her face, holding her, keeping her. She would trust him. She would trust him. She still did not feel lust, in that sheer moment. She felt tenderness. Jamie's hands lower, stroking her neck, gently. Like a Catherine wheel suddenly sparking in her gut, she felt desire so sharp she felt it would tear her apart. Shimmering, luminous, *glamorous* desire. His whole face was more beautiful than any Hollywood star before or since. His whole flesh was glowing and since she was near him, touched by his light, she was glowing, too. And yet she was frozen. She couldn't move. She could only

201

shiver and tremble and his hands stroked and cajoled and sang on her flesh – under her coat, under her shirt, over the lace of her bra. When he twisted one of her nipples, she bit his lip from the crisp, sharp sweet pain of his hand there.

It was also like she suddenly awoke, for now her hands had power, too, and she wanted to feel his skin: she wanted closeness, intimacy with him. It had nothing and everything to do with sex. It was not sex like she had ever had before in her life. She was rapid; her fingers were at his waist.

It was only afterwards, as they lay blinking in the sunlight under the altering and moving trees, that Tesser realised that she had forgotten to bank her cheque.

Go figure.

Chapter Ten

*I*t was no good. No matter what he came up with, there was nothing that fitted the bill in terms of innovative art. And damn it, he just knew that, were he to win this show, his name would be made. It felt right for him to win it. Karmic. If only he could come up with a bloody idea.

Paintings were out. They were too conventional, and, even if his medium and subjects weren't, they were still – God forbid – *representational*.

That would never do.

Ditto for sculpture. He ran through the possibility list that he had worked out together with Trevor's help. New media was out, also for the reason of being too conventional. Even a formaldehyde tank of nude consensual cannibals would get a big yawn from the jury. He knew it. Film was in, but he didn't know enough about video or film to compile something and he was too proud to ask Tesser for help. He just wished he could think of something. Anything.

He walked down Essex Road from Islington. By the time he had reached Dalston in Hackney, the rubbish was starting to pile up in places. He kicked a Coke can out of his way. The rubbish collectors in Hackney worked hard, but he also knew that (a) there weren't nearly enough of them because of the budget cuts made by the local ruling body, and (b) people often just threw their rubbish on to the ground after devouring the Big Mac or the parcel of chips. Perhaps that group Tesser was filming the other day – what did she say they were called? The Hackney Litter Brigade or something? Perhaps they should do a blitz round here.

He wondered whether he oughtn't give her a call and ask for innovative and imaginative art suggestions. She was a girl of ideas, after all.

Her mobile rang. Tesser checked the number and then answered. 'How's it going, Mr Outsider Artist?'

'It's going OK. What are you up to?'

'I'm making spring rolls for my fellow squatties. We have a communal lunch on the twentieth of each month and it's my turn to cook.'

'Is this a bad time to call?'

Tesser folded a parcel into a nice, compact vegetarian spring roll. 'Well . . .'

'I could call back later.'

'Yeah, cool! I am a bit busy at the moment. Call me at –' she suddenly remembered the meeting with Noriko '– call me tomorrow, yeah?'

'Yeah.' He sounded kind of disappointed.

'It'll be good to see you, Jamie.'

That seemed to cheer him up and he got off the phone without any further moping.

The spring rolls were a success, and even Jana was full of compliments. Which was good, because Tesser had borrowed her carrots, her bean sprouts, her soy sauce, her sugar, her cabbage and her oil to make them. She chose not to tell her this, however.

* * *

She hadn't seen Noriko in months, not since the girl had broken her heart and broken it bad. She tested herself to see whether she had any residual hurt feelings. Nope.

The greenhouses were where they used to meet, before Tesser had had enough of Noriko's philandering ways, which trumped even her own philandering ways. There was slutty and then there was *slutty*.

'You're looking good, girl. The single life agrees with you,' was Noriko's opening line as she came up behind Tesser and put her hands over her eyes. 'I know you can guess who.'

Noriko's body was warm and insinuating, pressed against her back. Tesser could smell the other woman's perfume: the smoky, masculine cedar tones of Gucci's Rush. Tesser couldn't distinguish Gucci from Charlie and she remembered how Noriko had had to identify it for her. Now she found herself remembering it very well. Yeah, Noriko had expensive taste, even though she wore a toned-down urban streetwear look of band T-shirts and expensive designer jeans. At the moment she was wearing a frail, pastel-yellow chiffon skirt with a T-shirt: a commodified punk moment. She had her short black hair cut in expensive salons that she could ill afford on the income of an accountant in training.

Noriko stood on her toes and nibbled at Tesser's ear. Tesser felt very confused as a sizzling rush of desire hit her square in the stomach – *pow!* – right where it did the most damage. This wasn't why she had called up Noriko. Or was it? She couldn't even remember clearly why she had contacted her ex-girlfriend in the first place. Noriko blew lightly on the short hairs at the nape of Tesser's neck, just the way she knew Tesser liked it. Oh, that's right. She remembered now. She had called up Noriko in order to both practise and gain insight into romantic detachment. Noriko was a pro in that arena.

Noriko was nudging her slowly, nearly imperceptibly, towards the inside of the greenhouse, a former venue for their many trysts. At first Tesser thought the other woman had romantic intentions, but she knew this wasn't the case. Noriko hadn't had a romantic intention in her life. Sexual intentions, sure, but romantic – *nada*. Actually, that had been part of the problem, aside from the fact that Noriko had dumped her big time on their two-month anniversary. She had wanted a little romance, just a little, and Noriko was a dyed-in-the-wool realist. Maybe – Tesser had never considered this, but maybe – she had been attracted to Jamie because he was a romantic, too. Not because she was a stay-at-home, monogamous cuddly type. You didn't have to be those things in order to be a romantic.

Once they got inside the greenhouse, things went quickly. Off with Tesser's trousers, off with Noriko's dress-down *Queens of the Stone Age* T-shirt, in with Noriko's fingers.

The light coming into the greenhouse was filtered, green and eerie. Tesser liked it. It felt like fucking in a science-fiction movie. *Day of the Triffids* or something.

'Fuck me harder,' she insisted to Noriko, who swiftly obliged. Noriko was a cute, rough piece of ass, a really in-your-face Riot Grrl type with fashionista aspirations. Tesser should thank her lucky stars for the shag opportunity.

Noriko bit at Tesser's tit.

'Ouch!'

'You're such a wimp,' said Noriko, who admittedly was more of a hard-nosed type than Tesser herself. She removed her wet fingers from between Tesser's pussy-lips, but Tesser was confident she would put them back, so she didn't complain. 'Come on, suck *my* tits, and I'll show you how a true lady handles a little pain.'

Well, Tesser didn't need much convincing because Noriko had truly lovely breasts, small and full with dark, triple-pierced nipples. One of the piercings was a green clear piece of zirconite hanging from a silver hoop.

Tesser immediately and carefully took it between her teeth, pulling gently.

'Harder!' Noriko ordered. Tesser did so. When Noriko reached her pain threshold – indicated by a slight, barely audible wince – Tesser lovingly licked around the nipple itself, slathering it with tenderness. In her experience, a mix of gentleness and cruelty was a potent and sexually lethal cocktail. Besides, Noriko was a good egg.

'Bloody hell, isn't it about time you fucked me?' Noriko complained in a petulant but somehow still charming voice. Tesser was already dreaming about the slickness of Noriko's creamy, sweet pussy and considering exactly how it would feel to slide her fingers up inside the other woman's hole and really get down to some serious fucking.

They slid on the gritty, grainy dirt of the greenhouse ground, Tesser running her hands over Noriko's ass. The scent of the place was rich and loamy; it made Tesser's nostrils flare. She thrust herself on top of the other woman and kissed her, feeling against her the sleek, compact body. She nearly lost herself in the sensation – that was how good it felt. Until Noriko said, 'Come on, Tesser, tribadism's a myth. Found only in the *Penthouse* letters pages and on Channel 5. I don't want any of that gently-gently smooth stuff or any soft-core pussy-lickin', for that matter. I want you to fuck me like a dyke does, even if you are a turncoat bisexual.'

Noriko grinned.

Tesser felt up to the challenge. She ripped apart Noriko's chiffon skirt with her bare hands.

'That was Donna Karan!' Noriko yelped. But she was into it and when Tesser without any preamble at all stuck four fingers up her cunt, she sighed happily. Jesus, she was burning hot liquid up there – like she had sex ever or something – and, as her flow hit Tesser's fingertips, Tesser's stomach flip-flopped with desire.

'I – want – you – to – fuck – me,' Noriko said, carefully

enunciating each word as she sighed and moved her pussy up and down, against and around Tesser's fingers.

'Believe me,' said Tesser, 'the feeling is mutual.' She kissed Noriko deeply. Their mouths were glued together, the other woman's hot tongue spinning lovely little circles around her own, causing her whole body to tremble, causing her own pussy to get wet, wet, wet.

'Harder!' insisted Noriko, and so Tesser really got down to business, fucking the other woman hard with her hand. Noriko screamed and sighed and wiggled wetly all over Tesser's fingers. Tesser wasn't fisting her, exactly, but she *was* fucking her mighty fiercely, with four wide-spanned fingers. She knew herself that this felt exactly the same as the widest, thickest cock, and wished that more men bothered to find out this little technique. Because then they wouldn't be so hung up on the cock-size thing. They had hands too, didn't they? Dykes were also usually much better at just getting right down to it and touching their clits unashamedly as Noriko was doing now, something that 'straight girls' – and Tesser had slept with a couple of girls in this so-called category – seemed strangely averse to, like it was an insult to the person fucking them. Men wouldn't dream of not involving their pricks in the sex action. Ditto for Tesser's clit. Viva la clit.

'Fuck me, fuck me, fuck me,' Noriko panted, and Tesser, grimy with dirt and sweat and in the middle of a greenhouse full of fertile bulbs and budding sprouts and damp, organic scents, fucked Noriko as brutally as she could ever remember fucking someone. She fucked her properly, as a dyke would. She didn't want to give Noriko any space for complaints afterwards.

Noriko put her mouth up to Tesser's ear and licked and licked at her, and Tesser felt white-hot desire kick in again, a warm shoot of fireworks all the way down from the sensitive flesh of her ear to her cunt.

Noriko in her turn squirmed and rubbed and shouted

and wiggled and eventually came, grabbing Tesser to her in a one-armed bear hug surprisingly gruff from one so petite. She didn't let go until Tesser eased herself away.

She was surprised to see tears forming in Noriko's eyes. She held the other woman close and made soothing sounds. 'What's the matter?' she said. 'Is something wrong?'

'No,' Noriko said, 'I just always feel emotional after I come. It's some form of weird release.'

Tesser was surprised. She had never noticed. Hey, maybe she was the one who had been insensitive. No use crying over spilled milk now, though. 'It's because you're such a tough cookie the rest of the time, maybe.'

Noriko smiled and kissed Tesser tenderly on the nose. 'Maybe,' she said. 'Soft-centred, and all that.'

'*Very* soft-centred.' Tesser thought of the gorgeous, delicious softness of Noriko's cunt and how it had trembled and swelled and retracted round her fingers when the other woman had come. 'I didn't even know you had a romantic side, if you really want to know.'

Maybe she could talk to Noriko about Jamie. 'Look,' she began, 'I'm kind of hung up on someone at the moment.'

'What's her name?'

'His name.'

'You really *are* a turncoat, aren't you?'

'Yeah, yeah, yeah. Lay off,' Tesser said good-naturedly. Then she told Noriko all about him.

When she was done, Noriko was cool about it. She didn't have weird hang-ups about exes the way some people did. At the end of the day, Noriko was a pretty good friend. She was a pretty good friend, and she gave some pretty damn good advice.

Which was: give the guy a chance.

* * *

Tesser took a ride to cool down after the greenhouse interlude. Inevitably, she found herself alongside the canals, as if a magnet was drawing her there again and again.

She cycled quickly past AMI Industries three and then four times, back and forth, trying to figure out what piece of the puzzle it was that she wasn't able to link together. The first time she glided past she was nervous that she would be overseen, but there was no one out there in front of the Victorian building, and she was pretty sure that the trees hid the path view from Dr Sharkey's window. So she went past the second, third and fourth times, still not able to figure out why she was hanging around in the area. It was only on her return trip the fourth time that she slowed down to a stop so she could check her tyres for air. Her head hanging down, she happened to look up again at the building, this time from a different perspective. The domes looked like valentines from this position. She looked up and then saw the domed cupolas at the top of the building.

Domes were weren't strictly Victorian, now that she thought about it. Domes that looked more like they would be correctly placed on top of a Russian-shaped church. Onion-topped domes. Yes – her heart was starting to beat fast now as she cycled away from the building as quickly as she possibly could – domes that might just look like upside-down hearts, with a bit of artistic licence.

Jamie's brother. Artistic licence. The Outsider Artist, the famous and devious Jamie Desmond. Oh shit.

Her legs made comic-book blurs as she pedalled for her life.

Jamie plopped down on the beige beanbag and clasped his head in despair. There was no way he was going to get a piece together. And, if he didn't get a piece together, that was his one chance at true fame gone.

There was something inside him that told him that he wasn't going to get another chance. He was too depressed to get up and take out his sketchbook in order to work out yet another sure-to-fail idea.

He was even too depressed to smoke.

He looked over his varnished floorboards and felt glumness seep through his entire being. At least his floor was shiny, he thought, trying half-heartedly to cheer himself up. He wasn't the manic depressive type, so a bout of self-enforced snap-out-of-it was usually effective. It didn't seem to work this time, though. The floor shone at him, expensive, glossy – a mockery of the money he had always had but that had never helped him attain the things he had genuinely wanted. Kudos. Respect. Artistic admiration from the world at large.

A huge, depressing, shiny floor, strewn with the detritus of his frantic and fruitless artistic efforts, bits of paper and the odd hair. It had been a while since he had swept.

The odd hair.

The odd red hair, the odd blue hair, the odd green hair, the odd blonde hair, the odd black hair.

The odd, multicoloured hair. Tesser's hair. Discarded hair. Hackney rubbish. Spiky, complicated, anticorporate Tesser. Multicoloured, anticorporate refuse.

Jamie gave a wild whoop and leapt up from the beanbag. He knew *exactly* what his submission was going to consist of.

Chapter Eleven

*P*ut the pieces into place. Come on, Tesser, put 'em into place.

Noriko had suggested that she trust Jamie, but how in hell could she 'trust' him now? Tattoo on his stepbrother's boyfriend; tattoo on the man next door. Onion-shaped dome logo for AMI Industries that looked identical to the tattoos. Coincidence? I don't *think* so.

She sat in the kitchen drinking Jana's peppermint tea and then rang AMI Industries. And again Frightful Fiona told her that Dr Sharkey was in a meeting. Would she care to leave another message? Dr Sharkey had been in a meeting for the last five hours. Even if it was the same kind of meeting that she had had with Tesser, at some point she would come up for air. Tesser declined to leave yet another message. At 3 p.m., after six hours of periodic calling, she came to the conclusion that Dr Sharkey was ignoring her calls. Also that her pay-as-you-go mobile was about ready to run out. Also that the next time Fiona saw her, Tesser was probably going to be mercilessly throttled.

What options did she have?

Then she remembered that she still had the key to

AMI Industries. She could sneak into the laboratory on the floor above Dr Sharkey's office and find out what the hell was going on all by herself, the lousy hypocrites. AMI Industries wanted a filmmaker to record their virtuous sponsorship of underprivileged schoolkids, and all the while they were dumping toxic stuff into the environment. They would get what was coming to them, though.

She made up her mind to sneak in tomorrow night. It was unlikely that Dr Sharkey would ask for the key back before then, particularly as she seemed to be avoiding all of Tesser's calls. Tonight Tesser had plans to meet with Jamie at the Vortex. She would play it real cool and not let on that anything was up. To think that she had come so close to trusting the two-faced artist. Con artist, more like.

Stoke Newington was one of the few ritzyish areas in the borough of Hackney. It bordered on slightly more ritzy Islington. It was famed for good and decently priced restaurants as well as for having a slightly bohemian, artistic air. Tesser usually judged areas on coffee-hangout appeal. There was more than one good café in the Stoke Newington area, but Tesser's favourite place to chill when she had money – and sometimes even when she didn't, because you could buy a herbal tea for under a pound and hang out all day on it – was the Vortex. Not only was it a bloody good jazz bar in the evenings, but there was a second-hand bookstore down below where a person could browse to their heart's content.

The coffee house was moodily lit, broken in by years of smoky performances. Tesser loved it. Even when she had to entertain the attentions of two-faced liars.

Playful jazzy rhythms bounced around the café as she and Jamie held hands in the darkened upstairs restaurant area. Tesser disentangled her fingers and took a long swig of her coffee. She remembered the other time they had been in a café together, that time in Old Street when she was on the lam from the ghost walk. It seemed like such a long time ago now.

How can you deceive me like this? Tesser thought, looking at Jamie. He had the least guilty conscience of anyone she had ever met. In fact, instead of slinking around with his tail between his legs like he ought to be doing, he was bubbly with excitement. Tesser observed him from underneath her lashes. He was putting one over on her; that was her gut feeling. She kept looking at him. It was time to start trusting her brain and not her clit. But he was a good-looking guy, no doubt about it.

Maybe she should exploit his physical qualities, though, while she still had a chance.

Yes.

She snaked her hand on to his lap. He wasn't hard, but as soon as she stroked across the crotch of his trousers there was a sudden reaction – as if an electric charge had jumped from her fingers to his cock.

'We can reverse the situation,' Tesser suggested.

'What do you mean?' The Judas. The beautiful quisling. He had sleepy, half-closed eyes and was leaning back in his chair, his mouth half open, his tongue suggestively licking his gorgeous lips. Tesser reckoned even this was calculated.

'I mean that I could return the favour and get *you* off, sweetie. Or don't you remember the café episode?'

'I remember.' His voice was slow and heavy. God, but he was devious. He seemed at peace with himself – content! – and this bugged her. 'You think I'm going to forget something like that? It made me hard for a week straight, just thinking about it.'

'Well, then . . .' Tesser increased the pressure on his crotch and felt his response: he was now erect, achingly so. The music had changed. The easy blues tones added to the ambience. No one was looking.

Except for the pretty but sharp-faced girl sitting in front of them. The girl staring at them. The girl otherwise known as Fiona.

Tesser felt a distinct thrill. She could imagine what Fiona was thinking: what a cheap little slut Tesser was, doing such things in public, disgusting! For her part, Tesser had never considered that Fiona might have a social life and actually do normal things like go to restaurants or cafés. It turned her on something rotten to think that at last she had a perfect opportunity to *really* get on Fiona's nerves. Ha ha, this was *greeeeaaaat*. The fact that she couldn't care less what Fiona thought of her behaviour just made it all the more perfect. Fiona was sitting there with her date – although it was probably a pity date from a brother or cousin. Tesser was playing with Jamie right under the stuck-up bitch's nose. She squeezed Jamie's cock again; it was firm and stiff through the fabric. She waited for Fiona to say something to her male companion but, to Tesser's surprise, she didn't.

So then Tesser looked Fiona straight in the eye and unzipped Jamie's trousers. Then she pushed her hand down his briefs so that she could feel the hardness of his warm, erect cock. His flesh was silky, rock-solid. She mentally dared Fiona to say something and never once broke her gaze from that of the receptionist from hell. But Fiona's only reaction was that her patrician face paled a bit, and then she took another sip of her coffee.

'Are you all right, darling?' said Fiona's male companion. His voice sounded familiar, but he had his back to Tesser. Christ! It was a date after all. Would wonders never cease?

'I'm just fine, thanks very much,' Fiona assured her date, and coughed politely into her napkin. It was only too evident that she was watching what would happen next. Eagerly.

So Tesser would give her a show. She began to jack off Jamie right in front of her employer's receptionist's carefully made-up eyes. She felt herself going sticky and wet; felt her clit beginning to buzz. Ah, yes. She was putting one over on Jamie, too. And there *was* pleasure to be had in deceit.

'Slide your hips lower,' Tesser whispered to Jamie, and he did.

'Is anyone watching?'

She had a view of the entire restaurant. A harried-looking waitress started towards them and then turned away. Embarrassed or aroused or both. It was hard to tell. She kept turning around to ensure that she was really seeing what she was seeing, but she didn't say anything. Tesser mentally thanked her. 'Nah,' she lied. Served him right for his own prevarications.

The new angle now gave Fiona an unencumbered view of the action, and Tesser made sure she got an eyeful. She slid down Jamie's briefs even further and then she leisurely began to work her hand back and forth along the length of him. Fiona would be able to see his thickened cock, his proud bush of dark hair. Tesser stroked him, nice and easy. She loved to give a good handjob. Hell, yes. She caressed him until his breath was coming fast and then, accidentally on purpose, she dropped a spoon and got down on her knees and slurped him up for few seconds, her lipstick ringed around his cock. She retrieved the innocent spoon and sat back up in the chair, checking for Fiona's reaction. The receptionist looked impressed. Impressed and nervous.

'Your mouth felt good,' Jamie whispered to her, his face creasing with intense pleasure. Fiona was also wiggling around uncomfortably. He was very hard. He pressed Tesser's hand down against his groin for a second. He groaned. Some people turned around for a moment, but didn't see anything untoward from their line of vision. Only Fiona and the waitress, who now also was watching avidly, knew. Then, exhibiting great self-control, Jamie pushed his pants and trousers back up, heaved himself up from the chair and walked, not too quickly and not too slowly, to the toilet. It made her panties go moist to think of him finishing up there in the loo, wanking while she and Fiona and the waitress knew exactly what he was doing. Tesser imagined his fist stroking up and down over his stiff dark prick until he came with a muffled groan in a wad of toilet tissue, hitting satisfaction at last. She squirmed in her seat. Maybe she ought to take a trip to the loo as well.

She wondered whether Fiona was thinking exactly the same thing, because it had to be said, she was looking awfully flushed and flustered. It was always those prim little missies that wanted it the most. Tesser sat demurely and batted her eyelashes at Fiona, mockingly folding her hands in her lap like the little lady her Italian grandmother had always coached her to be.

She wasn't *exactly* sure, but for a moment she could have sworn that she saw Fiona give a flutter of a smile. But then things moved too quickly for Tesser to be sure, because Fiona and her oblivious date picked up their respective coats and headed out. Tesser lowered her eyes, but Fiona didn't even glance at Tesser as they brushed past. Tesser couldn't help noticing that the receptionist had left a ten-pound tip on the table.

For once, the waitress's attention was not directed towards their area of the restaurant. Tesser considered pocketing the note herself. But then she glanced towards the poor harried girl working the counter and smiled: it was a fine piece of hush-money for a very discreet waitress, a little pay-off for allowing the show to go on, the show that Tesser and her – boyfriend? lover? fuck? personal traitor? – had just given.

After Fiona left and the happy waitress retrieved the tip, though, Tesser felt deflated. Then she felt angry. And then angrier. She was going to make him spill the beans. The time had arrived.

He was coming towards her, now. He was looking at her, his expression guilty – oh, no. Oh, no, Jamie. How could you? She felt the pain of his betrayal seeping throughout her body.

'Tesser, listen to me. I don't want you to get mad. I have a confession to make. I swore to myself I would tell you today.'

Please, no. And why the fuck was he grinning?

She had told herself that she would have to keep a cool head later. She knew she wasn't acting very cool now, being so pissed off, but she just couldn't help it. She would have to leave immediately, before she started blabbing out of sheer anger and revealed to him that she knew for a fact that he was involved in this whole weird toxic-dumping, tattooing, attempted hit-and-running conspiracy.

She would leave.

She got up to go, tears springing to her eyes, blindly reaching for her backpack.

'What's the matter, Tesser?' At least he wasn't smiling any more; that stupid grin had been wiped off his face. 'Do you already know?'

Don't let him know you know that he's involved. That's what he's presently trying to find out: how much you know. Just keep your mouth shut and get out of here.

'Tesser, please listen and try to understand –'

'I've done enough listening to you. In fact, I think I've done enough with you altogether.' She picked up the pink bill and for a moment she considered paying for the meal, in some sort of grand blow-off gesture. Then she thought better and handed it to Jamie. 'Here you go,

218

rich boy. Consider this your pink slip – your P45. This relationship, such as it was, is officially terminated.'

She grabbed her backpack and stalked out.

'Tesser!'

She tried to ignore the sound of Jamie back inside the restaurant, plaintively calling out her name.

She walked down the stairs, through the hallway papered with various music and art-exhibition posters. One of the flyers caught her eye with its big red letters:

UNDERSTATED® – FEATURING THE WORK OF JAMIE DESMOND.

Without breaking her stride, she tore it off the wall and hurried out the door.

As she walked down Church Street, she gave herself the space to take a big breath and then looked down at the piece of paper she was crushing in her hand. The gallery was in Hoxton. The biggest sell-out, phoney competition of the year, as well. Even she had heard of it. Then her eyes narrowed as she read the fine print below his name: DESMOND EXAMINES SCRAP-CULTURE, POLLUTION AND CAPITALIST PACKAGING.

The nerve of him! She *knew* he was involved in this whole pollution thing. She just *knew*. You know, to hell with that whole trendy pretentious art thang. She was shaking with rage. She checked the address. Hoxton, East London again.

She had half a mind to go over and expose him to the gallery as a polluting toxic hypocrite, even if she couldn't make the exact link. She found that her heart was thumping madly as she turned on to Stoke Newington High Street.

You know, maybe she would do exactly that.

She boarded a No. 149 bus.

The spring rolls were multicoloured, every shade of the rainbow, and strewn all over the floor of the gallery room. The spring-roll pastry itself obviously had been tinted with food colouring, and subsequently everywhere the eye looked was a huge, heaping pile of green or blue or violet or apricot or grey or crimson or hot-pink egg rolls.

'Goddamn.' Tesser stared stunned at the accompanying notes that were placed, conservatively and inauspiciously, to the side of the display room, so as not to assert themselves too much on the artistic integrity of the work. No doubt. In complete horror, she began to read said notes. The spring rolls, the notes explained, represented the commodification of current Western culture, the quick and easy junk-food approach of capitalism. Each diamond-shaped pastry packet actually contained real rubbish, culled from the dump heaps of Hackney. This, the notes further informed, were indicative of 'scrap culture', and both the human instinct to pollute the environment and also the rubbish packaged up by capitalistic forces and sold to the masses.

She couldn't fucking believe it.

Best in show, as well. What a scam. He had even trodden on her ideals. She wasn't the only one who had had the wool pulled over her eyes by him.

'Tesser!'

And there he was, right on schedule. She turned away from him, drained of all energy. She had shown up at the gallery, thinking that she was going to expose him to the cultural masses, but now she just wanted to wash her hands of him.

Jamie caught up with her. 'Tesser! Didn't you hear me calling for you down Church Street? I saw you get on the bus holding the flyer and I thought you might be going here. I had to wait ages for a cab. This is what I wanted to talk to you about!' He was pleading. 'Come on into the bar with me, and we can talk about it. I understand you're a little mad, but it's not *that* big of a deal. I admit it, I'm a sell-out – but I'm a nice sell-out.'

She stared at him, speechless. In a haze, she let him lead her into the bar area.

'I have you to thank,' Jamie continued, after he had ordered her a Bailey's and a pint of wheat beer for himself. 'You're the one who gave me the idea. The way you rant on about commodification and McJunk. The spring rolls you were cooking the other day. Your hair colour gave me the final inspiration – I thought it was just that extra colourful touch that would make the display appealing to the eye. Thank you.'

'Please tell me you're joking,' Tesser said. 'Come on, Jamie – tell me you're pulling my leg.'

'Would I joke about my art, Tesser? I thought you would like it, actually. It's kind of a tribute, actually. I thought you would like the message.'

She didn't know the answer. She downed the whole shot of Bailey's to earn some time to think. 'I can't believe you would betray me so totally,' she said finally. 'Go to hell, Jamie Desmond.'

'Hold on.' Jamie was moving quickly towards her; too quickly. 'Just a bloody second. The *only* thing I've betrayed you about is the art. That's the only deception I've made. With everything else, believe me, I'm on your side.'

'And you expect me to believe that?'

'I do.' She looked at him. He was so gorgeous. She wanted to believe him. But that meant just getting hurt again. And she couldn't let him know what she knew.

'Sorry, mate,' she said, and for the second time that day she left him sitting on his own with a bill to pay.

This time, though, he didn't call after her.

It was as dark as sin. She bicycled to the factory, aware the whole time that cycling through Hackney after dark as a young woman was not considered sensible behaviour. She was more powerful than if she were walking, but all it took was a gang on similar cycles or a person on foot with a gun and that was it: goodbye, Tesser has left the building. Even her swans were not keeping watch tonight the way they had done when she was down in the canals with Jamie – the water was eerily undisturbed, not a ripple of birdlife marring the steady tug-tug-flow. She shivered on her bike; it was starting to rain now, too. In a way, this was good – she always assumed, but wasn't sure, that rain discouraged muggers and rapists the same way intense summer heat encouraged them. Thank Christ for the protective fall of typical London July rain. And it was the last day of the month, too, wasn't it? The season was sliding into late summer as of tomorrow.

Right before she reached AMI Industries, she felt down with one hand to touch the key through the fabric of her trousers, like an amulet. Her hand felt clammy. The moon had come out from behind the clouds.

There was no one around the building: no lights, no sounds. This made her feel worse; she knew now that she had to go through with what she had planned. The old Victorian structure stood isolated like a haunted mansion does in horror flicks and she felt a corresponding sense of trepidation as she pushed her bicycle quietly, quietly around to the back and hid it deep within the bushes. She felt more exposed now. Anyone could see her crossing the parking lot in the moonlight: anyone watching from the canals; from across the water from Hackney Marshes; from within the dark bushes; even from within the building.

There was no point in locking up her bike. The locking process itself would make too much noise and draw attention to her if there actually were others about, and if someone saw her then it would be too late anyway. This way she had a chance at a getaway.

She kept close to the building as she edged closer to the back door entrance and avoided the wide expanse of the parking lot.

The key was hot in her hand, now moist with perspiration. She hadn't even used it yet, because the door had been unlocked during the day. What if it was the wrong key and she was out here in the canal system risking her life? Again. And this time on her own, without even the presence of the traitorous Jamie.

Her hand trembling, she inserted it into the lock. It worked.

The door reverberated as it shut automatically behind her and she shuddered at the noise. She waited for an interminable half-minute, but throughout the entire building there was no response. So she began to ease her way up the stairs. All the way up to the third floor: Dr Sharkey's office. Now up to the fourth floor that encapsulated the lab, the floor upon which she had never yet set foot.

She entered the darkened laboratory gingerly. There were a variety of labelled jars and canisters and a glass cage with several lazy-looking mice. Yuck. Other than those and the fact that there was a wide table that looked like that of a forensic scientist, it still didn't look like the lab setting she had in her mind. She remembered her disappointment her first day at AMI Industries. Her expectations of a place full of bubbling blue liquids and strange mechanical apparatuses were probably garnered from watching too many crap sci-fi films. There was a strange smell in here, though, and Tesser recognised it as the scent that always made her dizzy when she was in the reception room downstairs. It didn't seem to affect Fiona at all, but then of course Fiona was not human.

But there was a desk over there against the far wall of the room. Tesser smelled for gas, couldn't detect any, and then lit a flame with her lighter and moved towards the well-organised desk. It belonged to someone who obviously had a near compulsive nature when it came to tidiness. Her first thought was Dr Sharkey, but she wasn't sure. She started to rifle through the drawers quickly, hoping to find something that would hold up in court as evidence of toxic dumping. She really ought to have grabbed Kitty in a spare moment and asked her what kind of stuff would suffice as legal proof. She really ought to have told someone about her whereabouts tonight, too, but hindsight was always 20/20. No one knew she was here. No one at all.

Then her eyes were drawn up above the desk, to a poster that caught her eye. COMPANY PARTY, it read. THE JUNE BALL FOR AMI EMPLOYEES AND FAMILIES. FREE BALLOONS. FREE SILVER TRINKETS. FREE DRINKS. FREE FORTUNE-TELLER. FREE FAKE TATTOOS. FREE, FREE, FREE. EXECUTIVE DIRECTOR RICHARD DESMOND WILL BE PRESENT GETTING DOWN WITH THE LITTLE FOLKS – NOW MIGHT BE THE TIME TO ASK HIM FOR THAT RISE!

Free fake tattoos? Hold on now. Richard Desmond? That had to be Jamie's father. He *owned* AMI Industries? She thought quickly about the logo on Eric's upper arm and on the upper arm of the bald guy who had been her neighbour for such a short time. Fake tattoos? Temporary tattoos? She supposed it was possible – after all, AMI Industries probably employed local people. The bald guy and the woman had had the look of a couple recovering from a night of shagging as well. Maybe they had just had a wild night of it, the way people did at office Christmas parties, and had continued screwing way into the next day. Eric dated Jamie's stepbrother. Assuming Jamie's family weren't homophobic – and there was no reason to suspect that they were – he would have been invited along to that party as well. Oh, Jesus. It was all starting to come together now. No wonder Eric had chased her for the Super-8 camera – it wasn't homosexual panic. He was having an affair, and it was pure infidelity panic! Jesus mother-of-God fucking Christ. Oh, Shit. What a dummy she had been.

Still, the toxic dumping! Jamie wasn't off the hook. Not yet. His father still owned, or ran, this joint.

Suddenly Tesser heard a distant sound; it could have come from a great distance away, but it terrified her. She had to hurry and get something on AMI Industries now, while she had a chance. She skimmed through the papers in her hand and then she found it. She read as rapidly as she could with the help of her cigarette lighter. She was right after all: AMI *was* polluting. And Dr Sharkey knew all about it. Engrossed and horrified, Tesser sped through the text. They manufactured chloroform, which was what had been making her dizzy at AMI. They had been dumping as a form of waste management for the last three years, under the direct management of Dr Sharkey. And look: there was more stuff in the drawer, lots of stuff – it looked like a bunch of videos, and a reel of Super-8 film and –

There was a beam of light in her eyes and Tesser's heart stopped.

'I'd put those papers straight down, if I were you.' The male voice was familiar, but since she was blinded by the torch, Tesser couldn't make out who it was.

Then it clicked. Kevin. From the Geyser Festival. And his voice. She'd heard it recently – in the café with Fiona! Why, oh, why, was she so oblivious to her past shags? She was worse than the most laddish bloke in that respect. Her mind was whirring now: that's right, young Kevin's mother was a friend of Dr Sharkey's. Judging by the lab coat, Kevin worked here, too.

'Kevin.' Tesser made her voice as soft and seductive as she was able to, remembering somewhere deep in her mind that Kevin had a crush on her. Hold on to that, she told herself. Use that.

'What are you doing here?' Kevin's voice was trembling. He was going to crack at any second. If only Tesser could distract him.

'Come over here, Kevin. I was only doing some research that Dr Sharkey asked me to do. Why don't you come a little closer?' She tried to make her voice steady.

'No, you're not researching. I can tell. You're going through her things.'

'Well, if you're convinced of that, Kevin, why don't you come over here and apprehend me.' Tesser tried to push out her cleavage as a million sexual clichés raced through her head. Trouble was, Kevin was behaving just like a cliché.

'Stop saying my name! Quit saying it!'

'Why, Kevin? Do I make you nervous?'

She put her finger in her mouth and sucked on it, hoping that there weren't any stray chemicals around the place. Of course there were. So instead she hoped they wouldn't kill her right off the mark.

Kevin was staring at her. He lowered the beam so that it no longer shone in her eyes. His many freckles were now visible on his blanched, nervous face in the moonlight. She was just about ready to give up and maybe make a run for it when she heard him say in a low, ashamed voice, 'Yeah. You do make me nervous.' Progess!

'Then why don't you drop the flashlight, come a little closer over here and we can talk about it.'

'I – I'm not sure that I should.'

He was still holding out against her, poor lamb.

'Kevin.' She made her voice very strict. 'Come over here, right now.'

That did the trick, as she supposed it would for someone who was employed by a disciplinarian like Dr Sharkey.

He stood before her, too ashamed to raise his eyes.

'Now, this isn't the way to treat a lady, now is it, Kevin?' Tesser tilted his head up so that he was forced to look her straight in the eye. 'Did Dr Sharkey ask you to come and make sure no one is going through her papers tonight?'

He hung his head and didn't answer.

'Kevin. Answer me.'

'Yeah. She's been paying me twenty quid every night for the last week to come in and make sure no one's been snooping around. I think she's nervous about something. And it looks like she had reason to be,' he suddenly added, self-righteously.

'And what did she ask you to do if you did find someone?'

'Well, she told me not to call the police. She told me to call her up on the mobile directly and that she would deal with it herself.'

'Did she now? What else did she say?'

But Kevin was giving her a stubborn, frightened look now, as it finally appeared to dawn on him that he might have said too much. Suddenly he twisted out of Tesser's grasp and ran several feet away. He took out his phone and brandished it. 'I'm not kidding. I'm going to call her right now, you know. I've dialled her number, see, and I've got my finger on the CALL button.' It was like he was testing her.

'Give me the phone, Kevin.' Tesser took a step towards him, not breaking his gaze in the erratic light of the torch he was waving around. 'I think we could have a lot more fun if you just gave me the phone.'

'I'm warning you . . .' His eyes looked scared. He was panicking. Tesser knew she could get him under her thumb in just a few more minutes, but she didn't know if she had those few more minutes. Jesus! She watched as his thumb, as if in slow motion, lowered on the call button. She was upon him now, and she bumped his hand, but the phone was searching the network, holy hell – she grabbed the phone just as Dr Sharkey answered.

'Hello?'

Calm down, Tesser told herself. Calm down. Kevin, by some act of God, was keeping quiet for the moment.

He seemed frozen with horror at the very idea that someone might intercept a missive meant for the doctor's own ears. 'Hi, Dr Sharkey? It's Tesser.'

'Ms Roget? Do you know what time of night it is?'

'I do, Dr Sharkey. I'm sorry.' She made her voice low and suggestive. Blast! Kevin looked like he was about ready to start hollering. She had to do something. 'I really had to hear your voice, though, Doctor,' she murmured into the mobile phone.

Dr Sharkey sounded disgruntled. 'That's all very well and good, Ms Roget, but there is a time and place for everything.'

Tesser had to distract Kevin. In a moment of inspiration, she started to unbutton her shirt. Thankfully, that seemed to hold his attention. One button. Then another one.

'But I never got a chance to thank you personally for the, the, uh – the Leda thing. And I was trying to get hold of you all day yesterday, wondering if we could meet up.' That was an inspired embellishment! Fiona had to have told the doctor how many times she had called. She bent over, so Kevin could see straight down her shirt.

'Oh, that's right.' Dr Sharkey sounded a little mollified. 'I'm sorry I didn't get back to you. I thought it was concerning something else. It's still an inappropriate hour, I might add.'

Tesser stroked her bra, and then pulled the top of the fuschia-coloured lingerie down a bit, so Kevin could just see a bit of her nipple.

'Wouldn't you like me to lick you again?' Tesser stared at Kevin as she said it, holding the phone to her ear.

'I beg your pardon?' Dr Sharkey said on the other end of the line.

Kevin's cock was hard; Tesser could see it from where she was. He was fucking hard.

228

'I said, wouldn't you like me to lick you – taste all your juices, run my tongue all over you –' Tesser reached over to Kevin and pulled him closer by one of his belt loops, then rammed her hand down his pants, grabbing his stiffening cock – 'put my pussy in your face, wave it back and forth so you can really smell me, smell all my hot wet juices, my pubic hair dripping with scent and juice, inches away from your face? Just like you did to me?'

'Hmm. That's interesting, Ms Roget. Why don't you elaborate?'

'Then I would, um, put my hand down on you –' Tesser pulled on Kevin's cock, slowly at first and then more and more quickly '– and touch you really nice and slow at first.' She removed her hand and immediately Kevin replaced it with his own. 'And then, Dr Sharkey, then I'd tell you to play with yourself.' Kevin began to masturbate with the quick, lusty wrist action of a very young man, and Tesser found her own hand creeping down to her groin. No! she told herself. Now is not the time!

But she unzipped her trousers and thrust her hand down on her bush, searching for her clit. Oh, that did feel so good. She was all creamy and stirred up from hearing Dr Sharkey's voice and watching Kevin's self-fondlings. She just needed a good fiddle herself.

'Uh, yes, that's what I'd do,' Tesser said lamely into the phone, totally losing her train of thought. She rubbed her clit round and round, faster and faster, looking Kevin straight in the eye. Her fingers were soaked. Her cunt was humming with the fast, steady friction. It felt so good. It felt so very, very good. She didn't want to stop. At the same time, she was mortally embarrassed that she was wanking while Dr Sharkey listened in, but she just had to play with herself and there was no sense in improving her phone manner at this late stage in the game.

Oh! She thought of Dr Sharkey's high, firm tits underneath that tight turtleneck and a little wave of dirty pleasure passed through her. Oh! When she saw how Kevin had taken his hand away from himself and was looking at her with something like desperation, another pulse of pleasure shot out from her clit through her entire body.

'Ms Roget? Ms Roget? You've become very silent, although I can observe that your breathing is becoming more and more laboured. You're not touching yourself, are you? Between your legs? Because you know I require your sole concentration. Why don't you elaborate on what you are doing?' the doctor requested, for the second time.

Tesser could detect that, far away on the other end of the line, the doctor's breath was quickening. She was nearly panting for it, the horny stuck-up bitch. God! She was sexy, though. For a moment Tesser nearly wished Dr Sharkey was here in the room too, until she remembered her mission. Augh! She was losing it. She made her voice low and confidential, and looked down at Kevin's shining green eyes as she spoke. 'I'd love to elaborate, Dr Sharkey. But I'd rather elaborate in person. Maybe tomorrow at noon? At AMI?'

Dr Sharkey chuckled. 'You're rather naughty, Ms Roget, for calling me at this hour. I have to admit that you've made me rather . . . moist. In fact, even as we speak, I'm fingering myself rather indecently. I will look forward to talking to you.'

'Ohh . . .' Tesser hated the fact, but the truth was that Dr Sharkey made *her* pretty moist as well. So the doctor was masturbating even now? Oh, the thought made Tesser break out in a light perspiration. She wanted to fuck and suck and lick. No! She wanted to get out of this situation. Kevin was still looking at her pleadingly; Tesser made an O out of her thumb and forefinger and began to wank Kevin in careful, light little pulses of movement.

230

'What's the matter, Ms Roget? Cat got your tongue?'

She remembered Jamie once using the same phrase. 'No . . .' No, I just want to listen to your voice and jerk off this teenager and touch myself frantically, when really I ought to be worrying about the environment and, more importantly, my life. 'No, I'll see you tomorrow.'

'Don't wear yourself out,' Dr Sharkey said dryly, and rang off. Tesser was just too horny to speak. She put her head down and began to lick and then blow Kevin. He took the cue, pulling down her pants and going to work on her, too. His tongue flickered all over her hole, sometimes dipping in, sometimes slurping up the juices. When Tesser touched herself she felt raw – raw and horny and so, so wet. She jerked herself to a climax just as she sucked him off, swallowing his sweet thick juice down her throat. He lapped at her pussy the whole time he came, and it seemed to make him shoot even more inside her mouth.

Suddenly there was another blinding light from the door. Not again! All in disarray on the floor, her mouth still wet from Kevin's cock and her own sex juices smeared all over his face and hair, Tesser struggled to stand up. This time she probably *would* have to fight her way out – no delays.

But no: receptionist from hell was holding a gun. Tesser pulled up her trousers, trying to preserve a little of her dignity even if she was going to croak. Damn. She wished she had listened to what her mother had said about always wearing her nicest underwear.

'Jesus, Fiona, you fucking bitch!' she couldn't help saying. If she was going to die, it didn't matter *what* insults she threw at the evil blonde.

'Calm down, all right. Just calm down.'

As Fiona talked, she inched into the room. Tesser realised that the gun, for some fucked-up reason, rather than being aimed at Tesser, was trained on the far corners of the room, where the shadows made it difficult to see. What the hell?

'Tesser, this is not what you think.'

'Isn't it?' Tesser was going to bolt. She was going to save her own juicy ass.

Fiona looked nervous; her hands were shaking as she held the gun. Nope, it wasn't cocked on Tesser and Kevin. Didn't she know how to use one? How crazy was she? 'Is there anyone else in the room here? Tell me!'

'Why should I tell you?'

'I'm not the enemy here, Tesser.'

'Hey, try telling that to those thousands of people you screw over through environmental destruction. Tell that to Jamie Desmond's father. Better yet, why don't you tell Jamie, being as he certainly seemed to catch your eye yesterday at the Vortex? I think you might even have a little crush there, Fiona. Best of luck with it. You're a pair made in heaven.'

'Why don't you tell him yourself?' Fiona didn't look as embarrassed as Tesser had hoped she would. In fact, she was still keeping her hands firmly on the gun. 'You're sure there's no one up here but you and Kevin?' Thankfully, she at last began to lower the firearm.

Tesser edged towards the door. Contrary to TV-cop logic, she didn't face Fiona, reasoning that it would look bad if she were shot in the back. Maybe even Crazy Fiona wouldn't risk the time behind bars that particular action would buy. She could see the wispy shadow of someone standing just by the stairwell, could just make out someone's profile. She could practically smell him . . .

Whoever it was, he was wearing cinnamon aftershave.

Jesus fucking mother-of-God bollocks gob Christ.

It *was* Jamie there in the stairwell, leaning casually against the wall. Leaning far too casually.

'You bastard!' she screamed. 'You betrayed me!'

'No, Tesser! I'm the one that went and called up Fiona to come down here.'

'I'll just bet you called her up.'

'I'm serious. I've been trailing you all day.'

'Why doesn't that surprise me?'

'Why don't you listen? My dad owns some businesses. We're pretty well off.'

Like that's news, buster.

'He holds stakes in quite a few companies, actually. Fingers in many pies, you know.'

'Yeah?' She was dreading what was coming, but she already knew what he was going to say –

'He owns a company called AMI Industries, a standard mechanics firm, which has a subsidiary named Blairstone Chemicals. They farm stuff out to them, but Blairstone has a fair amount of autonomy.'

He said it.

'Listen, Tesser – I knew you were doing video work for them but I didn't want to tell you I knew, because maybe you would think I had got you the job or something.'

'Yeah, much better to think you're lying scum trash. Hold on, I'm sorry – you still are. Nothing's changed.'

'No, listen – my dad's not so bad. Not for a suit, anyway. He's the guy that signed up for the charity sponsorship, actually. Not Blairstone. He's been suspecting that there's some polluting going on for some time – that's why he hired Fiona. She's an undercover cop, linked with the Department of the Environment.'

Tesser turned quickly around to face Fiona, who had crept up behind them. 'But this means that you're actually helping me out!'

'I am, Tesser. But it doesn't mean I like you even one smidgen of a little bit more.'

'That's a relief, perhaps,' Tesser said dryly.

She walked over to the room where Jamie was. Fiona's hand was still on her gun. Kevin was trying to pull his trousers back up. 'You fuckhead, Jamie!' Tesser screamed. 'How could you lie to me about all that stuff?'

'I didn't lie to you. And anyway, an artist must follow only the rules of his art,' Jamie said sanctimoniously.

Oh, she wasn't going to believe this bullshit from him for a second. There was no way she was going to risk trusting him again.

Suddenly Tesser remembered what she had missed; she glanced over at the open drawer of the desk. She thought quickly and, without warning, she dived over Jamie's lanky body and retrieved the short film. 'Or *her* art,' she replied, and she took off running like a bat out of hell. Yes! *The Passion Flowchart* was in her possession once again.

'Cover my back,' Tesser screamed to Fiona as she ran out of the room and towards the flight of stairs. If Fiona really was on her side, then she could start to prove it now. She could hear Fiona screaming 'Stop!', but then there was no sound of gunshots. And Jamie was there behind her now! How the fuck did he get out of that room?

Fuck! Fuck! Fuck! Down the spiral staircase, Jamie dashing behind her, Fiona screaming something at them both, down and down and down. She had to beat Jamie Desmond down the stairs; she had to make it; she had to make it; she had to make it –

Bang!

What the fuck was Dr Sharkey doing there with a gun?

'Hello, Tesser. You're a bit slow today, aren't you? Didn't you consider that Kevin's mobile number might show up on my caller display? Though I must say, I enjoyed your rather desperate attempt at phone sex. I had to have a nice good wank after I hung up the phone, that's how hot you got me. Delayed me for ten minutes or so, but now here I am.'

Tesser's heart sank. She was done for. She was a

goner. And so, she realised, was Jamie. 'What, no "Ms Roget"? "Wank"? Pretty informal, Dr Sharkey, don't you think?'

'Get back up the stairs, Tesser, with your boyfriend and my dear, traitorous Fiona.'

'Tesser!' Jamie was screaming behind her.

And all of a sudden Tesser realised that it might have been a good idea to trust Jamie, after all.

She didn't run. She stood her ground. She gave Dr Miriam Sharkey a good bollocking, as the British say. Even in the face of impending death, never let it be said that Tesser Roget held her tongue.

'You! Your company is dumping toxic waste in Hackney Canals – not only that, but I found a memo that stated that you were close to winning the bid for the care of the European canal systems, as well as those in Third World countries. And do you know what, *Miriam*?' Tesser spat the name out. 'Do you know what? That same memo states that Blairstone intends to use exactly the same disposal process that it's been using in Hackney! The same disposal process that means you're not only going to pollute the canals of East London with foul toxic waste, as you've already been doing, but that you intend to do this on a worldwide scale! I'm reporting you, Miriam! I'm in control now!'

'Really, Tesser? And just who are you going to report this to?'

'She'll be reporting this to me, actually.' It was Fiona, from up above. 'She'll be reporting it to me, Dr Sharkey,' Fiona continued, 'because I'm sure that's information that I'll want to have in my own report to the Environmental Protection League. What's more, I hear the girl has video evidence – which is great, because despite the fact that I pored over the other tapes, I had nothing concrete on Blairstone Chemicals. Nothing concrete until now, it is.'

Without lowering the firearm, Fiona rustled through

her pocket and threw a badge out towards Dr Sharkey and Tesser. The wallet landed open in the middle of the floor, and Tesser saw that it said EUROPEAN ENVIRON-MENTAL PROTECTION LEAGUE, INVESTIGATIONS.

Fiona was a spy? No way!

Way.

'You never were the brightest crayon in the box, were you, Fiona? Perhaps I should just delicately add at this point in time that you were a truly awful receptionist. Inefficient and rude.'

Despite her better intentions, Tesser found herself nodding along with Dr Sharkey.

'No matter now,' the doctor continued. 'I hold all the cards, you see – you may be up above me with a gun, but one hint of movement and I'll blow Tesser's brains out down here.'

Tesser stopped nodding.

'I know you were never particularly fond of her, anyway,' Dr Sharkey added. 'Now I, on the other hand –'

But just then, a crack shot rang out from below, one that blew the gun itself away from Dr Sharkey's hand, but spared her marvellous fingers.

'Hands up, Sharkey!'

Tesser hardly dared to look below, even when the police backup team further down in the stairwell raced up and forced the doctor down at gunpoint.

Tesser watched in shock. Half a floor above her, Jamie was still frozen in place on the stairs. And above him stood Fiona and Kevin. All three of them seemed stunned.

As Dr Sharkey was handcuffed and led away, Tesser couldn't help but have an image of the doctor being trussed up in silver twine, begging for orgasms, begging for sexual release. Look who's crying now, eh, Doc? Well, Tesser was only human.

* * *

It was a shock to find out that Kevin was undercover, as had been his 'mother' at the festival. He was actually a nice married man of twenty-five who looked very young for his years. Oops. He certainly had gone far in the name of duty. But Tesser kept silent about that. Apparently, she had been under surveillance as an accomplice to Blairstone Chemicals; it was widely believed that her filming was only red-herring work to distract from the real-life activities of the subsidiary company. At least until Fiona had apparently convinced most investigators working on the case that Tesser didn't have the balls or brains to deceive at such a high level, a statement that once revealed would irritate Tesser for weeks. Fiona might be one of the 'good guys', but she was still suffering from a seriously mutated personality disorder.

Kevin, at least, had thought Tesser capable of mischief. While still undercover, he had convinced Dr Sharkey that it might be a good idea if he checked in nightly at the laboratory in case Tesser planned a break-in. What he really wanted to do was see which team Tesser was playing for, so to speak. Along with Fiona, Kevin had been investigating Blairstone for months and had completely fooled everyone with his naïve act. He had attended all company functions – like the company June Ball. He had even been the one who had trailed Tesser to the zoo, which was where he had accidentally dropped Finna's card (Finna had been distributing the cards quite freely at the company party).

There were two more puzzle-pieces that clicked into place once the dust had settled, pieces that made sense in a weird sort of way. The first was that Jamie's father wasn't such a bad guy, as Jamie had said. He had tried to keep an eye on the rumours of toxic dumping and had initially alerted the Environmental Protection League of his own volition. He was a popular boss. He sponsored parties for his employees, like the June Ball – which Tesser's short-term exhibitionist neighbours had indeed attended. The bald guy, a Mr Mickey Rogers, had received a fake tattoo. He had left his address in the company guestbook, as was the custom at the annual party. Then Baldie had become very drunk, picked up the redhead and left the party. It was revealed in later questioning that Dr Sharkey had cross-referenced the guestbook with Tesser's own address, noticed a similarity and, due to that coincidence, had suspected Tesser was a spy from the very start of her employment. So she had tried to trip Tesser up, hoping that she would be caught illegally filming, making the evidence inadmissible in court. When it appeared that Tesser was too subtle, Dr Sharkey had set her personal goon squad on Tesser no fewer than three times: the nearly snatched film at the festival, the squat robbery, the Ford Mondeo. The man in the green-hooded sweatshirt was one of Dr Sharkey's little friends, as well. But nothing had been found – mainly because Tesser actually was no double agent. Apparently, Dr Sharkey had become convinced that Tesser was a mastermind of great intellect.

At last, a flattering character analysis.

Back to Jamie's father. He had an interest in the occult. He always had the same fortune-teller – Finna – for company parties.

Anyway, it was the androgynous Finna who first turned Trevor on to the concept of ghost walks. Which led to the second revelation: Trevor was Alistair. He had been too chicken to give out his real name on the ghost walk. He and Eric had just been cruising for cheap thrills to spice up their relationship, and Eric was a hotheaded drag artiste who didn't take kindly to being filmed or photographed without his express permission. Just as Jamie hadn't had the heart to tell Trevor that Eric was having an affair, Trevor hadn't had the heart to tell his stepbrother that he had had sex with his new girlfriend.

And so what about Finna? It turned out that she was actually quite shy. Rumour had it that she found it difficult to face former paramours straight in the face. She might have been shy, but she still liked to reminisce. She had once scored with a very nice person on a ghost walk, a nineteen-year-old with rainbow-coloured hair, and after one too many flirtinis at the June Ball, the seer had drunkenly divulged to Trevor and Eric that if they wanted to spice up their sex life, they should go on a ghost walk.

Which was, of course, what Tesser had always said.

So that was sorted: a promise from Richard Desmond to keep an eye on clean water as well as sponsoring a new group of Hackney schoolchildren on boat rides; bliss for Trevor and his beau; £1,000 reward for Tesser Roget for capturing the polluters (plus, Dr Sharkey's cheque didn't bounce!); a £10,000 art prize for Jamie – like he needed more money – and a citation for Fiona Curew, Detective Inspector Extrabitchonaire.

Jamie might be a sell-out, but he was a happy sell-out and Tesser had decided to forgive his need for mainstream approval. Besides, he promised her that he would still be putting on his hybrid cyborg art show, so that was a bit of a sweetener.

Tesser had already started on *Chain of Lurve* – the idea that love and sex affect everything, and everyone is culpable (be it in regard to love of boyfriends or love of nature); the idea that we are always less than six degrees of separation away from sex and love; the idea that the wavering wings of besotted butterflies in China may affect infatuation statistics in small hamlets in Alaska; the idea that everyone and everything in life is connected. Boy, didn't she *know* it?

She was at Jamie's in his bed, where she had been for the past five hours. She forced herself to send a quick text message to Kitty before she got up out of the sheets to get ready to go back to the squat.

IM AT JAMIEZ. WE'LL B HOME FOR DINNR.
MAKE SURE U TAKE A FEW T BAGZ FRM JANAS
CUPBOARD IN PREPARATION FOR TRIUM-
PHANT ARRIVAL. SHE'LL MISS ME 2 MUCH
OTHERYZ.

Tesser pushed 'SEND' and then, as an afterthought,
quickly punched in a second message:

WE'LL CELEBR8 W/ PEPPERMINT T COS
YOU'VE PROBABLY HAD ALL THE BOOZ.

'Are you sure Jana won't mind you borrowing her
peppermint tea?' asked Jamie, reading over her shoulder
as she keyed in the text message.
She kissed him lightly on the nose. He was pretty
lovable.
'Let me see that for a second.' He took the phone from
her and added a few more lines. Then he kissed her
warmly, deeply, tenderly. Tesser peeked and saw the
message just before he pressed 'SEND'.

ON 2ND THOUGHT, [it read], WE'LL B A BIT L8.
C-YA. T & J.

His arms went round her and the phone dropped to
the floor.
'If this is what happens with the third-time shag, what
happens with the hundred-and-third-time shag?' Jamie
asked when he came up for air.
'I don't know,' said Tesser. She looked him squarely
in the eye. 'I'm willing to find out. All I ask is that you
don't expect that the odd numbers are with you.' It was
as close as she was able to discuss her unfaithful nature
without hurting his feelings. If Jamie wanted to be
faithful to her, that was his damage. It only meant she
could have her cake and eat it, too.

240

'I would never expect that, Tesser Roget. Although I do believe this is shag number ten, and that means tonight is my night.'

He laughed and he kissed her again.

Several minutes later, the phone on the floor beeped with a new message that read:

WHERE R U GUYS? COME OVER IMMEDIATELY.

It was quite some time before Kitty got an answer.

BLACK LACE NEW BOOKS

Published in August

MINX
Megan Blythe
£6.99

Spoilt Amy Pringle arrives at Lancaster Hall to pursue her engagement
to Lord Fitzroy, eldest son of the Earl and heir to a fortune. The Earl is
not impressed, and sets out to break her spirit. But the trouble for him
is that she enjoys every one of his 'punishments' and creates havoc,
provoking the stuffy Earl at every opportunity. The young Lord
remains aloof, however, and, in order to win his affections, Amy sets
about seducing his well-endowed but dim brother, Bubb. When she is
discovered in bed with Bubb and a servant girl, how will father and
son react?

**Immensely funny and well-written tale of lust among
decadent aristocrats.**

ISBN 0 352 33638 2

FULL STEAM AHEAD
Tabitha Flyte
£6.99

Sophie wants money, big money. After twelve years working as a
croupier on the Caribbean cruise ships, she has devised a scheme that
is her ticket to Freedomsville. But she can't do it alone; she has to
encourage her colleagues to help her. Persuasion turns to seduction,
which turns to blackmail. Then there are prying passengers, tropical
storms and an angry, jealous girlfriend to contend with. And what
happens when the lascivious Captain decides to stick his oar in, too?

**Full of gold-digging women, well-built men in uniform
and Machiavellian antics.**

ISBN 0 352 33637 4

A SECRET PLACE
Ella Broussard
£6.99

Maddie is a busy girl with a dream job: location scout for a film company. When she's double-booked to work on two features at once, she needs to manage her time very carefully. Luckily, there's no shortage of fit young men, in both film crews, who are willing to help. She also makes friends with the locals, including a horny young farmer and a particularly handy mechanic. The only person she's not getting on with is Hugh, the director of one of the movies. Is that because sexual tension between them has reached breaking point?

This story of lust during a long hot English summer is another Black Lace special reprint.

ISBN 0 352 33307 3

Published in September

GAME FOR ANYTHING
Lyn Wood
£6.99

Fiona finds herself on a word-games holidays with her best pal. At first it seems like a boring way to spend a week away. Then she realises it's a treasure hunt with a difference. Solving the riddles embroils her in a series of erotic situations as the clues get ever more outrageous.

Another fun sexy story from the author of Intense Blue.

ISBN 0 352 33639 0

CHEAP TRICK
Astrid Fox
£6.99

Tesser Roget is a girl who takes no prisoners. An American slacker, living in London, she dresses in funky charity-shop clothes and wears blue fishnets. She looks hot and she knows it. She likes to have sex, and she frequently does. Life on the fringe is very good indeed, but when she meets artist Jamie Desmond things take a sudden swerve into the weird.

Hold on for one hot, horny, jet-propelled ride through contemporary London.

ISBN 0 352 33640 4

FORBIDDEN FRUIT
Susie Raymond
£6.99

When thirty-something divorcee Beth realises someone is spying on her in the work changing room, she is both shocked and excited. When she finds out it's sixteen-year-old shop assistant Jonathan she cannot believe her eyes. Try as she might, she cannot get the thought of his fit young body out of her mind. Although she knows she shouldn't encourage him, the temptation is irresistible.

This story of forbidden lusts is a Black Lace special reprint.

ISBN 0 352 33306 5

Published in October

ALL THE TRIMMINGS
Tesni Morgan
£6.99

Cheryl and Laura, two fast friends, have recently become divorced. When the women find out that each secretly harbours a desire to be a whorehouse madam, there's nothing to stop them. On the surface their establishment is a five-star hotel, but to a select clientele it's a bawdy fun house for both sexes, where fantasies – from the mild to the increasingly perverse – are indulged.

Humorous and sexy, this is a fabulous yarn of women behaving badly and loving it!

ISBN 0 352 33641 2

WICKED WORDS 5
A Black Lace short story collection
£6.99

Black Lace short story collections are a showcase of the finest contemporary women's erotica anywhere in the world. With contributions from the UK, USA and Australia, the settings and stories are deliciously daring. Fresh, cheeky and upbeat, only the most arousing fiction makes it into a *Wicked Words* anthology.

By popular demand, another cutting-edge Black Lace anthology.

ISBN 0 352 33642 0

PLEASURE'S DAUGHTER
Sedalia Johnson
£6.99

It's 1750. Orphaned Amelia, headstrong and voluptuous, goes to live with wealthy relatives. During the journey she meets the exciting, untrustworthy Marquis of Beechwood. She manages to escape his clutches only to find he is a good friend of her aunt and uncle. Although aroused by him, she flees his relentless pursuit, taking up residence in a Covent Garden establishment dedicated to pleasure. When the marquis catches up with her, Amelia is only too happy to demonstrate her new-found disciplinary skills.

**Find out what our naughty ancestors got up to in this
Black Lace special reprint.**

ISBN 0 352 33237 9

To find out the latest information about Black Lace titles, check out the website: www.blacklace-books.co.uk or send a stamped addressed envelope to:

Black Lace, Thames Wharf Studios,
Rainville Road, London W6 9HA

Please note only British stamps are valid.

BLACK
lace

BLACK LACE BOOKLIST

Information is correct at time of printing. To avoid disappointment check availability before ordering. Go to www.blacklace-books.co.uk

All books are priced £5.99 unless another price is given.

Black Lace books with a contemporary setting

THE TOP OF HER GAME	Emma Holly ISBN 0 352 33337 5	☐
IN THE FLESH	Emma Holly ISBN 0 352 33498 3	☐
SHAMELESS	Stella Black ISBN 0 352 33485 1	☐
TONGUE IN CHEEK	Tabitha Flyte ISBN 0 352 33484 3	☐
SAUCE FOR THE GOOSE	Mary Rose Maxwell ISBN 0 352 33492 4	☐
INTENSE BLUE	Lyn Wood ISBN 0 352 33496 7	☐
THE NAKED TRUTH	Natasha Rostova ISBN 0 352 33497 5	☐
A SPORTING CHANCE	Susie Raymond ISBN 0 352 33501 7	☐
TAKING LIBERTIES	Susie Raymond ISBN 0 352 33357 X	☐
A SCANDALOUS AFFAIR	Holly Graham ISBN 0 352 33523 8	☐
THE NAKED FLAME	Crystalle Valentino ISBN 0 352 33528 9	☐
CRASH COURSE	Juliet Hastings ISBN 0 352 33018 X	☐
ON THE EDGE	Laura Hamilton ISBN 0 352 33534 3	☐
LURED BY LUST	Tania Picarda ISBN 0 352 33533 5	☐
LEARNING TO LOVE IT	Alison Tyler ISBN 0 352 33535 1	☐

| FORBIDDEN FRUIT
£6.99 | Susie Raymond
ISBN 0 352 33306 5 | ☐ |

Black Lace books with an historical setting

PRIMAL SKIN	Leona Benkt Rhys ISBN 0 352 33500 9	☐
DEVIL'S FIRE	Melissa MacNeal ISBN 0 352 33527 0	☐
WILD KINGDOM	Deanna Ashford ISBN 0 352 33549 1	☐
DARKER THAN LOVE	Kristina Lloyd ISBN 0 352 33279 4	☐
STAND AND DELIVER	Helena Ravenscroft ISBN 0 352 33340 5	☐
THE CAPTIVATION £6.99	Natasha Rostova ISBN 0 352 33234 4	☐
CIRCO EROTICA £6.99	Mercedes Kelley ISBN 0 352 33257 3	☐
MINX £6.99	Megan Blythe ISBN 0 352 33638 2	☐

Black Lace anthologies

CRUEL ENCHANTMENT Erotic Fairy Stories	Janine Ashbless ISBN 0 352 33483 5	☐
MORE WICKED WORDS	Various ISBN 0 352 33487 8	☐
WICKED WORDS 4	Various ISBN 0 352 33603 X	☐

Black Lace non-fiction

| THE BLACK LACE BOOK OF
WOMEN'S SEXUAL
FANTASIES | Ed. Kerri Sharp
ISBN 0 352 33346 4 | ☐ |

------✂------------------

Please send me the books I have ticked above.

Name   ....

Address   ....

....

....

.... Post Code ....

Send to: **Cash Sales, Black Lace Books, Thames Wharf Studios, Rainville Road, London W6 9HA.**

US customers: for prices and details of how to order books for delivery by mail, call 1-800-805-1083.

Please enclose a cheque or postal order, made payable to **Virgin Publishing Ltd**, to the value of the books you have ordered plus postage and packing costs as follows:

UK and BFPO – £1.00 for the first book, 50p for each subsequent book.

Overseas (including Republic of Ireland) – £2.00 for the first book, £1.00 for each subsequent book.

If you would prefer to pay by VISA, ACCESS/MASTER-CARD, DINERS CLUB, AMEX or SWITCH, please write your card number and expiry date here:

....

Please allow up to 28 days for delivery.

Signature ....

------✂------------------